"This is a wowzer. Intricate plotting, appealing locations, unusual characters, and a touch of humor combine to make this one amazing debut novel."

—Stacy Alesi, a.k.a. The BookBitch

"★★★★. This novel hits the ground running and never lets up. Maleeny takes a lush, San Francisco–style noir and turns it on its head with plenty of gusto."

—Sheila Leitzel, *Bookfetish*

"I curled up and couldn't put it down."

—Barbara Peters, The Poisoned Pen Bookstore

"Don't let yourself miss Tim Maleeny's *Stealing the Dragon*."

—The Mystery Bookstore, Los Angeles

"Tim Maleeny gives us an exercise in pulp, noir, and kung fu, all rolled into one: three great tastes that go great together."

—Bruce Grossman, *Bookgasm.com*

"Cape and Sally are fascinating characters. I'll look forward to further books in the series."

—Maggie Mason, *Deadly Pleasures Magazine*

"*Stealing the Dragon* is a no-holds-barred delight from the get-go."

—Cornelia Read,
Edgar-nominated author of *A Field of Darkness*

BEATING THE
BABUSHKA

ALSO BY TIM MALEENY

Stealing the Dragon

A CAPE WEATHERS INVESTIGATION

BEATING THE BABUSHKA

TIM MALEENY

MIDNIGHT INK
WOODBURY, MINNESOTA

FIRST EDITION
First Printing, 2007

Book design by Donna Burch
Cover design by Gavin Dayton Duffy
Cover photograph © AsiaPix / Asia Images Group / PunchStock

Midnight Ink, an imprint of Llewellyn Publications

Library of Congress Cataloging-in-Publication Data
Maleeny, Tim, 1962–
  Beating the babushka : a Cape Weathers investigation / Tim Maleeny.—1st ed.
    p. cm.
  ISBN 978-0-7387-1115-7
 1. Private investigators—Fiction. 2. Murder—Investigation—Fiction. 3. Motion picture industry—Fiction. 4. Organized crime—Fiction. 5. Russian American criminals—Fiction. 6. Triads (Gangs)—Fiction. 7. San Francisco (Calif.)—Fiction. I. Title.
PS3613.A4353B43 2007
813'.6—dc22

                                                                    2007018873

Midnight Ink
Llewellyn Publications
2143 Wooddale Drive, Dept. 978-0-7387-1115-7
Woodbury, MN 55125-2989, U.S.A.
www.midnightinkbooks.com

Printed in the United States of America

For Kathryn,
Far better than my better half.

1
—

Tom Abrahams was flying to his death.

That's what he told himself as he plummeted through the fog with his arms outstretched, the wind roaring in his ears. He was flying, not falling. He could turn and glide safely back to the bridge at any moment. All he had to do was concentrate.

No problem.

He felt surprisingly calm, his mind clear. The night air was invigorating. A sudden image from his daughter's video collection flashed across his consciousness: Peter Pan and Wendy soaring above the London Bridge. They'd watched that scene a thousand times—what was the secret Peter told the children?

Think of a happy little thought.

Two hundred feet was a long way down. Plenty of time to think of something.

He thought of skydiving in Florida when he was eighteen, the rush of air so intense the only sound was his heart pounding somewhere inside his head, then silence once he reached terminal velocity and everything stabilized. One hundred twenty miles per hour, the white noise enveloping him like a protective blanket, the world literally at his feet.

A happy little thought?

Tom worried for an instant over the morbid sound of *terminal velocity*, wondering who invented the term. Realized too late he should have paid more attention in high school physics.

An object falls from the center span of the Golden Gate Bridge, which sits approximately two hundred and twenty feet above San Francisco Bay. Since all objects accelerate at the same rate under gravity, and taking into account air resistance, how long before the object hits the water below?

Tom didn't know the answer, but he hoped it was a long, long time.

The fog parted for an instant, revealing the black water below. Whitecaps appeared and then vanished from the surface, a distant Morse code warning him to turn back.

Just a happy little thought.

Tom spread his arms wider, arching his back to keep from spinning. The crush of air felt like it was going to break him in half. He spread his fingers, willing them to grow feathers and turn into wings.

Then he remembered the catch. Peter Pan got it wrong—you needed pixie dust to fly. Until Peter grabbed Tinkerbell and shook pixie dust on the kids, they dropped like stones onto their bed. Without pixie dust they were just another physics experiment, all victims of gravity. Without pixie dust they were fucked.

Like Tom was now.

His eyes watering, Tom squinted to make out a flash of light piercing the fog. He wondered briefly if it was Tinkerbell, come to shake her little fairy butt in his direction, give him a lift.

You can fly, you can fly, you can fly!

A gust of wind flipped him upside down as Tom realized the flashing was the lighthouse at Alcatraz. No Tinkerbell, just a run-down jail holding tourists prisoner.

Head down, Tom strained to see through the fog, thicker now and backlit by the distant beacon. Then everything turned a blinding white, as if he'd fallen into a ball of cotton. He spun again, no longer sure if the water was below or above him. He just knew it was close.

With his eyes shut tight, Tom thought he could hear the sound of waves breaking against the base of the bridge tower. He thought he could smell salt spray through the dampness of the fog. He thought he heard music. Then he thought about his daughter.

Tom had no more happy little thoughts after that.

2

C APE W EATHERS LOOKED UP from the newspaper before there was any knock on his door. These days it wasn't too hard to tell when he had a visitor.

His office sat on the third floor of a building along the Embarcadero, the gently curving road that separated downtown San Francisco from Fisherman's Wharf and Pier 39, two of the more dubious landmarks in a city known for its good looks. One short trip across the asphalt and you went from urban paradise to tourist hell. Cape liked to think of his office as purgatory.

A couple of years ago, the other offices in the building were bustling with tech start-ups, the hallways buzzing with entrepreneurial fervor and breathless whispers of pending IPOs. Now they were all but deserted, the dot-com acolytes back at their old jobs, making Cape one of the few remaining tenants who paid the rent on time. Most months, anyway.

The door was open, so there was no mistaking the footsteps echoing down the hallway. Sounded like a woman wearing heels, average weight, confident stride. Not a fast walker, but zero hesitation at the end of the hall. She knew where she was going.

Cape reflected that it could also be an underweight man who cross-dressed. This was San Francisco, after all. He'd just have to wait and see.

It was worth the wait. The woman standing in the doorway was wearing heels and probably was average weight, but there was nothing else average about her. She filled the room with her presence before she'd even cleared the threshold.

The word that came to Cape's mind was *intense*.

She had long black hair with matching eyes, her hair pulled back into a no-nonsense ponytail. She wore jeans and a blouse that looked casual but elegant, the kind of thing Cape figured cost roughly what he paid in rent, even before she added up the dry cleaning bills. She stood in the doorway with a posture that suggested she didn't really want to be there but had nowhere else to go. When she smiled at Cape, her face radiated warmth everywhere, except her eyes, which looked like they belonged to a woman who hadn't slept in a week.

"Cape Weathers?"

Cape returned the smile. "Welcome to purgatory."

"Excuse me?"

"Never mind," he said as her smile vanished. "Have a seat."

She remained standing.

"Rebecca Lowry said I could trust you," she said pointedly, watching him.

"That's nice of her." So much for small talk. *Let the interview begin.*

"She said you could find anyone."

Cape shrugged. "Most people don't know the good hiding places."

"She also said you almost got killed trying to help her."

"Rebecca was somewhat prone to exaggeration," replied Cape. "I got a little airsick traveling back and forth to Mexico. But I'm not really in the habit of talking about past clients."

"She also said you were modest."

Cape gestured toward the client chair again. "She mention that I was charming?"

"Never."

Cape nodded. "Rebecca was also prone to understatement."

The corners of her mouth turned up slightly. "How do I know I can trust you?"

Cape shrugged again. "Do you trust Rebecca?"

"Rebecca and I were roommates at school." She said it as if they'd scaled Everest together or survived a tour in Vietnam. Cape figured he must have gone to a different school.

The woman nodded as if he'd said something, or maybe she'd made a decision and said something to herself. She stepped around the chair and extended her hand. Her grip was firm, her hand surprisingly large. Up close, she smelled faintly of strawberries.

"I'm Grace Gold," she said. "And just so we're clear from the start, I can't stand men who lie to me."

"I'm lactose intolerant," said Cape. "Anything else you want to get on the table?"

That got a full smile, if only for an instant. "When I told Rebecca about my situation, she told me it was your kind of problem."

"OK, Grace," replied Cape, raising an eyebrow. "Since assertiveness isn't one of your problems, it must be something else."

"I'm having trouble with the police."

"Which police?"

"The San Francisco police—they won't listen to me."

"I find that hard to believe," said Cape. "You strike me as, well, *persistent.*"

"I've talked to six different people in two different departments, and no one's listening."

"I have the same problem with cops but always thought it was me. Have you tried a bullhorn?"

"Are you going to help me or not?"

"With *what?*" Cape spread his hands. "Don't take this the wrong way, Grace, but are you typically this obtuse? Why were you talking to the police in the first place?"

Grace sighed, dropped her hands to her lap. Took another deep breath before looking up. Now her face matched her eyes, and she looked ten years older than a moment before, as if what she was about to say would stop her heart.

"A friend of mine was murdered."

"When?" Cape glanced at the discarded newspaper on his desk. He didn't recall reading anything about a murder.

Grace followed his gaze and turned the paper toward her, scanning the front page. She flipped it around and pointed to the headline in the lower right corner.

Movie Producer Takes a Dive.

Cape frowned. The local paper had become more like the *New York Post* every year. He'd just read the story and seriously doubted the man's family took any solace from him *taking a dive* off the Golden Gate Bridge. He quickly scanned the article for the name.

"Tom Abrahams?" he asked. "The producer—that's your friend?"

"Yes," she said. "We work—worked—together."

"It says he jumped," said Cape. "They found his abandoned car. I know this is upsetting, but—"

"It's *bullshit!*" Grace almost came out of her chair, slamming her right hand on the desk. "You don't jump off a fucking bridge in the middle of a movie!"

"Suicides don't always choose the most opportune times..."

"Bullshit," repeated Grace, her nostrils flaring. "Tom called me the night he—" She stopped, staring at the newspaper. "The night this happened."

"What did he say?" asked Cape.

"I was out." Her mouth was a straight line of frustration. "He left a message asking me to call him back."

"Did you?"

Grace shook her head. "It was late—I figured I'd just catch up with him in the morning."

Cape nodded, understanding her absolute conviction that he didn't jump, or at least her need for it.

"So you might have been the last person he tried to speak to," he said deliberately, watching her across the desk. "Before he died."

"Yes," said Grace bitterly. "Only I wasn't there for him."

"That doesn't mean you could have saved him," said Cape. "If he was really depressed about something—"

Grace cut him off. "I know Tom—I've worked with him on three other pictures. He was always mooning over his daughter, couldn't wait to see her again after a shoot. And he loved the business—he lived for it. He was *not* a jumper, plain and simple."

"Was there a note?"

Grace nodded reluctantly. "Typed into his computer."

"What did it say?"

"*I'm sorry.*"

"That's it?" Cape couldn't help himself. "That's not much of a note."

"*That's because he didn't jump.*"

Cape held up his hands. "You knew him, I didn't. Fair enough. What do the cops say?"

Grace relaxed only slightly, her arms back in her lap. "The police don't know what they're talking about."

"That wasn't my question."

Grace blew out her cheeks. "There was no sign of foul play. There's every indication Tom drove onto the bridge by himself, abandoned his car, and jumped."

"Anything else?"

"Yeah," she replied disdainfully. "The police said they'd notified the family, so it was their concern, not mine. And unless there was a basis for an investigation, they had to put their energies into solving real murders with real suspects."

Cape wasn't surprised. Cops wanted evidence, not theories or hunches. It was one of the reasons he wasn't a cop.

"So what do you want me to do?" he asked.

"Find them a suspect," Grace replied.

3

THE DEAD MAN'S EYES stared accusingly at the two policemen. Strangulation had caused the eyes to bulge and turn outward, giving the illusion that the corpse was scowling at both men simultaneously, angry at being excluded from their conversation.

"Who did you say he was again?"

Vincent Mango looked almost as annoyed as the corpse, but anyone who knew him would swear that was his normal expression. Even with risers in the heels of his Italian loafers, his wiry frame stood just over five and a half feet tall, so he compensated by acting testy. His short black hair was slick above a high, pale forehead, and he was dressed impeccably, right down to the Glock on his right hip, his detective shield clipped on his left side so he'd look symmetrical.

"Real name was Otto Metzger. Most people called him Otto the Kraut, but never to his face."

The voice that answered nearly rattled the windows. Beauregard Jones stood very still as he spoke, as if worried about crushing his diminutive partner. At six-five and almost 240 pounds, all he had to do was fall over. His face was a mahogany mask that would have been inscrutable if not for the eyes. Twenty years on the force had given him cop eyes that could go from open and friendly to flat and deadly in a heartbeat. He wore high-tops, jeans, and a black T-shirt with a weathered shoulder rig stretched tightly across his chest, holding a Springfield forty-five stainless. A sizable firearm, it looked like a toy against Beau's massive frame.

"Otto was the man in the middle," added Beau, as if that explained everything.

Vincent scratched his right ear. "Middle of what?"

Looking at the smaller man with a hint of amusement in his eyes, Beau leaned forward and pointed at the table in front of them. "Those are drugs, Vinnie—heroin, if you want to get specific."

Vincent glanced at the worktable in front of them, taking note of the scarred Formica, the four steel legs running to the cracked and faded tile floor. Scattered across its surface was everything you needed to make a sandwich, including cold cuts, sausages, string, plastic—and Otto, his feet splayed and hanging off the edge.

He wore a butcher's apron over brown canvas pants, his leather shoes stained from years of animal blood and worn from miles of pacing behind a deli counter. His hands were thick and coarse, the veins prominent even in death. But beyond those simple observations, it was impossible to tell what the man had resembled in life. Beneath the protruding eyes, his nose flared angrily, a last attempt to draw breath into failing lungs. His tongue jutted obscenely between cracked lips, a thin line of blood visible where he'd bitten down in agony. The right temple looked bruised, a purplish welt visible above the eye. Otto had not gone quietly, but to determine the cause of death you only had to look at his throat.

His neck looked raw where a coarse brown string cut across the Adam's apple and disappeared where it broke the skin. The chosen instrument of death appeared to come from a small pile of cord near Otto's leg, the thick strands coiled next to a broken pyramid of sausage links.

Finally Vincent let his eyes follow the line of Beau's enormous arm to a spot on the table just above Otto's swollen face where a sausage lay snapped in half. The sausage itself was a good foot and a half in length and four inches in diameter. It had split laterally, but instead of the normal mottled coloring of pressed meat, the broken sausage revealed a stark white interior, a plastic tube hidden within its length. From the end of the broken tube spilled a brown powder with the consistency of flour.

"I know it's heroin," said Vincent. "Just 'cause you used to work Narcotics doesn't mean—"

A uniformed cop with more pimples than bullets interrupted with a short step forward and a cough. "Detective?"

"The ME here?" asked Beau.

The cop shook his head. "No, sir, but the techs would like to start tagging and bagging, if you don't mind."

Beau looked at Vincent, who took one more glance at Otto before moving over toward the deli counter about ten feet away. "Be my guest."

Beau started to join him when his phone rang, the vibration making him jump. He pulled the phone out of its holster and stepped away as a choreographed swarm of crime-scene technicians buzzed around the worktable, gloved hands and tweezers moving back and forth with practiced ease.

"Who?" said Beau, holding the phone to his right ear. "Send him here. Yes, to the deli." Beau took a deep breath but kept his voice mild. "I know it's a crime scene—it's *my* crime scene—I'll arrest him myself if he disturbs any evidence. And tell him I'll only be here another thirty minutes." He snapped the phone shut and stood next to Vincent, who was leaning against a refrigerated display cabinet containing as many different meats as there were animals on Noah's Ark. Proudly stenciled in orange and black lettering across the glass was *Otto's Meat*.

"So it's heroin," said Vincent. "Which tells us Otto probably didn't pay his taxes."

Beau shook his head. "It doesn't matter *what* it is, Vinnie. What matters is *who* it belongs to."

Vincent sighed—there was no stopping Beau when he was in his element. Vincent often wondered why his partner left Narcotics in the first place.

"So who does it belong to?"

Beau rubbed his hands together. "You ready for Narcotics 101?"

"The suspense is fuckin' killing me."

"You might have noticed that Otto's little deli sits right at the intersection of San Francisco's two most popular neighborhoods, North Beach and Chinatown."

"I live here, too, asshole."

Beau continued, unfazed. "The tongs run Chinatown—the gangs get their smack from the Triads in Hong Kong, who bring it in from the Golden Triangle. Got it?"

"As long as there's no pop quiz later, we're good."

Beau ignored him. "Then in North Beach, the Italians—"

13

"Hey," snapped Vincent. "Don't start with the ethnic generalizations—I'm Italian, you know."

"With a name like Mango?" said Beau, laughter in his eyes. "I always thought you were named after a fruit, Vinnie. And seeing as how you dress, I just figured—"

"Funny, coming from a guy whose socks don't match."

Beau looked down at his ankles, frowning.

"OK, Vinnie," he said calmly. "From North Beach, *the mob*—an organization primarily run by Italian-Americans like yourself—distributes the heroin."

"Much better," said Vincent. "And Otto was the bagman?"

Beau nodded. "Narcotics watched his place for years, but Otto was too slippery."

"Never heard of him."

Beau shrugged. "Not surprised—both his business partners own plenty of judges in this town. They needed Otto—the Italians and Chinese don't always get along so well—turf wars, that kind of nonsense."

"We haven't had any of that shit for years."

"Didn't happen very often. One side would cut into the other's action, then all hell would break loose. That is, until they agreed the drug trade was too important to be disrupted."

"So?"

"So we have Fat Frank Alessi on the Italian side of Broadway distributing smack bought from Freddie Wang in Chinatown. And then you have Otto the Kraut." Beau gestured at the table. "Whose German deli became the neutral ground where all controlled substances could be exchanged."

"Germany as the neutral party," mused Vinnie. "That's gotta be a first."

"Was that some kind of *ethnic generalization*?"

"What do you care?" said Vincent defensively.

"Seems like a double standard," replied Beau. "'Specially from a politically correct guy like you."

Vincent started to respond when Cape ducked under the police tape stretched across the entrance. The uniformed cop gave him a dubious glance but let him pass.

Cape lingered for a moment next to Otto and the technicians, his blue eyes darkening as he studied the corpse. After a moment, he tore himself away and gingerly stepped around markers and photographic equipment before shaking hands with both detectives. "When you told me to meet you here instead of your office, I figured you were going to buy me lunch."

Beau chuckled, a seismic tremor deep in his chest. "Dream on. You want to meet me, you come to me. I'm a cop—the street is my office."

"*The street is my office?*" said Cape. "Is that this year's bumper sticker for the police cruisers?"

Beau scowled. Cape gestured toward the corpse. "What happened to him?"

"You saw the body," said Beau. "Someone choked the shit out of him after smacking him over the head."

"Smacked with his own smack," said Vincent.

Beau nodded. "Poor Otto was *KO'd by a kielbasa*."

Cape shook his head. "Summer sausage."

"What?"

15

"I'm pretty sure that's a summer sausage," said Cape, gesturing toward Otto before turning and pointing at the glass case behind them. "My mom worked in a butcher shop her whole life, remember? A kielbasa is a Polish sausage, like that one."

Beau look bemused. "So?"

"It's more narrow and usually curved—it lacks sufficient tensile strength to be used as a bludgeon."

Beau looked at his friend with heavy-lidded eyes. "Whatever. I just liked the alliteration—you know, *KO'd by a*—"

"No, he's right." Vincent chimed in. "No way that's a kielbasa. Might be a bratwurst, though. They're nice and thick—you could definitely stun a man with a bratwurst."

"They're usually shorter than that, though," said Cape. "And wider. But you're right. You could do some damage with a bratwurst."

"How about a *chourica*?" suggested Vincent. "I once had one at a Spanish restaurant. Had heartburn for a week."

Beau frowned. *"Chore-eek-uh?"*

"It's Portuguese," explained Cape, squinting through the glass. "A heartier, spiced meat. Pretty good size, too."

Vincent bent over the glass case next to him. "Is it that one?"

Cape nodded. "I don't think you could kill a man, but you'd definitely get his attention. And there's a *linguica*—that's another possibility."

"What's that?"

"Another Portuguese sausage. About the same size, but made of pork."

"It would make a pretty good weapon," said Vincent admiringly.

16

"Much milder than the chourica," said Cape. "You should try it sometime."

"I'll tell my wife," said Vincent, pulling a notebook out of his suit jacket. "How do you spell that?"

"Will you two knock it off?" Beau snatched the pen from Vincent and threw it at Cape, who ducked. It flew across the deli, narrowly missing one of the uniformed cops.

"Hey," said Vincent. "That was my good pen."

Beau ignored him. "While you two are comparing recipes, our friend Otto is getting stiffer and smellier by the minute."

"He's not going anywhere," muttered Vincent, waving at the uniform to retrieve his pen.

Beau turned his bulk on Cape. "Don't make me sorry I invited you down here, brother—you said it was important."

"It is."

"Well then, since your little seminar on deadly meat by-products is over, maybe you could cut to the chase and let us get back to work."

Cape looked from Beau to Vincent. "I need a favor."

Beau opened his eyes wide and made the letter O with his mouth. "I'm shocked," he said.

"Stunned," added Vincent.

"Speechless," said Beau.

"Fuck you," said Cape. "Fuck you both."

Beau laughed. "I think we hurt his feelings, Vinnie."

"You done?" said Cape. "Or just warming up to do 'Who's On First?'"

Beau looked at Vincent, who shrugged. "We're done, but this better be good."

"It is," said Cape.

"What's the favor?"

"I want you to arrest my client."

4

"YOU WANT ME TO go to jail?"

"No, I want you to get arrested."

"And you're sure there's a difference?"

"Pretty sure."

Cape sat across from Grace at a small window table in Town's End, a breakfast place along the waterfront not far from Cape's office. He ate breakfast there more often than most people eat breakfast, and the owners let him meet clients after they closed up for the morning. Even at eleven o'clock, the smell of freshly baked pastries hung in the air like a fat man's narcotic.

Though running had kept the calories from doing too much damage, Cape had developed a severe addiction to the miniature scones, which were complimentary and served in a basket on every table. He'd considered seeking professional help but lost his resolve at the first sight of wicker and checkered cloth.

Grace took a bite from a cranberry muffin and talked around it. "No offense, but when you say you're *pretty sure*, it doesn't inspire a lot of confidence."

Cape looked at his client before answering, gauging her stress. He also liked looking at her. She was wearing black pants made from some fabric developed at a NASA research lab, a gray sweatshirt with *UCLA* across the front, and a pair of low black shoes that Cape suspected cost more than his car. Her dark hair was pulled back into a ponytail, revealing diamond-stud earrings. Cape noticed she didn't wear any rings on either hand. He couldn't decide if she was dressed to work, dance, or ride a motorcycle.

Grace frowned. "As far as the police are concerned, there is no case."

"True."

"So why would they arrest me?"

Cape palmed another scone. He'd already lost count. "Because I asked them to."

"Are the local police always this accommodating to city residents?"

"Only if you pay your taxes."

"Can they be trusted? There's a lot of police corruption on *Law & Order*."

"Then it must be true," said Cape. "But you can trust this cop."

Grace looked skeptical. "How well do you know him?"

Cape shrugged. "He arrested me once, so I guess you could call us friends."

Grace waited for an explanation. When none came, she just stared. Cape stared back, a pleasant expression on his face.

Grace blinked.

"And why should he do you a favor?"

"I did a favor for him once."

"What did you do?"

"You must have missed that episode of *Law & Order*."

Grace took the hint. "I guess you wouldn't have many clients if you weren't discreet."

"I don't have many clients."

"Maybe because you want them to get arrested."

"Now we're getting somewhere," said Cape. "The police will either say they got a tip, or maybe we'll have you walk into the precinct and confess."

"Confess?"

"If you do that, then legally they have to question you, which means they've started a murder investigation."

"Confess?" repeated Grace, shifting in her seat. "But I'm the one trying to get an investigation started, remember? I had nothing to do with Tom's murder."

"*If* it was a murder—"

"It *was* a murder," Grace snapped, her nostrils flaring.

Cape held up his hands.

"What I was explaining," he said evenly, "is that if it *was* a murder, then by definition there must be a murderer somewhere."

"OK," said Grace cautiously.

"A murderer who thinks he—or she—got away with it. Most murders are solved within forty-eight hours or never solved at all."

Grace nodded. "I saw that on *CSI*."

Cape started to say something sarcastic but caught himself. She was paying his day rate, after all, and she had a natural disadvantage—she worked in Hollywood.

He said, "So the murderer is watching for any sign of trouble even as we sit here eating scones."

"I haven't had any scones," said Grace, picking at her muffin protectively. "You've eaten them all."

Cape smiled apologetically.

"We'll order more."

"I'm confused," said Grace.

"I want to send a message—we want the killer to know that the cops think Tom was a murder victim and not a suicide. It's more important that the cops *are* investigating a murder than *who* they're investigating at this point."

"I get it," said Grace. "Then what happens?"

"I call a reporter who works at one of the local papers and say the cops think maybe the jumper was murdered. They might even take your picture coming out of the precinct."

Grace sank down in her seat. "Is that really necessary?"

Cape shrugged. "If the bad guys can read, they'll know someone's nosing around their business."

"And you're pretty sure this will work?"

Cape shrugged again. "It's all about provoking a reaction."

"You sound more like a pain in the ass than a detective."

"I don't have the lab equipment they use on *CSI*," replied Cape. "A common misconception from TV and the movies is that clues are just lying around, waiting to be followed back to the villain's lair."

"Villain's lair?" Grace arched her eyebrows.

"I read a lot of comic books as a kid."

"So what do you think will happen?"

"No clue," said Cape. "I'm a pretty straightforward guy—to figure out what's going on, I usually have to piss someone off."

"Who are you trying to piss off?"

"The person or persons who threw your friend off the bridge," said Cape. "Or maybe the people who paid them to do it."

It was the answer Grace was waiting for. She took a deep breath and let it out, the tension in her face disappearing for the first time since Cape met her.

"So you believe me." She made it sound like a statement, not a question.

"I trust you," said Cape. "There's a difference."

Grace smiled.

"Do you think you could give me a ride to the police station? I have to confess to a murder."

"Sure," said Cape.

5

THE ZOO WAS IN an uproar.

Every time the panther roared, the antelope jumped—kicking and snorting—clueless about the fences separating them from the great cat. One or two invariably ran headlong into the metal fencing, which made a metallic sound that scared the shit out of the birds in the surrounding trees, causing them to fly in panicked circles. The squawking of the birds sounded like human screams.

The panther roared again.

It paced hungrily beneath the man tied to the rope, a guttural sound replacing the roar as it licked its lips. It was a primal sound, heavy with bass that hit you deep in the gut, telling you to run, get the hell out of there. Death was coming to dinner.

But there was nowhere for the man to run. With one leg tied to a rope secured with enough duct tape to fix the economy, all he could do was scramble around the cage, hoping to stay out of reach of the enormous black cat.

"The problem with the zoo is that most of your big jungle animals are nocturnal."

Frank Alessi spoke slowly from outside the protective bars of the panther's cell, careful to make every word heard over the animal buzz all around him. "Nocturnal means they wake up at night, by the way. So when busloads of kids pour through the gates to see the ferocious lions, tigers, and bears, all they see are big piles of fur, asleep in the corner."

Frank took the chewed cigar from his mouth and pointed at the man dangling above the panther.

"If you ask me, it's all a big scam."

The man on the rope said something in Chinese and spat, twisting his body to aim at Frank. He'd managed to climb one of the tall boulders the zoo designers had placed inside the supposedly natural habitat, but his perch was precarious, so his options for a dignified response were limited.

Frank leaned forward solicitously. "Sorry, I didn't quite catch that." He turned toward two men standing by the fence, gesturing once again with his cigar. They yanked the rope, dragging the man to the edge of the boulder. The panther growled as it suddenly vanished, then reappeared as it moved in and out of shadow. The man twisted frantically but only succeeded in swinging wildly back and forth.

"I asked you a question," said Frank, his belly pressing against the iron fence that separated the general public from the African veldt during normal visiting hours. Beyond the fence was a cement ditch twenty feet deep and maybe ten feet wide, too far for the panther to jump, and too smooth for the man to climb. Trees stood on both sides of the fence, their branches intertwining to form a latticework of leaves overhead. The boughs were thick enough to support the strain on the rope as it pulled back and forth, held fast by the two goons.

The man closest to Frank was maybe six feet tall but wide as a refrigerator. The guy to his right was tall and lean with a beak for a nose, so hooked it made him look like a hawk with a sinus infection. They watched impassively as Frank continued his lecture.

"My good friend Otto the butcher got himself killed." He strolled casually away from his captive, running his hand along the fence, then turned back and switched hands. "Now it looks as though Otto might have been socking away some product for a rainy day, maybe cutting his own deals on the side. It's not like we ever asked him to stuff his sausages. But be that as it may, none of my guys would have done something so—" Frank paused, looking over his shoulder at the two men.

"Rash," said the hawk-nosed thug.

"Right," said Frank, smiling. "My guys would never do something so *rash*. And neither would any of our business associates, not without telling me first."

The man on the rope twisted around like a spent yo-yo, then spun in the opposite direction without saying anything.

Frank shrugged. "To kill Otto like that was, well, it's … " His voice trailed off.

"Imprudent," whispered the hawk.

Frank shook his head, annoyed.

"Unwise?"

Frank smiled.

"It was *unwise*," he said.

The man on the rope said nothing. His eyes darted frantically around the cage, but he'd already run around its perimeter looking for a hiding place. Anytime he moved out of sight, the rope was pulled violently, dragging him to the ground. His face was covered in cuts and bruises and his nails had torn off trying to break through the tape, but only a serrated knife could cut that rope.

And now the great cat was not only awake but pissed. It was tired of the chase. The panther had stopped pacing and was sitting in a crouch, its paws moving excitedly, a big cat waiting for the catnip mouse to come within reach.

Frank cleared his throat. "Which brings me to the logical deduction that you and your Chinese pals had a little disagreement with Otto about his cut, so you decided..."

"To cut Otto out of the picture."

"Exactly." Frank nodded. "You wanted a bigger cut, so you cut him out. I like that."

The hawk man looked at his partner and raised his eyebrows, a smug look on his face. The refrigerator just shook his head.

The man didn't answer. He'd managed to scuttle back from the edge of the boulder but his legs were wobbling, the surface too narrow for him. He'd gained a few inches but was still only three feet from the swinging paws.

"Why go and do a thing like that?" demanded Frank. "Otto's deli was the perfect drop site—not your turf, and not mine. Why would you *stupid tong bastards* ruin something so sweet, unless you decided you didn't need Otto anymore?"

The man on the rope caught the tone in Frank's voice and spun around, tearing his eyes away from the shifting ground in front of him.

"And if you don't need Otto, then maybe you don't need Frank either."

The man's eyes were wide, the fear visible even in the dark.

"Not—not us," he said in halting English. "Not Chinese."

Frank screwed up his face and scratched his cheek, looking about as contemplative as an angry hippo.

"I didn't ask *if* you did it," said Frank. "I asked *why*."

Before his captive could answer, Frank walked away from the fence, past his two men.

"Pull the rope," he muttered. "I'm going home to get some sleep."

The two thugs obliged, putting their backs into the effort.

The panther roared and the zoo exploded with sound. The antelope ran, scaring the birds, which screamed just loudly enough to drown out the sounds of a man being eaten alive.

6

CAPE HEARD A GROWL and realized it was coming from his stomach.

Golden Gate Park is a good spot for a picnic. It's roughly three miles long and half a mile wide where it runs into the Pacific Ocean on the western edge of San Francisco, so even on the weekends there's plenty of room to spread out. A free patch of grass for residents of a city where housing is too expensive for anyone to afford a backyard.

Cape considered it the perfect rendezvous point for meeting his friend from the newspaper. Though Linda Katz lived and worked in the city, she spent all her free time away from office buildings, restaurants, and most public transportation. She wasn't claustrophobic, nor did she dislike people. What she hated was electricity.

While everyone else in town worried about earthquakes, Linda was convinced electromagnetic radiation would be the end of her. One conversation on a cell phone and tumors would blossom in her brain like dandelions. A ride on one of those electric buses hooked to the power lines above the streets and all her hair would fall out.

This last concern was considerable, since Linda's hair practically had its own zip code. Never tamed by a hair dryer or electric shears, her hair moved seemingly of its own accord, expressing Linda's feelings more clearly than anything she ever said or did. Right now it was shifting unsteadily in the breeze, moving suspiciously back and forth as Linda looked at the picnic spread before her.

"You're feeding me. How big is this favor you're asking?"

Cape looked up from the cheese and crackers with a wounded expression.

"Isn't this nice?" He swept his arm toward the field around them. "No antennas, no high-tension wires."

Linda shrugged. "We're still in a nexus," she said, reaching into the basket for a bottle of water.

"A what?"

"A nexus," she repeated. "An electromagnetic vortex caused by the surrounding transmission towers for cell phones, the nearby power generator for the park lights, not to mention the radiation from the cars passing by."

"You seem awfully calm for someone sitting in a nexus."

Linda shrugged again. "I'm not a Luddite, you know. I just try to limit *unnecessary* exposure. Compared to someone who makes a living trying to get people to shoot at him, I consider myself quite balanced."

"I usually don't ask them to shoot at me—it just happens."

"I even agreed to use an electric typewriter at work."

"Not a computer?"

"Don't push it." Linda's hair assumed a menacing posture. Cape decided to change the subject.

"How are things at *The Examiner*?"

"It pays the rent," she said. "And every once in a while, it feels like you're making a difference."

"You've always been an optimist." Cape first met Linda when they were both working as investigative reporters at *The San Francisco Chronicle*. Linda was already a veteran when Cape arrived. He was a transplant from New York with a knack for finding people who didn't want to be found. He also had a talent for pissing off his editor. Linda took him under her wing, taught him some manners, and had mothered him ever since. He smiled briefly at the memory. "By the way, sorry that vegetarian paper you were editing on the side had to fold."

"That was the problem—it *wouldn't* fold." Linda snorted in disgust. "The paper was made from corn husks, more environmentally friendly than recycled paper, which rarely gets recycled anyway. So the publishers found someone who made this vegetable papyrus for the paper stock. But you couldn't fold it, the pages would stick together, and the ink would run. It was a paper you could boil and eat, but you couldn't read it. Even I thought the publishers went too far."

"Sounds very San Francisco," said Cape.

"Very stupid," said Linda as she grabbed a carrot stick. "The experience proved that being a vegetarian does wonders for your body, but unfortunately very little for your IQ—so I kept my diet and quit the job."

"You seem happy with your day job."

"*The Examiner*'s a kick," replied Linda. "Since they changed to a tabloid format they've been willing to take risks. The city desk editor is willing to push the boundaries."

"Then you'll love this story."

Linda took a sip from her water. "You said it had something to do with the bridge jumper?"

Cape outlined his meeting with Grace, smiling to himself as Linda's eyes grew wide and her hair stood on end. She was hooked.

"So the suicide's a murder?"

Cape shrugged. "That's what my client says."

"And you believe him?"

"Her," said Cape. "My client's a *she*."

Linda frowned, a worried crease appearing between her eyes. "Uh-oh."

"What's that supposed to mean?" said Cape indignantly.

Linda looked at the blanket while her hair shrugged noncommittally.

"Nothing. It's just that you have a tendency to … well, you know …"

"What?"

"I think it's called a *paladin complex*," said Linda. "Every woman is a damsel in distress, and you're the knight in shining armor—you feel a moral obligation to help them. It probably has something to do with your mother."

"Oh, *Christ*."

"Good point," said Linda, nodding, "You probably have a *Christ complex*, too. You want to save everybody and you're willing to sacrifice yourself to do it. So maybe you'd be just as obsessive if she were a man."

Cape sighed.

"You have to admit," pressed Linda, "that every time we go to lunch or dinner, you fall in love with the waitress."

"I have a healthy appetite."

"Forget I said anything."

"Can I get off the couch now?"

Linda kept her mouth shut but her hair laughed silently.

Cape blew out his cheeks. "As I was saying, my client worked with the guy who jumped. They worked together for almost ten years and co-produced four movies."

"Co-produced?"

"The way she described it, Tom typically handled shooting at the studios, on the big sound stages in Hollywood."

"OK."

"Grace handled scouting and location shooting. And Tom handled most of the budgeting."

"Most?"

"Grace manages her segments of the movie, but Tom managed the overall budget, making sure everyone's segment added up to the same bottom line for the studio."

"Which studio do they work for?"

"Empire Films."

Linda sat up straighter. "Didn't they make that gay astronaut movie?"

Cape nodded. "That's one of theirs."

"I loved that film."

"So did everyone else," said Cape. "The last American male archetype, shattered."

"That's what they said about the gay cowboy movie."

"Yeah, but when you're gay in space, there's no one to hear you scream."

Linda's brow furrowed. "Wasn't that the line from *Alien*?"

"Not exactly."

Linda's politically correct instincts kicked in and she frowned disapprovingly. Cape thought her hair liked the joke, but he couldn't be sure.

"It was a great movie," said Linda.

Cape nodded. "Yeah, it was. And Grace tells me it made a fortune for the studio. The big actors treated it like an art film, so they all cut their salaries."

"So the box office receipts went to the bottom line."

"Yeah. And they bought the script for next to nothing, because all the studios in Hollywood had already passed on it."

"That's right, Empire is based in New York, aren't they? I read an article in the *Times*—it referred to them as Hollywood outsiders."

Cape nodded. "Two brothers—Harry and Adam Berman."

"I saw their picture, standing on their yacht in New York Harbor," said Linda. "Is Harry the fat one or the tall one?"

"I'm not sure," replied Cape. "For all I know, he might be the tall, fat one."

"Do they know you're working on this?"

"Not yet."

"Have you talked to anyone from the studio besides your client?"

"No," said Cape. "Before she went to the police station, Grace called the head of operations at Empire—a guy named Angelo—and told him what she was doing."

Linda raised her eyebrows. "How did that go over?"

"I guess he was pissed—Grace said he's kind of a control freak."

"Your favorite."

"Well," said Cape, "I can understand his reaction. They are in the middle of a movie, and they're down one producer."

"Who might have been murdered."

"I have a feeling we're the only ones who believe that."

"We?" said Linda, her eyebrows once again heading north.

"I meant Grace and me—but I'm glad you're on our side already."

Linda smiled, knowing exactly what he meant.

"So what do you want me to do?" she asked cautiously. "I may work for a budding tabloid, but I do have standards."

Cape tried to look vulnerable but gave up. No one could bullshit Linda, and he didn't have it in him anyway.

"The studio is screwed if Grace walks from this picture, so they have to indulge her murder theory, at least for now."

"OK."

"But they don't know *me* from a key grip on one of their sets."

"I always wondered what a key grip does," mused Linda. "You think the studio may not be entirely forthcoming."

"The studio doesn't want to risk too much publicity, let alone an investigation."

"What if there really was a murder?"

"To hear Grace describe it, there could be ten murders a day and the studio wouldn't launch an investigation if they thought it would interfere with production. That's apparently Angelo's real job—keep things running, no matter the cost."

"Sounds like his idea of an investigation and yours might be a little different," said Linda, her hair bouncing in anticipation.

"But my approach is to stir things up as much as possible, since you never know who might be hiding something."

Linda nodded. "You're a pain in the ass."

"That's what they're afraid of," said Cape. "Grace wants me to proceed with the investigation but somehow stay off Angelo's radar."

"How are you supposed to do that?"

"I think it comes down to two things."

"The first?"

"Don't do anything that interferes with the production of this movie."

"And the second?" asked Linda.

"Keep the investigation as low-profile as possible," replied Cape.

"Not likely."

"That's the hard part," said Cape. "My guess is Angelo won't like it if I do anything to embarrass him."

"So what do you want me to do?"

"Embarrass him for me," replied Cape.

Linda smiled.

"Do you think you can do that?" asked Cape.

"You bet."

7

IF YOU ASKED BOBBY McGhill to tell you the best thing about a trip to the zoo, he'd tell you without hesitation it was the yellow slide. Some kids in his fourth grade class hung out at the snack bar, others loved riding the train, and most liked looking at the animals. But the food was gross, the train went too slow, and the animals always slept during the day. Bobby thought it was dumb to pay five bucks admission to watch a lion snore. For Bobby, the slide was the only reason to come to the zoo.

The yellow slide was awesome because it wasn't just a slide—it was a giant plastic tube, so once you jumped inside you disappeared. Hidden from view until you hit the sand below. And today was going to be even better, because Bobby and his mom were first in line at the zoo's entrance. So before any other kids tracked sand and pebbles down the slide that would slow you down, Bobby would be at the top of the ladder, the first to reach the bottom.

But Bobby never made it to the bottom of the slide, because after he jumped inside he just ... *disappeared.*

His mom waited a full thirty seconds for him to come out, anticipation turning to anxiety until she heard her son's muffled cries. Without hesitation, Mrs. McGhill scampered up the ladder and dove after her son. Her legs were still sticking out of the top of the tube when their combined screams got the attention of a young couple watching their two-year-old play in the sand.

The couple ran to the nearby concession stand, where the woman behind the counter called the front office. When a security guard finally arrived and looked up the tube to see what was blocking the McGhill family's descent, he dropped to his knees in the sand and vomited.

Pretty soon after that, the zoo was closed. It wasn't much longer before the police arrived.

Cape showed up an hour later, ducking carefully under the yellow tape marking the crime scene. Two uniformed officers were carefully removing the top half of the plastic tube from which they'd already extracted a hysterical mother and son. A guy from the medical examiner's office was yelling at them to not disturb the body. Cape couldn't see a body from where he was standing, but as the officers shifted position he noticed a dark patch of sand at the base of the slide. Vincent Mango was kneeling and poking tentatively at the sand with a pencil. When he saw Cape, he nodded but stayed where he was.

Beau detached himself from a pack of techs and walked over, smiling.

"Welcome to the San Francisco Zoo."

"How come you're always inviting me to these little get-togethers of yours?" asked Cape. "You and Vinnie need a chaperone?"

"You called me, dickhead, or don't you remember?"

"I forgot—*the street is your office.*"

"Sorry I don't have regular office hours, but I'm workin' for the taxpayers."

"I'm a taxpayer," said Cape defensively.

"Not enough so I'd notice."

"What's in the slide?"

"Don't you mean *who*?"

"I'm not sure from here," replied Cape. "Are you?"

"Pretty sure," said Beau, scratching his head. "Not that you should give a shit, but I'm pretty sure it's Cecil Yun."

"Yun?" Cape's brow furrowed. "'Cecil' doesn't strike me as your typical Chinese name."

"Cecil wasn't your typical Chinese guy," said Beau. "He handled the business side of Freddie Wang's business."

"You mean the drug business."

Beau nodded. "Among other things. Freddie has a diversified portfolio of unsavory business."

"Cecil was a money guy?"

"Uh-huh. Pretty hands-on in the drug trade."

"So what's that mean for your other investigation?"

Beau frowned, the lines in his face like cracks in obsidian. "I hate to admit it, but it might mean Frank Alessi didn't whack Otto the Butcher."

"Payback?"

Beau shrugged. "Cecil wasn't treated so well before he got shoved in the tube. There's a blood trail from the panther's cage, and the body's definitely been mauled—you can tell just looking down the tube at his legs, but give the ME ten minutes and he'll confirm it."

"If the panther killed him, why drag him over here?"

"He was probably still alive." Vincent had walked over to join them. He bent over to brush sand from his slacks. "Hell of a view up that slide—half the head is missing. Someone shot Cecil in the face before they stuffed him down there."

"Somebody was pretty pissed off at Cecil," said Cape.

Beau shook his head. "Someone wanted to send somebody else a message. I'd bet my left nut that someone is Fat Frank, telling Freddie Wang he's pissed about Otto."

"What about your right nut?" asked Cape.

Beau shrugged. "Holding on to it for collateral—might need it for my next case."

"Can we talk about something other than Beau's balls?" said Vincent.

"How'd it go with Grace?" asked Cape. "I'm meeting her at my office later and wanted to check your gut."

Beau raised his eyebrows. "You saying you don't trust your client?"

"I trust her," replied Cape evenly. "I just want to know if you trust her."

"My … my." Beau smiled. "Has experience made you wiser?"

"What's that supposed to mean?"

"Well, you forgot to mention your new client was so damned attractive."

Vincent nodded. "A looker."

"Maybe I didn't notice," replied Cape. "I am a professional."

Beau snorted. "A professional investigator's *supposed* to notice things."

"I guess I'll have to investigate further."

Beau laughed. "That's what I'm worried about."

Cape held up a hand in warning. "Don't *you* start. I already got an earful from Linda."

"I'm starting nothing—and make sure you don't, either. Just because the lady needs your help doesn't mean you get your white horse out of the stable."

"Was that a metaphor?" asked Cape. "Or an analogy?"

"You're a lost cause," replied Beau. "You know that, don't you?"

Cape ignored the bait. "You didn't answer my question."

Beau spread his arms and stretched, blotting out the sun. "Grace was cool when we questioned her, but the story didn't track. Just a list of reasons why her partner wouldn't want to go swimming in the bay. But we'll toss the guy's hotel room, maybe ask around the movie set."

"Standard follow-up," said Vincent.

Cape nodded. "Not surprised. She's more hunch than fact right now."

"Well, it's on you," said Beau, putting his hand on Cape's shoulder. It felt like a titanium catcher's mitt. He raised the arm and waved it in an arc around the playground. "As you can see, the police got real murders to investigate. No way we'll give your client's hunch more than a day's worth of looking."

Cape held out his hand. "More than I deserve—I owe you one."

"You definitely owe me," agreed Beau. "But I'm pretty sure it's more than one."

"Put it on my tab. And good luck hunting Fat Frank."

"I ain't interested in hunting anymore," said Beau, his cop eyes hard and flat again. "I plan on *catching* next time."

Being hunted by Beau was not something most people survived. As Cape crossed the police tape and headed for the exit, he almost felt sorry for Frank Alessi. The feeling was gone by the time he reached his car.

The fog had crept over the hills to wrap the zoo in a wet blanket. Cape turned up his collar and wondered whom he was hunting and whether they even existed outside his client's imagination.

8

—

"How does it feel to be famous?"

"Don't you mean infamous?"

Cape didn't answer, gesturing at the newspaper on his desk. Long shadows swam across the walls of his office as the sun sank into the bay outside. Grace was almost in silhouette, the circle of light from the small desk lamp not quite reaching her face.

Cape made no move to turn on the lights. Even in the dark he was reminded of Beau's astute observation—she was attractive. Better to keep the lights low. The last thing Cape needed right now was another distraction.

"This is embarrassing," said Grace. Her right index finger came down hard on the paper, her polished nail glowing in the small pool of light. The headline said it all:

Movie Mogul Murder Mystery!

Four *M*s in a row had to be a tabloid record for alliteration. When Cape called Linda to congratulate her, she told him she wanted to add *Mayhem* at the end, but her editor said four was the limit—stringing five words together in a single headline might call into question the paper's journalistic integrity. Cape admired their restraint. It was important to have standards.

Despite the bombastic opening, the article hit all the right notes. Grace was described as having been brought in for questioning, but the article gave the impression she was the first of many interviews—neither the instigator of the inquiry nor a suspect. Cape was mentioned as an independent investigator hired by the studio. Linda had agreed that any heat should be directed toward him and not his client. They even spelled his name correctly, something his own bank couldn't seem to manage.

"It's not so bad," said Cape, absently turning the front page. "You came across exactly as you should—a colleague of the victim who wants to help the police in their investigation."

"Will there be an investigation?"

"They said they'd look into it."

"That's it?" asked Grace. "There's nothing else you can do?"

"There's plenty I could do," said Cape calmly. "But it would be a waste of time."

"Why?"

"The police are better at this than I am," he said simply. "They have more resources and more legal means of finding out what your friend Tom was up to—warrants, badges, that sort of thing."

"Then why am I still paying you?"

"I bet you're a good producer."

"Nothing personal—just curious."

"The studio should have put you in charge of the budget instead of Tom."

"Well, now they don't have any choice," said Grace. "But you didn't answer my question."

"Fair enough," replied Cape. "The cops in question are doing this as a favor, but they'll give it maybe twenty-four to forty-eight hours, tops. If it still looks like a suicide, they'll close the file."

"And then?"

"I'll be there to open it up again."

"OK," said Grace cautiously.

"Besides, I don't think we'll have to wait forty-eight hours."

"Why not?"

"Because the police will either find something right away, or nothing at all. Either way we'll learn something."

"What do we do in the meantime?"

"You should go back to work," replied Cape. "When do you start shooting again?"

"The end of the week, but there's a lot to do before then, not the least of which is to reassure the neurotic director that his movie is still on track."

"What's the director like?"

"Michael?" Grace grimaced. "I worked with him on his first film, when he was an up-and-coming talent."

"And?"

"He was great, but the last movie made a ton of money, so now he's an *auteur*, which translates from Hollywood-ese to royal pain in the ass."

"Sounds as charming as your head of operations—Angelo?"

"Asshole."

"How'd he like the article?"

Grace laughed, a sound like wind chimes laced with nicotine. "He threatened to fire me."

"Can he do that?"

"Not a chance. Only Harry and Adam Berman can do that. Angelo's just their resident bully. Besides, if they fire me in the middle of this picture, they are *fucked beyond recognition*."

Cape raised his eyebrows. "Nice turn of phrase."

Grace laughed again.

"It's a tough business, especially if you're a woman."

"You've been doing this a long time."

"Was that a statement or a question?"

"A statement, unless you tell me otherwise."

"You must be a detective," said Grace. "I started as a PA right out of college."

"PA?"

"Acronym foul," said Grace, holding up her hands. "I should have said 'production assistant.'"

"Tell me about the movie you're producing. I'd like to understand what you and Tom were doing before he—" Cape stopped himself just before saying *jumped*, adding, "died" halfheartedly before Grace noticed the slip.

She leaned back and looked at the ceiling while she talked.

"It's a forty-five day shoot, three locations, lots of green screen, thousands of extras." She moved her hands as if counting them off on her fingers. "From a production standpoint, it's a big film."

"Should I have said *film* instead of movie?" asked Cape. "Or don't distinctions like that matter?"

Grace laughed again. Cape had to admit he liked the sound.

"Actually they matter quite a bit. Most producers would claim that *film* is the celluloid equivalent of literature. It makes you think differently about the world, maybe changes some preconceived notion you had. A film stays with you long after you've watched it."

Cape's right eyebrow arched skeptically. "And a movie?"

"Two hours of entertainment," said Grace. "Fun but disposable. Pop culture at its most overt."

Cape feigned comprehension by keeping his mouth shut.

"Let's put it this way," said Grace. "Critics love films but hate movies. The Oscars love films—audiences love movies. Producers want to be known as *film* producers, but they want to be financially linked to a blockbuster *movie*."

"So what are you working on—a film or a movie?"

"Depends on who asks. The studio tells the press that it's financing a film but tells the producers to make sure it's a blockbuster movie."

"So what does that make you?"

"A film producer working on a movie."

"I have a headache," said Cape.

"Hollywood can give you one."

"But you're from New York."

"When you're in this business, everyone's from Hollywood," said Grace. "Even me."

"So what exactly are you working on?"

"The movie's called *The Revenge of Icarus*," said Grace. "Remember that big asteroid movie that broke all the box office records?"

"Which one?"

"The good one."

"Not the one with the kid on the bicycle at the end, trying to outrun the cataclysmic tidal wave?"

"God, no—that was ridiculous. Our studio made the one where the team of construction workers fly into space, land on the asteroid, and set off a nuclear bomb to save the Earth."

"Much more believable."

"We did over $300 million at the box office," replied Grace. "Do you believe that?"

"No, but what do I know? My idea of a movie is *The Maltese Falcon*."

Grace lowered her voice and slouched in her chair. *"I like talking to a man who likes to talk."*

"Sydney Greenstreet." Cape smiled. "Great movie."

"Great *film*."

"So what's *The Revenge of Icarus*?"

"The second big blockbuster from Empire Films."

"That sounds like the press release. What's the plot?"

"In the last movie, the hero died when he detonated the nuclear bomb on the asteroid to save humanity."

Cape nodded. "I wept."

Grace ignored him. "In this movie, the daughter he saved gets called by NASA to save the planet from—"

Cape cut her off. "Another asteroid?"

"Good guess."

"I am a detective."

"Only this asteroid is bigger than the last one—a lot bigger—and it's headed straight for the sun. An impact will trigger a supernova that will destroy the sun."

"Hence the title."

"Exactly. And of course, if the sun is destroyed, it will mean the end of all life on Earth."

"So it's a family picture."

"Don't be a smart-ass—it's a summer movie."

"It's not a movie," said Cape. "It's a sequel."

"You sound like a critic."

"I'm a guy who likes movies. But I'm tired of all the sequels, prequels, and movies based on old TV shows."

"Actually it's more than that. I'm producing the next installment in the *Asteroid Franchise* from Empire Films."

"You're kidding."

"That's what Hollywood is all about these days—everyone wants a *franchise*."

"So tell the studio to go buy a McDonald's."

Grace shrugged apologetically. "'Franchise' is the movie industry's euphemism for revenue stream. Batman, Star Wars, Bond, Spider-Man—those are franchises. The studio gets a built-in audience who will see the movie no matter what."

"No matter what?"

"It's basic marketing—familiarity leads to loyalty."

"I thought familiarity breeds contempt."

"Only with critics, and they don't buy enough tickets to matter anymore. And don't forget merchandising, video games, DVD sales. You can get five or more movies out of a single franchise if you know how to work it."

Cape shook his head. "So you're not making movies, you're manufacturing them."

"Welcome to Hollywood."

"Seems a shame," said Cape. "I go to the movies to see something I haven't seen before."

"But you're not the seventeen-year-old male the studio is targeting."

"Don't remind me," said Cape, looking up at the ceiling and briefly trying to remember what it was like to be seventeen. He remembered being stupid and horny, but not much else, and not necessarily in that order. He turned back to Grace.

"So doesn't anyone make original pictures these days?" he asked. "What about that gay astronaut movie your studio made?"

"That was all Harry's doing."

"Harry Berman, the guy who runs Empire Studios."

"Yeah, Harry and his brother, Adam, though it's hard to believe they're related."

"Why?"

"Harry loves movies," explained Grace. "I mean *films*—the more artsy the better. He's the one who put the studio on the map by courting stars, convincing big names to act in small films."

"How?"

"He's a visionary," said Grace. "He wanted to prove a studio could make it outside of Hollywood, so he based Empire in New York. Then he ignored all the scripts that were piling into the big studios and instead bought the rights to award-winning foreign novels, which he turned into contemporary screenplays. Then he'd tell the actors they'd get an Academy Award if they starred in one of his films."

"Pretty big promise."

"Which he's delivered on *every year*," said Grace. "Harry figured out the awards circuit. He was the first to run ads in *Variety* promoting his films around the time the judges voted. He'd re-release the films into local art theaters in the neighborhoods where the judges lived. He'd invite critics to his yacht for a movie opening and cruise around New York Harbor, plying them with drinks. He had them eating out of his hand."

"So how did they go from being the darling of the critics' circle to the giant killer asteroid?"

Grace hesitated as if trying to find a simple explanation. She bit her lower lip, working it thoughtfully between her teeth.

"Adam happened," she said finally.

"The brother."

"Yeah," said Grace. "But like I said, you'd never believe they came from the same womb. While Harry loves movies, Adam loves the movie *business*. He doesn't give a damn about awards—he just wants the biggest opening weekend in July."

"That must create a certain amount of tension around the office," said Cape.

"It used to," replied Grace. "It kept things interesting, that's for sure. And it gave people like me a chance to work on a serious film every once in a while, then go back to paying the bills with an action film. That was the financial strategy behind the studio."

"A balanced portfolio?"

"Same idea, yeah," nodded Grace. "Adam would make action flicks to get the box office and generate enough cash for Harry to make his art films with big stars."

"You keep using the past tense," observed Cape.

Grace smiled. Cape thought she looked sad but couldn't be sure in the half-light.

"Harry has become—," she hesitated for an instant, then plunged ahead. "Harry's become strange."

"Define strange."

"I mean *strange*, even by Hollywood standards," replied Grace. "He makes odd requests, then changes his mind, then calls to demand why you haven't answered his original question."

"Sounds like my ex-girlfriend."

Grace forged ahead. "Harry's alienated a lot of the celebrities he courted in the early years. And when you go to talk with him in his office, he's not even there."

"You mean he's not working?"

"I mean he's not physically there," said Grace.

Cape peered through the growing dark. "Now you're sounding strange."

Grace shook her head, annoyed. "The only thing in his office is a giant TV monitor perched on top of his desk with a remote-controlled camera on top. And on the screen is Harry—looking at you, talking to you, all via satellite."

"From where?"

"Nobody knows," replied Grace. "Harry's not telling, and neither is Adam. Sometimes the background looks like a beach house and Harry looks tan and relaxed, other times he could be in a hotel room in Berlin, for all I know. He's always looking off camera, as if he expects someone to interrupt him at any minute. Like he's paranoid."

"That's kind of strange."

"What did I tell you?" said Grace. "They say it's *sociophobia*—fear of people and normal social interaction. Greta Garbo had it.

So did Howard Hughes. They say a lot of powerful people get it. But I think it's just fucking *strange*."

"So Adam's in charge," said Cape. "Because he's there, and his brother's nuts."

Grace nodded. "So it would seem."

"Any chance either of them had anything to do with your colleague Tom's murder?"

Grace answered without hesitation. "No way."

"Convince me."

"Because Harry didn't really know Tom," she said. "Tom worked exclusively on the big action movies with Adam. And if something goes wrong with this picture, then Adam loses a lot of money for the studio."

"How much?"

"Over $200 million in production alone," said Grace. "And that's not including the cost of screwing up the franchise."

"OK," said Cape. "But I might ask Harry and Adam what they think anyway."

"If you meet them," said Grace. "Angelo may not even allow it."

"I can be very persuasive," said Cape reassuringly.

"I'm sure."

Cape noticed the crow's-feet around her eyes as he met her gaze. They sat like that for a minute, not saying anything. It was a comfortable silence on the verge of getting awkward when Grace spoke up.

"Just don't get me fired, OK?"

Cape stood up. "You're the client."

Grace stood next to the desk for a moment as if she were going to say something else, then suddenly extended her hand.

"Thanks."

"Sure." Her grip was as he remembered, strong and firm. Cape walked her to the door and listened as she went down the hallway. He flipped on the overhead lights as he stepped back into his office. He blinked against the sudden glare as he sat down and idly moved some papers across the desk.

When he heard the footsteps coming back down the hall, he felt a small knot forming in his stomach. *Excitement, anxiety, or just the lack of dinner?* Cape shook his head and smiled at his own stupidity, remembering Linda's advice. *Leave your white horse in the stable.*

As the footsteps came closer, Cape stopped smiling, discerning the staccato pattern of two sets of shoes.

Klip-klop, klip-klop.

Heavy shoes. Two men were coming down the hallway toward his office.

Or a horse, Cape thought.

It could be a white horse.

9

THE FIRST MAN INTO the office was bigger than a horse, even a Clydesdale. He actually ducked to clear the frame. The man who came second was average height but seemed as small as a child, as if Cape's brain couldn't comprehend the true size of the giant.

The smaller man wore a dark overcoat, black leather gloves, and a fedora, the kind of hat you saw in gangster movies from the fifties. Cape had always wanted one but looked ridiculous every time he tried one on. Somehow his guest managed to pull it off—maybe it was the unnaturally high forehead. Cape noticed the butt of a medium-frame automatic sticking out from a shoulder holster as the man spread his arms as if in greeting. When the man smiled, the creases alongside his mouth became black crevasses. Cape was guessing this was the bad guy.

"You are Cape Weathers," said the man deliberately. "And you are working on movie case." The accent sounded Russian or Eastern European, aggressive consonants stomping on slippery vowels.

Cape shrugged, noncommittal.

"This case," the man continued, "will be dropped."

Cape looked the man in the eye.

"Was that a question?" he asked. "Because, you know, with your accent it's kind of hard to tell if there was a question mark at the end of that sentence."

"You will drop case." It was a statement.

Cape shifted his gaze from the man in the hat to the giant. Leaning back in his chair, he smiled broadly at both of them.

"Sure," he said. "Why not?"

10

ANGELO TOOK A MOMENT to adjust the athletic cup so it didn't show under his trousers. The thing pinched like a lobster when he walked, but why take chances? Angelo believed in being prepared, even if he probably wouldn't need it today. The boss couldn't hit the side of a barn after two o'clock in the afternoon.

Michael Angelo took a lot of shit for his name when he was growing up. Other kids would ask him to paint their ceilings, do their portraits, that sort of thing. What made it worse, years later, was learning that his mother didn't even name him after the famous painter—she just adored Charlton Heston. She'd seen *The Agony and the Ecstasy* the night before going into labor and thought Charlton was just dreamy, so the next thing you know, her baby boy is named after some dead painter she'd never heard of until that fucking movie. She briefly considered naming him Moses but thought that might be a little odd, their family being Italian and all.

These days Michael just went by his last name. His mom—the dumb bitch, God rest her soul—had passed on a few years back, so why put up with the aggravation? And it was very Hollywood. All the big stars were known by a single name, even if they had two to begin with. *Arnold. De Niro. Spielberg.* Why not Angelo? It was just a matter of time.

He knocked lightly on the massive oak door and let himself in.

Adam Berman, co-chairman of Empire Studios, sat behind his desk talking on the phone. He was maybe five-six, with a waistline that reflected his success and a neck that rolled past the collar of his black shirt. When he saw Angelo, he hung up in mid-sentence, grabbed the stapler off his desk, and hurled it across the room. Before Angelo could duck, it slammed against the door behind him and broke in half, staples flying like shrapnel around his head.

Adam stood and snatched a silver letter opener from a base made of crystal, a gift from a screenwriter. With a snap of the wrist he sent it flying. It stuck in the door, vibrating back and forth like a tuning fork next to Angelo's ear. He managed not to flinch as his thighs tightened involuntarily around the cup.

If you show fear it only encourages him, Angelo repeated silently. *He's just like a dog that way. Hold your ground.*

Adam was panting, eyes gleaming with malice. He reached for the nearest thing on his desk, which happened to be an Oscar statue, then hesitated. He reached for the next item, which was a Golden Globe Award, then looked at Angelo standing stone-faced against the door. Glancing at his desk, Adam moved his hand and grabbed an Emmy, cupping it in his palm to test its weight.

The wings of the Emmy snapped like the tail section off a crashing plane as it hit the door. Angelo winced despite his mantra.

"You wanted to see me, Mr. Berman?" he asked.

Adam breathed through his nose, sweat trickling down his forehead. When he spoke, it was a dry rasp, cigars and bourbon mixed with rage.

"What the fuck is going on?" yelled Adam, the veins in his neck bulging. "I open the paper today and the headline says one of my producers was murdered. Is that correct?"

"No, sir."

"You saying I didn't read that?" Adam asked, picking the newspaper off the desk and flinging it at Angelo. The pages scattered across the room before they reached him.

"No—I mean, yes," said Angelo. "You did read that. But no, that's not right."

Adam was scanning for the next projectile.

"He jumped," stammered Angelo. "You remember—Tom jumped off the bridge."

"What an irresponsible little shit," muttered Adam. "Guy kills himself in the middle of a movie—it's unprofessional."

"I never thought of it that way."

"If he wasn't already dead I'd sue the bastard."

"He's definitely dead," said Angelo in a tone meant to imply this topic had come up before.

"So this whole movie is riding on Grace?" asked Adam, rubbing the back of his neck.

"Pretty much," nodded Angelo.

"So what the fuck is she doing?"

"Being questioned by the police, apparently."

"Why?" snapped Adam. "Did she kill Tom?"

"Not that I know of—she told me they just wanted to ask her a few questions."

Adam sat down heavily, reaching for the glass on his desk. His eyes looked dull, as if he was suddenly bored with the conversation.

"But we're still on schedule?" he asked in a tired voice.

"Well, we might have a problem."

Adam swiveled around slowly in his chair, and when he looked at Angelo all the menace had returned to his gaze.

"*We* don't have problems, Angelo," he rasped. "*You* have problems to solve. That's what I fucking pay you for, remember? To solve problems."

"Right," said Angelo, nodding.

"So what's the problem?"

"A detective." Angelo looked at his hands. "Grace has hired a detective."

Adam threw back his drink and swallowed in one gulp, baring his teeth as he exhaled.

"A detective," he repeated dully.

"She wrote him a check on the studio's account," said Angelo. "So technically *we* hired him."

"You're not serious."

"Grace insisted," said Angelo, anxious to deflect heat onto someone else. "Said she won't be able to focus on the picture if Tom's death isn't getting the attention it deserves. She also said she might not be able to keep the production on schedule if we don't let her do this."

Adam sat up in his chair, his eyes wide with disbelief.

"She said that?" he asked, his voice rising with each word. "She said she might not make the schedule?"

"Yes."

Adam stood, glass still in his hand. Before Angelo could say anything it sailed across the room and caught him square between the legs. There was the sound of glass hitting plastic and Angelo grunting, followed by glass shattering on the hardwood floor.

Adam raised his arms above his head. "Is she threatening me?"

"Sure sounds like it," gasped Angelo, his hands on his knees. The cup had shifted from the impact and was pinching like a motherfucker.

"That fucking cunt," barked Adam, pacing behind his desk. "Can we fire her?"

"Not without paying her contract," replied Angelo. "I already had legal check into that. Besides, we won't make the schedule if we change producers at this stage."

At the sound of the word *schedule* Adam stopped pacing.

"Fuck it," he said. "Let Grace do whatever she wants. The schedule stays the same."

"You sure?" asked Angelo.

Adam looked at him as if he were a cockroach.

"Am I sure?" he asked sarcastically. "Do you know what it means if we're behind schedule?"

"Money."

"Money," said Adam, smiling. "Do you know how much money?"

"A lot," replied Angelo, thinking it was a safe guess.

"No, asswipe," snarled Adam. "Not just a lot of money—*all* the money."

Angelo nodded but didn't say anything.

"You know what the movie business is, Angelo?" asked Adam.

Angelo looked questioningly at Adam but declined to comment.

"The movie business is a game of chess," Adam continued. "You probably don't play chess."

"Actually—"

Adam cut him off. "In chess, timing is everything. You move a piece to a position on the board, and it might be genius one moment, but it might cost you the game on your next turn. It all depends on what your opponent is doing. You understand what I'm saying?"

"I think so," said Angelo, hoping it wasn't too obvious he was lying.

"Let me put it this way," said Adam, pressing his hands together. "We're making a summer movie. Do you remember a few summers back—that movie about the talking dog that solved mysteries?"

Angelo nodded, pleased to finally know the answer to one of his boss's questions. "Based on an old cartoon."

"Right, a movie about a talking dog that solves mysteries, based on an old television cartoon."

Angelo laughed. "Pretty stupid."

"Stupid?" said Adam incredulously. "You think that was stupid? It was fucking brilliant!"

Angelo retreated to the safety of silence.

"You know why it was brilliant?"

Angelo shook his head mutely.

"Because of timing," replied Adam. "They launched that movie during the lull between *The Lord of the Rings* and *Harry Potter*. A dead zone for summer movies, because all the studios were afraid to compete with those two blockbusters. So along comes the talking dog when those shows are all sold out, and it gets every ticket sale for two weeks straight, with no competition." Adam paused for effect, adding "And it made *seventy million* dollars."

"Wow," said Angelo.

"Fuckin-A right, wow," said Adam. "But you launch that movie two weeks later in the same markets and the same theaters, and you know what happens?"

"What?"

"You get *crushed*. Annihilated. If a movie doesn't dominate its first week out, you *never* pick up the slack, because something better comes along to take your place. So all that production cost, all that advertising money, and all the salaries you paid to the actors disappears right down the fucking toilet, just because you screwed up the timing. And you know what you are then?"

Angelo raised his eyebrows expectantly.

"Then you're the asshole that thought it was a good idea to make a movie about a talking dog that solves mysteries," spat Adam vehemently. "Which has got to be the *stupidest fucking idea* anyone ever had since the invention of the motion picture." Adam shook his fists at the ceiling, angered at the gods of entertainment over the injustice of it all. "And your only defense is *umm, well, gee*—it seemed like a good idea at the time. You'll never get funding for another movie, and you'll probably need plastic surgery to avoid being ridiculed every time you go out to dinner. Just because you missed your launch date."

Angelo suddenly understood the chess metaphor. "I'll make sure we stay on schedule."

"And make sure that fucking detective keeps his nose where it belongs," said Adam. "Away from my business and away from my movie. I don't care who jumped or who got murdered—if some-one gets in the way of this picture, I'll kill them myself."

Angelo nodded.

"Anything else, Mr. Berman?"

Adam blinked slowly, looking almost reptilian.

"Fuck off," he said, dismissing Angelo with a wave of his hand.

Outside in the hall, Angelo clenched and unclenched his fists for almost a full minute before exhaling. He hated that son of a bitch, but no way was he going to quit this job. He'd worked too damned hard to get this far inside a major studio.

Taking a deep breath, he walked slowly toward the massive door at the far end of the hall. He may have to eat shit, but no one—not even Adam Berman—could stop him from spreading it around.

11

"I AM MAJOR YURI Andropov."

The man in the black coat took off his hat and held it lightly in front of him. Cape could still see the bulge under his coat, but the gun was no longer visible. The giant had moved to stand directly in front of the door, making it clear that the only exit was no longer available.

The man in the coat nodded at his companion. "And this is Ursa."

Cape grimaced involuntarily as Ursa smiled. He was almost seven feet tall and as wide as the door behind him, his massive head covered in black stubble. Running diagonally from the left side of his scalp to the right side of his chin were three parallel scars, livid tracts of raised flesh maybe two inches apart. The bottom scar crossed Ursa's lips, giving the first impression that he was swallowing an albino worm. The next broke his nose in half, compressing the cartilage just above his nostrils. The top and final scar bisected his right eye, which had turned a milky blue, the pupil faded and indistinct.

It moved in perfect sync with his left eye, which was black. They followed Cape's movements the way a shark tracks a seal.

Cape looked from the giant to the man in the coat, nodding at each in turn.

"Ursa … Major."

Ursa continued to smile, a malevolent grin promising a future of pain. His teeth were perfect, almost blindingly white. Cape smiled back at the giant.

"Do you floss every day?" he asked. "Or do you use those whitening strips?" Ursa leaned forward, but the Major waved his right hand in a gesture that was part wave and part Nazi salute, and the giant stopped in his tracks.

"Ursa spent fifteen years in *gulag*," said the Major proudly. "Every bone in his body broken."

"Congratulations," said Cape.

"Then after many years in prison, Ursa is released in Siberia with no shoes, no coat. He begins the long walk home. Two thousand kilometers."

Cape glanced at Ursa but didn't say anything.

"One night he is attacked by bear—Siberian grizzly, very dangerous." The Major paused for effect, then splayed his fingers and ran them gently across Ursa's ruined face. "Ursa kills bear and eats it."

Cape had to ask. "Did it taste like chicken?"

Ursa had no comment.

Cape figured as long as the Major kept talking, Ursa was less likely to start doing whatever it was that Ursa did, which Cape suspected wasn't anything nice. "So you guys are Russian?"

"Of course," replied the Major, as if the question itself was insulting.

"How'd you fellas meet?"

"I am ex-KGB," said the Major proudly. "It was me who put Ursa in *gulag*."

Cape didn't know what to say to that. Ursa was smiling again, clenching and unclenching his hands in anticipation.

"This case you are working on," said the Major. "It is dangerous."

"For whom?"

"It is dangerous," repeated the Major, enunciating each word carefully.

Cape shrugged. "Well, it was awfully sweet of you gentlemen to stop by and check up on me. Can I call you a cab?"

The Major narrowed his eyes and moved his right hand slightly, as if brushing lint from his lapel. Ursa took one giant step forward. Cape figured one more step and Ursa would be standing on top of him.

Cape held up his hands. "OK—OK. I'll drop the case."

The Major gave him a look that said *convince me*.

Cape dropped his hands to his lap with a sigh of resignation. "In fact, I had already decided to drop it—I was thinking of going to Hawaii instead."

The Major snapped his fingers lightly and Ursa stepped back, disappointment etched across the gargoyle face. Cape moved his hands forward and pulled a revolver from the holster mounted to the bottom of the desk drawer. He lifted the gun deliberately and pointed it squarely at Ursa's head.

"You know," said Cape, "now that I think about it, it's hurricane season in Hawaii."

The gun was a Ruger .357 magnum, blued steel with a four-inch barrel. The kind of gun designed to get your attention and hold it, and it seemed to be working on the Major. He rocked back on his heels in surprise, his head unconsciously turning toward his giant comrade.

Ursa had the opposite reaction and rolled onto the balls of his feet, a distinctly feral sound starting somewhere deep in his throat. Compared to going to prison for fifteen years and having every bone in your body broken, then dancing with a bear, the prospect of getting shot wasn't a big threat.

Cape shifted his aim to the Major's chest, pulling back the hammer with an exaggerated motion. "You go first."

The Major nodded and said something in Russian under his breath. Ursa stopped growling and blinked, as if awoken from a trance. Then he turned suddenly and pulled open the door. The Major looked over his shoulder at Cape as he was crossing the threshold.

"Hawaii would have been nice this time of year," he said quietly, a small smile playing around the edges of his mouth. Pulling on his hat, he turned and left. Ursa stepped into the hallway without turning back, pulling the door gently until it latched.

Cape brought the hammer down slowly and put the gun on his desk before releasing the breath he didn't realize he'd been holding. He was about to take another deep breath when the wall adjacent to the door exploded.

Plaster and bits of wood flew across the room as Cape grabbed the gun and crouched behind the desk, taking aim at the wall. His first thought was a shotgun blast fired from the hallway.

A massive fist protruded through the wall, knuckles red with blood and fingers white with plaster. As Cape stared, the hand disappeared, replaced a moment later by Ursa's milky eye glaring at him. Then the eye vanished and the hand reappeared, this time with the middle finger extended.

Cape heard the Major's muffled voice and the hand retreated back through the hole it had made. The heavy *klip-klop* of angry feet faded down the hallway.

Cape dropped the gun on the desk and sat down heavily. He looked around the office, now shrouded in a fine white mist of plaster. Outside the window the fog had rolled in, turning the city a pallor as dead as Ursa's sullen orb.

Cape put his head in his hands and muttered to himself.

"Maybe there's a direct flight to Maui."

12

ANGELO TOOK A DEEP breath as he reached the end of the hall. Set into the wall adjacent to the door was a small lighted button connected to an intercom. Before he could press the button, he heard a familiar voice asking him to come in.

Harry Berman's office was smaller and more intimate than his brother Adam's. The walls were lined with bookshelves instead of video cassettes, the chairs wood and leather instead of brushed chrome. It was a more human environment, even though it currently lacked a human occupant.

The television mounted behind the desk was fifty inches wide, a flat plasma display easily seen from almost any angle in the room. Above the screen was a camera, a red light above the lens announcing the presence of its owner even before he spoke.

The face on the screen was benevolent in close-up, the broad smile stretching a good thirty inches across the wall. The eyes were brown, enormous, and gentle. Lines around the eyes suggested that the man with the rugged good looks was older than he appeared, but his voice still sounded boyish and cheerful as it reverberated through the speakers mounted on either side of the screen.

"Hard day, Angelo?" asked Harry Berman.

Angelo shrugged, looking at the face on the screen instead of directly at the camera. "Just the usual, sir."

"I read the newspaper," said Harry, his smile spreading across the wall. "Quite a story."

"Mr. Berman—I mean Adam—the other Mr. Berman," began Angelo haltingly. "Adam's worried about the asteroid movie getting off schedule."

The smile disappeared, leaving in its wake a suddenly small mouth pursing its lips. The wall seemed to move as Harry's eyes shifted, glancing first to his left, then his right.

"A man might have been murdered," he said solemnly. "While working for this company. We have a responsibility to that man's family. Did he have a family, Angelo?"

"A daughter," replied Angelo. "He had a daughter. I understand he was a widower, so the child is being taken by her aunt and uncle."

Harry shook his head sadly, giving the impression the entire room was shaking in an earthquake.

"He was part of *our* family," he intoned. "The Empire Films family."

"Yes, sir."

"We need to set things right."

"But we don't know if there was a crime committed," protested Angelo, wondering if he sounded as unconvincing through the speakers.

The brown eyes hardened. "Then we must find out, Angelo."

"But the schedule—"

Harry cut him off, a giant hand appearing and then vanishing from the screen. Angelo felt like he'd almost been swatted.

"Damn the schedule," said Harry. "The integrity of this company is at stake, Angelo. That's more important than any movie." A wry smile spread across the screen. "Even one of my brother's asteroid movies."

"Whatever you say, sir."

"Harry."

"OK, Harry."

"I understand there is a detective."

"Yeah," said Angelo. "Grace hired him."

"But he works for us."

Angelo shrugged. "I told Grace to explain the ground rules to him—you know, when working on one of our productions."

"Good," said Harry, the giant face moving up and down. Angelo started to feel queasy, made a mental note to take Dramamine before his next visit. This fucking office was like an Imax theater.

"Take care of him, Angelo."

Angelo shifted uncomfortably. "Yes, Harry."

"And Angelo?" One foot-long eyebrow rose higher than the other.

"Sir?"

"Don't forget who you work for."

"I won't," said Angelo, careful not to look directly at the camera.

13

"He looks like a pretzel."

The man in the oven had his legs twisted behind his back and over his head, his arms bent to force his hands between his knees. The death grimace was so severe it looked as if he were about to laugh, his predicament unbearably funny. His back was broken just above the pelvis so he could fit into the oven. If there were yoga classes in hell, this is what they would look like.

"He looks like a Goddamn pretzel," repeated Vincent.

"That's the idea," said Beau wearily. It was six o'clock in the morning. Beau rubbed his eyes and looked forlornly at the empty coffee cup in his hand.

Vincent pulled a pair of latex gloves from his coat pocket and stepped closer to the oven. He was wearing a gray double-breasted suit with a yellow tie and shiny black loafers. He looked like someone who got up early and enjoyed it, even on the weekends. Beau suspected he'd been awake when they got the call and had already eaten a complete breakfast.

"Who did you say this guy was?" Vincent asked.

"Pete Pirelli, also known as Pete the Pretzel. That's the joke, Vinnie. Why just kill the man when you can twist him into a knot and stuff him into an industrial oven at a bakery? And here I was, beginning to think you had a sense of humor."

Beau's voice echoed faintly around the huge expanse of the bakery. The building was a converted warehouse in a neighborhood that had been nothing but warehouses until a few years ago, when the Internet boom pushed out the manufacturing companies to make room for residential lofts costing two million dollars and trendy restaurants serving fifty-dollar plates. Now the lofts cost less than half what they were built for and most of the restaurants were gone, but the manufacturing and warehouses were gone for good. The bakery was one of the few original buildings left.

Two uniformed policemen milled about near the entrance while two others marked off the area around the ovens. Each oven was six feet wide and maybe two feet high, able to handle everything from pizza to pretzels. The lingering stench in the air smelled like neither.

Vincent wrinkled his nose and frowned as he peered inside the oven. "And why was he called Pete the Pretzel?"

"The fuck should I know, Vinnie?" said Beau testily. "Maybe he ate 'em by the bag full. Maybe he was double-jointed. You never know with these mob assholes."

"So he was one of Frank Alessi's guys?"

"Yeah, Pete was a bagman. Made deliveries, took payoffs from the protection racket. Not very high on the *Mafioso* food chain."

"Drugs?" Vincent pulled a pencil from his jacket pocket and poked tentatively at the corpse's cheek.

"Oh yeah," replied Beau. "Frank's operation is pretty big for a small city—loan sharking, extortion, some construction—but drugs are definitely a staple. Poor Pete would have followed the traffic here in town, made deliveries here and there."

"So this was Freddie Wang's handiwork?"

Beau nodded. "I'd say it was payback for the zoo—why else would you kill a mug like Pete?"

Vincent rubbed the back of his neck. "We're in the middle of a war over the drug trade."

Beau shrugged. "Seems that way to me."

"Swell."

"Maybe we can let the scumbags kill each other," said Beau. "Go back home and get some sleep."

"Wouldn't that be nice?"

"Yeah, but I 'spect the captain might frown upon that sort of laissez faire attitude."

Vincent raised his eyebrows. "Did you say *laissez faire*?"

Beau scowled at Vincent. "What—you didn't think a brother could speak French?"

"*Do* you speak French?"

"Fuck no," replied Beau. "Don't know why *anyone* speaks French, do you?"

"They speak it at the Olympics."

"I thought the Olympics were Greek."

"I think the French bought them out."

"Another mystery," said Beau. "I can say *croissant* and *laissez faire* just fine, and that seems to cover about every situation I can think of. Around here it helps to know a little Spanish, some Chinese— but *French*? Let's be serious."

75

"Then why'd you get so defensive when I asked?" demanded Vincent.

"Just fuckin' with you, Vinnie. You got to learn to relax, especially at this hour."

"I get up at five every day—mornings are the best part of the day."

"I knew it," said Beau, shaking his head sadly. "You're a morning person, that's your problem. You know what the best time of the day is, Vinnie? *Night*—that's the best part of the day."

"That's Homicide. As soon as the body goes down, you get up."

"Never should've left Narcotics."

"Maybe we could ask Frank Alessi and Freddie Wang to kill each other after dinner."

"Then I'd be a happy man."

A uniformed officer walked over and mumbled a few words to Beau before handing him a phone. Beau listened for a few seconds, then put his hand over the mouthpiece.

"How long you think we gonna be here?" he asked Vincent.

"Depends when the ME shows up, as usual. Why?"

"We got another appointment," replied Beau. He moved his hand and spoke rapidly into the phone. "Fine. Stay there, and we'll meet you in an hour. That's right, an hour. And I want you to make a phone call for me." He grabbed a card from his wallet, read the number, and hung up, handing the phone back to the uniform.

"Who was that?" asked Vincent.

"Johnson," replied Beau. "Remember how that lady producer said the studio put the crew in corporate housing at Golden Gateway Apartments?"

"What about it?"

"The signed warrant came back, and Johnson tossed the dead guy's room."

"He found something?" asked Vincent, disbelief evident in his tone. Neither of them expected anything to come from the search, a bullshit favor for a nonexistent case.

"About ten kilos of heroin."

"Jesus."

"Never should have left Narcotics," said Beau.

14

"I'M WORRIED ABOUT A bear."

The man behind the counter looked skeptical. Over the years Cape had found that guys who worked in gun shops were like that—it took a while to earn their trust. All the political heat over the second amendment had made them paranoid. Cape might have been an ATF agent or government official posing as a customer, trying to catch them using the wrong registration forms or screwing up the background check. Cape hadn't bought a new gun in a long time, and apparently he didn't look like a serious hunter.

"You hunting moose or caribou?" asked the man, narrowing his eyes.

Cape noticed the man's name tag. "Well, Bill, I was thinking about hunting some moose, and I'm afraid a bear might attack me."

"Where you gonna find bear?"

"Alaska," said Cape. He'd checked Google earlier.

Bill visibly relaxed. He took a step back from the counter.

"That was a trick question, wasn't it?" asked Cape.

"Ain't no moose 'round here," said Bill conspiratorially. "What kinda firearm you want?" He swept his arm across the glass counter.

Every kind of handgun imaginable sat beneath the glass, arranged by manufacturer. Behind him, racks holding rifles and shotguns three and four deep ran the length of the thirty-foot wall of the store. Mounted directly behind Bill, just above the gun racks, was a plaque reading *Remember the Alamo*. This struck Cape as somewhat out of place in California. He looked around the store and decided that Davy Crockett would still be alive today if he'd had this many guns.

"Actually, I'm all set in the firearms department," said Cape. "I'm looking for more of a deterrent."

Bill's disappointment showed. "Deterrent?" He made a face that suggested the word tasted bad.

"Yeah, I understand the Department of Fish and Game doesn't want you to shoot a bear unless you absolutely have to. You know, only in self-defense, like if the bear comes at you suddenly while you're stalking the moose. They'd rather you scared it away."

Bill nodded sullenly, obviously displeased that a supposedly pro-hunting group like Fish and Game would discourage anyone from shooting anything. He squatted suddenly, disappearing for a moment behind the counter. When he emerged, he held a narrow canister in his right hand that looked like shaving cream.

"Wear this on your belt." He held it for Cape to examine.

Cape read the label out loud. "*Bear Be Gone*. Effective to almost thirty feet. One-time use only." He looked up at Bill. "What is it?"

"Concentrated pepper spray," said Bill. "Same as the police use, only in a bigger dose. Only get one shot, though."

"I'm hoping I won't need one," said Cape. "But I'll take it, just in case."

Bill leaned over the counter and dropped his voice. "You want my advice, you shoot that bear. Put him down."

Cape nodded solemnly as he took the canister. "Remember the Alamo."

"Fuckin-A."

Cape's phone started ringing as he walked back to his car. The theme song from *The Good, the Bad, and the Ugly* played itself out in high-pitched electronic tones until he thumbed the right button. The phone had come preloaded with the ringtone and he kind of liked it, though he wasn't crazy about cell phones. Though he had to admit it was useful, carrying the phone sometimes made him feel like he was on a leash. He'd only given his number to four people. Beau was one of them.

Ten minutes later he was driving across the Oakland Bay Bridge, wishing he'd pulled the top down. High taxes and restrictive city ordinances had chased all the gun shops out of San Francisco, which forced Cape to drive to San Leandro, where it was hot as hell, and the air conditioning in his car hadn't worked in years. But as he passed the sign reading *Welcome to San Francisco* at the midpoint of the bridge, Cape felt the vestige of the morning fog and a chill from across the water.

He pulled onto the first exit ramp and headed downtown, contemplating what Beau had told him and wondering how to tell his client something that she didn't want to hear.

15

"HE'S HERE."

The Major nodded in acknowledgement after a moment's hesitation. He'd also heard the door chimes but took an extra beat to process what Ursa had said. Though Ursa spoke only Russian, his ruined nose and throat made his voice a guttural rumble that even the NSA couldn't decipher.

"Get him," said the Major.

Ursa shambled through the door of the back office into the front of the store. *Medical Supplies* was stenciled neatly across the plate glass window, partially obscured by the silhouette of a man holding a box. Ursa made his way past an obstacle course of wheelchairs, canes, and metal walkers, ignoring their guest until he'd latched the front door and flipped a *Closed* sign so it faced the street. He looked right and left out the window but the block was quiet, a few parked cars and little traffic.

Nearly fifty thousand Russian immigrants lived and worked in San Francisco. The ten thousand or so that spoke only Russian at home had clustered in the Richmond and Sunset districts, where they had forged a tight-knit community. A surprising number worked in the medical industry as doctors, orderlies, nurses, and in medical supply stores. Though Soviet healthcare had eroded along with the rest of the country's infrastructure, the system had been large enough to have employed a great many men and women, training them sufficiently to get a decent job in the United States.

Most families were either Jewish or Russian Orthodox, both religions having flourished in exile and survived underground during the Soviet era. They had faith and a work ethic that would put the Puritans to shame. The Major had neither.

He'd come to the store earlier in the day and told the owner he was going to borrow it.

The owner was in his late fifties and had a family, but when he was younger and working in a Moscow factory, he had known men like the Major. Men who pretended to be your co-workers but were really KGB, men who smiled to your face but lied behind your back. Men with dead eyes who took pleasure in pain. The store owner left without a word, leaving the front door open and the keys behind.

Ursa shuffled through the orthopedic maze, the man with the box in tow. When they reached the back room, the man squinted through a haze of smoke at the Major, who was smoking an unfiltered cigarette, flicking the ash onto a cracked tile floor directly below a no-smoking sign. The squint didn't do anything to change the man's expression, which seemed to be a permanent scowl. He had large black eyes set too deep for his narrow face and small mouth, sinking beneath a wave of black hair that hung over his eyebrows and past his collar. His crooked teeth flashed in a feral smile as he greeted the Major.

"I am Marik."

The Major didn't respond, just gestured toward a folding card table against the back wall, which Ursa had cleared earlier with one sweep of his arm. Manila folders and stacks of paper were strewn across the floor.

"Show me," said the Major.

Before carrying the long box over to the table, Marik glanced over at Ursa. The giant had moved behind him and was leaning against the door, watching him with open disdain. Ursa didn't know Marik but didn't let that get in the way of his contempt. Marik was a little man acting the tough guy, a soldier in the *mafiya* looking to earn his stripes. Ursa knew men like Marik in Russia and they were all weak, selling their souls and betraying their comrades for a little cash or out of fear of the *gulag*. Ursa had never broken, but after years behind bars, he'd seen almost everyone crack. He realized the only man with a will to match his own was the Major, the man who had caught him, tortured him, and sent him to the *gulag*. Ursa could respect his enemies but not his friends. He stared until Marik broke eye contact and returned his attention to the Major and opened the box.

The rifle was almost four feet long, half the length taken up by a barrel that protruded from a worn, wooden stock like a bayonet. A short magazine extended from the square receiver just below the trigger, a capacity of five rounds. A short telescopic sight sat on top, a military mount with tapered edges. The shoulder stock looked skeletal, with sections carved out to reduce weight. The gun looked deadly just sitting in the box.

"Just as you ordered," said Marik, unconsciously rubbing his hands together.

The Major picked up the rifle with his left hand and stroked the length of the barrel with his right, his eyes following every contour with a look that bordered on lust. There was a long, uncomfortable minute before he set the rifle down and focused on Marik.

Reaching into his coat pocket, the Major took a white envelope and tossed in onto the table. Marik almost grabbed it in mid-air but managed to restrain himself, though he tore it open immediately and riffled the bills with a hungry look that matched the Major's from a moment before.

"There is more," said the Major.

That got Marik's attention. He jammed the bills into his jacket pocket. "Another delivery?"

The Major shook his head. "I want you to get dirty."

Marik smiled nervously and glanced at the rifle. "I can't shoot that thing."

"Leave that to me," said the Major. "This job, it is nothing." He reached into his coat and produced another envelope, this one fatter than the first.

Marik licked his lips. "What do you want me to do?" Behind him, Ursa's face twisted into a malicious grin. The Major returned the smiled but kept his eyes on Marik.

"I want you to go for a drive," he said.

16

WHEN IN DOUBT, BRIBE the guy in uniform.

Golden Gateway Apartments consisted of four white towers crowding the skyline behind the Ferry Building. As with most destinations in San Francisco, there was no parking except for the street, and all the meters were taken, so Cape spent the next five minutes trying to convince the doorman to let him park behind the police cruiser. It took ten dollars to settle the discussion, a bargain compared with the pay lot five blocks away.

Grace was waiting in the lobby of the north tower wearing a black T-shirt and jeans over leather boots. A simple silver chain hung around her neck, and her dark hair was pulled back in a ponytail. She wore lipstick but no other makeup, as far as Cape could tell. She smiled when she saw him, but her expression was pure anxiety.

"I got your message," she said. "What's going on?"

"Are you staying here?" Cape asked, ignoring her question.

"Yes. The studio put me, Tom, and most of the senior production team here—maybe twelve of us in all. The director, cinematographer, assistant director, and most of the cast are staying at the W Hotel, and the rest of the crew at the Hyatt a few blocks away."

Cape nodded and led her toward a bank of elevators. The nearest door stood open, the arrow glowing in anticipation of the next passengers. A happy chime sounded when Cape pushed the button for the eighteenth floor, the number Beau had given him.

"What floor you staying on?"

"Sixteen, but I'm in the west tower." She turned to force eye contact, which Cape had studiously been avoiding. "What's going on?"

Cape said it plainly, watching for a reaction. "There's a chance Tom was involved in drugs." He didn't have to watch very carefully.

"Bullshit!" Grace flung her hands out from her sides. "You think that wouldn't be obvious during a shoot?"

Cape held up a hand. "I didn't say *using*."

Grace was incredulous. "You're suggesting he was *dealing* drugs?"

The elevator stopped. Cape noticed they'd only made it to the fifteenth floor. The towers were over thirty years old, their age showing once you stepped beyond the newly renovated lobby. Cape glanced at the elevator's inspection certificate and saw it was expired. A short woman with blue-white hair and a cane stepped between them and smiled, reaching out slowly to push the button for sixteen. Everyone smiled but said nothing during the faltering ascent to the next floor. After the doors closed again, Cape put a hand on Grace's arm.

"Look, you hired me to find out why someone might have killed Tom. Now we're about to walk into a crime scene. There will be cops there, including some I don't know. They're going to ask you questions—that's what cops do. We can turn around and leave if you want, but I thought you'd want to see for yourself."

Grace breathed through her nose, a smoldering anger still visible in her eyes.

"Now is not the time to protest Tom's innocence," said Cape gently.

Grace nodded as the elevator doors opened. "Thanks for the advice."

About thirty feet and three apartments to the left, two uniformed cops stood before an open door. Cape gave them his name and the officer on the right disappeared inside, emerging a minute later.

"Mind your step," he said. "It's tight in there."

Cape let Grace enter first. Both of the door cops swiveled their heads and tracked her progress without being too obvious about it. Cape waited until she'd cleared the short hallway and then stepped inside, glancing back at the uniforms.

"If you guys even think about checking out my ass, you're in big trouble."

The apartment was a studio with a walk-in kitchen and a small bathroom off the hallway. It was claustrophobic even for San Francisco—maybe fifteen by fifteen—but the view almost made up for it. Directly across from the entrance, two sliding glass doors opened onto a small balcony overlooking the bay. Even from the hallway, Cape could see from the Oakland Bay Bridge all the way to Alcatraz.

A total eclipse occurred as Beau stepped from the kitchen and greeted Grace. His move revealed three men standing around the refrigerator, the nearest smoking a cigarette and knocking ashes into the sink. Cape recognized him from Narcotics division, a guy named Brewster. He was tall and skinny with red hair and freckles—a gangly, unimposing figure for a police detective. Vinnie stood to his left, immaculate in a pale green suit. The third man Cape didn't recognize, but the camera around his neck, tape recorder in his pocket, and harried expression suggested Forensics.

Beau didn't bother to make introductions. Instead he gestured to the right of the sliding glass doors, where a Sony TV sat atop a stand that also held a DVD player and a video playback machine that took three-quarter inch tapes instead of the standard half-inch videocassettes played on a VCR. To the right of the television was a stack of round film canisters about fourteen inches in diameter and two inches wide. Instead of the brushed silver Cape had seen in the past—in old movies about making movies—these were heavy industrial plastic, black with bright yellow latches on the sides. There were maybe twenty canisters in the stack.

"You know what those are?" Beau directed his question at Grace, his tone mild.

Grace nodded. "Sure. Those hold the raw footage we ship to L.A. for processing, before it's sent back for dailies."

"Dailies?"

"The film we shoot every day on the set," replied Grace. "You see, there's a video playback on the set so we can track our progress—we shoot simultaneously on film and digital video."

"Why both?"

"The most expensive mistake in production is thinking you got something on camera and then finding out later that you blew it. You have to get the talent back, secure the location again—you're starting over. So you watch the video as you go, but you don't really know what you captured on film until you see the *dailies*. The film from each day's shoot is shipped to Los Angeles every night for processing, then video or DVD transfers are shipped back. They're watched on machines like this one, so the producers and director have a sense of what they captured on film the day before."

"OK." Beau nodded slowly. "Was Tom in charge of sending the film to L.A.?" Cape watched Grace carefully. He'd known Beau long enough to know there were no idle questions.

"Now that you mention it, no." Grace looked at the film canisters and frowned, as if suddenly realizing how out of place they were. "A production assistant would've handled that. Tom would have the DVDs, but not the film." She took a step forward, but Beau extended his arm.

"Allow me," he said, kneeling next to the television. "Detective Brewster took the liberty of opening these earlier." Beau gingerly lifted the lid off the uppermost case.

Inside there wasn't a scrap of film. Twelve neat packets of aluminum foil filled the canister, each wrapped tightly into a triangle like a pizza slice. The packet in the two o'clock position had been sliced open, revealing a pale brown talcum. Cape exhaled slowly as Grace gasped.

"Not a bad way to move heroin from one city to another," said Vincent, leaning over the kitchen counter.

Beau stood up. "Nothin' serious in terms of quantity, but enough to keep a man in Italian loafers for a while."

Grace's knees buckled but she caught herself. Her lips moved but no sound came, her eyes fixed on the film canisters. Cape could feel the magnetic pull of the cops in the room watching her for a reaction. He caught Beau's eye and held it. Beau nodded and Cape took Grace by the elbow and steered her onto the balcony. He pulled the sliding glass doors shut behind them, then leaned against the railing and looked down, not saying anything.

The drop to the street was enough to cause vertigo, so Cape shifted his gaze to the water, where a massive container ship navigated the uncertain depths of San Francisco Bay. The bay was two hundred feet deep in some areas and as shallow as six in others, but it all looked the same on the surface. You never could tell.

Cape kept looking at the water as he spoke. "How long were you involved with Tom?"

Grace laughed—a short, sad flutter against the wind. "That obvious?"

Cape shrugged. "Well, I am a detective."

"Now you're being sweet."

"Yeah, it's obvious. It's understandable you'd want to do the right thing for a friend and colleague—I'd like to think I'd do the same. But some of your reactions have been …"

"Emotional?"

Cape shrugged.

Grace watched the wake from a ship fan out, lifting smaller boats far behind it. "We got involved on our last picture, maybe a year and a half ago. I'd just ended a four-year relationship, he was recently widowed. We were working together day and night to finish a movie, traveling together."

"And?"

"The production wrapped, and we decided to call it off," she said. "That was nine months ago."

"Just like that?"

Grace shrugged. "We worked too closely together—it felt claustrophobic."

"To him or you?"

"Calling it off was my idea. I've been told I have a problem with commitment."

"By whom?"

Grace almost smiled. "You want a list? Where should I start, with my mother or the ex-boyfriends?"

Cape turned his back on the view so he could face her. "I need to know more about Tom."

Grace brushed a stray hair out of her eyes. "If you mean more about what's inside that apartment..." Her voice trailed off until she found it again. "I don't believe it. Money wasn't a problem, believe me. You work just one of these mega-productions and you're doing great, and Tom produced a movie every eighteen months."

"Sometimes it's not about the money."

Grace stepped directly in front of Cape, nearly pinning him to the railing. Her hair smelled of lavender. His didn't.

"It's just not Tom. He wouldn't do this. I don't know how else to explain it."

"You notice any changes in his behavior recently?"

"The police asked me that when I went in for questioning."

Cape nodded toward the glass doors. "They're going to ask you again in about five minutes. So what's the answer?"

"I didn't think so before."

"But now?"

"I don't know." Grace shook her head in irritation and the wind caught her hair, whipping it behind her. In profile she looked more sad than angry. "Since he died, I've heard some of the crew making comments."

Cape remained silent.

"Like he seemed distracted lately, preoccupied. He was working too hard, not getting enough sleep. He was stressed out, short tempered."

"And you didn't notice?" asked Cape, thinking the cops inside would be asking the same question.

Grace looked down for a minute before answering. Cape wondered if she was visualizing the jump from the Golden Gate Bridge.

"The truth is we didn't spend much time together, and almost never alone. Remember, we were working on different parts of the movie." Grace looked up from the street below. "Tom was the kind of guy who'd deal with his own problems, not whine about them. And I think Tom was always putting on a good face, you know?"

"You mean for you—because of your past relationship. *Don't worry about me, I'm doing great* ... that sort of thing?"

Grace nodded. "I think I took that for granted when we were together. He was always there for me, and when he needed me to be there, I wasn't."

"Not answering the phone isn't the same as turning your back on a friend," said Cape. "You're here now." Cape shut himself up before he started sounding like Dr. Phil and turned to face the glass doors. He wanted to give her absolution but knew Grace was the only one who had it to give. She'd have to figure that out on her own, and the cops were waiting.

Grace caught the body language. "Time to go back inside, huh?"

Cape nodded. "I'll find out what's going on. I work for you, remember."

"Technically you work for the studio," said Grace. "They're the ones picking up the tab, and they may not want this to go any further, now that drugs are involved. I want to find out what happened to Tom—they want to protect their movie."

"You're the one who hired me."

Grace smiled and slid open the doors. Inside the room was unchanged, except Brewster and the Forensics guy were gone. Beau sat on the sofa and Vincent stood at the kitchen counter, scribbling something on a pad.

Beau gestured toward an overstuffed chair facing the couch and Grace took a seat. Cape leaned against the sliding doors and kept his mouth shut. The questions were short and pointed, and the answers shed no light whatsoever on the case.

They wrapped it up after fifteen minutes. "We're gonna need a list of contacts in the crew, people working with Tom who might know something or may have been involved. You OK with that?"

Grace nodded. "If it helps catch the killer."

Beau didn't say anything, which said something to Cape. He knew the drugs made the case more interesting—hell, it made it an actual case—but he also knew the drugs didn't prove that Tom was murdered. The drugs might be the reason Tom jumped, especially if he thought he was losing control of the situation. Who wanted to tell his daughter he was going to the big house for drug trafficking?

Beau rubbed the back of his neck with his hand. Despite the breeze from outside, the room had grown stifling in the afternoon sun, and his massive head gleamed with sweat. "You don't have any plans to leave town, do you?"

"I have to be here to finish the movie," said Grace.

"Fair enough," said Beau.

Grace stood and extended her hand. "Thank you."

Beau rose, towering over her. "Nothin' to thank us for—we haven't done shit, and we don't know a damn thing."

"That's true," said Grace. "But I'm sure you can do better."

Beau's eyebrows rose in amusement. "I set myself up for that, didn't I?"

Grace smiled as she released Beau's hand. "Yeah, you did."

Cape left with her, neither saying anything until the elevator doors had closed.

"Will they find out what happened?"

"Yeah," said Cape. "They're good cops. But it will take a while—they have to follow the drugs, see who's involved."

"Tom wasn't," said Grace. "I don't care about the drugs."

"The cops do, and it's the only place to start."

They reached the lobby, where Grace would make her way to the adjoining tower, and Cape would exit to his car.

"I want you to keep investigating," said Grace.

"Don't worry," said Cape. "I'm committed to solving this."

"I know you are."

Grace hugged him, then turned and walked away, leaving Cape with the lingering scent of lavender and a lot more questions than answers. As he stepped onto the street, he reflected on what he'd just promised, wondering if maybe he didn't have a commitment problem of his own.

17

CAPE PICKED UP THE tail two blocks from the apartment building.

In a town with no parking, where the favored car was small and trendy—a Mini, BMW coupe, or anything made by VW—the black Lexus sedan with the tinted windows stood out like an ink stain. Considering how it was being driven, Cape was embarrassed he didn't notice the tail sooner. He watched in his side-view mirror as the sedan swerved past a VW bug, getting a blast from the VW's horn. Cape almost laughed out loud when the sedan honked back. *Maybe this guy never followed anyone before.*

Cape drove up the Broadway hill to a point where the incline blocked a view of oncoming traffic, then took a sharp right onto Sansome and hit the gas. He heard the squeal of tires and someone on the sidewalk shouting "*asshole*," then the sedan appeared again in his rearview mirror about one block back. Cape eased off the gas and cruised down Sansome until it connected with the Embarcadero, the wide street running along the water, then turned onto Bay Street, heading west. Bay was two lanes in each direction, so he picked up the pace, passing three cars on the right as he cleared the first light. The sedan closed the distance to maybe half a block, clearly worried about getting cut off at the next light, but so close Cape started to doubt whether someone was really tailing him. *Maybe a drunk tourist just wants to get close enough to ask directions.*

Or maybe the driver of the sedan didn't give a shit if Cape saw him. That seemed more likely, and Cape didn't like the implication. He decided to play out the tourist angle and followed Bay up a hill to Larkin, where he took a right and scraped the car's undercarriage as the street dropped sharply down toward the water. Only in San Francisco—a street so steep you felt a wave of vertigo just driving. See how the tourists liked that.

At the bottom of the street was every postcard you've ever seen of San Francisco crammed into one square mile. Ghirardelli Square, a sprawling panoply of restaurants, art galleries, and water—a genuine tourist attraction complete with its own cable car station, historic three-masted ship, and a small white-sand beach curving around an inlet in the bay. If there were confused tourists in the sedan, they'd be jamming on the brakes and pulling out their Instamatics any minute now.

As the sun bounced off the water, Cape was temporarily blinded. He hit the brakes, blinked rapidly, then double-parked at the bottom of the street. "This will have to do," he muttered, taking one last look in the rearview mirror. He jumped out of the car and stepped across the sidewalk onto a field of grass that fronted the beach.

The field sloped sharply until leveling off onto a brick retaining wall that divided the grass from the sand and water below. Just before the retaining wall was a small stand of scrub pine, trunks bent from the constant ocean breeze, branches from different trees twisted together. From the perspective of the street, the cluster of pines was the only thing blocking an otherwise unbroken view of the beach.

Hiding behind a tree wasn't the most dignified move, but Cape didn't have any better ideas. He racked his memory for examples of other detectives debasing themselves but came up empty. *Travis McGee never hid behind a tree. Sam Spade didn't lurk behind bushes. Nero Wolfe never even left his apartment…*

The train of thought continued as Cape peered between two twisted trunks. The black sedan perched precariously halfway down the hill. From that vantage point, there was no way to tell whether Cape had jumped the retaining wall for the beach or had gone right toward the cable car. Their next move would tell him everything—they either had to leave the confines of the sedan or pick him another time. It was either his imagination, a tail job, or something more serious.

The driver's door opened and a man about six feet tall emerged wearing black jeans, a black leather jacket, and driving gloves. Overdressed for the weather. He absently pushed the door shut and started walking toward the grass, scanning right and left with all the subtlety of a flying cow. As he walked, he unbuttoned his jacket with his right hand.

Marik reached under his jacket and scowled as he walked unhurriedly across the street. This fucking climate was miserable. This morning he was freezing his ass off, the city covered in fog, and now it was sunny, this leather coat an oven. But the gun wouldn't fit under his shirt, so he was fucked. He'd be sweating like a pig with menopause by the time he reached the sand.

Cape stepped behind the largest of the trees. *If that guy's a tourist, I'm a desperate housewife.* He figured maybe three minutes before the guy reached the retaining wall, more if he took a detour toward the cable car and came up empty. Cape turned toward the ocean and tested his theory, squinting against the sudden glare off the water. The dance of the sun off the ocean was impossible to ignore, and when it hit the right angle, it hit hard. Anyone walking down the hill would be blinking away spots the whole way.

Marik raised his arm to block the glare from the water. *Fuck me, this would never happen in Russia. At least in Moscow you could count on the weather. Freezing cold in winter, maybe rain in spring, always gray with smog. Reliable, not this fairy-tale place with its cable cars and chocolate factory. No wonder America has so many homosexuals.* Marik squinted and cursed under his breath, thinking he should have taken the money for the rifle and gone home.

Cape peered around the trunk, catching another glimpse of the man striding across the grass. He made no effort to conceal himself, resigned to the fact that he was walking across an open field. Tourists moved around in small packs, chatting and sometimes stopping to take pictures, but the nearest batch of sightseers was twenty yards away. The man in the black coat was only fifteen feet away now, approaching from the right. Cape moved to the left, matching the man's progress, trying to keep the trees between himself and the stalker in the black coat.

When Marik reached the retaining wall, the ocean glare hit like an anvil, the white-sand beach multiplying the intensity. He involuntarily jerked his head sideways and raised his right arm across his eyes. It was the moment Cape was waiting for. He waited a heartbeat before circling the trees to stand directly behind Marik.

Marik was silhouetted against the white sand, his back to Cape, arm raised as he stood on the wall and scanned the beach. He had passed within a few yards of the trees but obviously thought Cape had sought refuge with the people on the beach, out of sight beneath the wall. Had he been asked, Marik would have agreed that hiding behind trees was undignified for a detective.

Cape let a full minute pass before closing the gap between the two men.

"Quite a view," he said.

Marik had good reflexes. He instinctively reached for his gun as he spun around, just in time for Cape to punch him squarely on the nose. Cape felt the cartilage give way as Marik tumbled backward over the retaining wall. Cape jumped the wall and landed on the sand.

Marik landed on his back and used the momentum of the fall to roll into a crouch. Cape kicked him in the face, catching Marik's chin with his right heel. When Marik hit the sand again, Cape sat on his chest, pinning Marik's arms with his knees. Before he lost any leverage, Cape started digging under Marik's coat for the gun he knew was there.

Someone was yelling about calling the police, and in his peripheral vision Cape saw people running. He ignored them. Marik bucked and spit, blood streaming from his broken nose. He glared balefully at Cape as he struggled.

Cape felt the handle of the gun—it had slipped sideways and was partially trapped under Marik. Cape punched him hard in the stomach, Marik twisted sideways, and the gun came free in Cape's hand. Marik unleashed a torrent of curses and spit blood as far as Cape's chin.

Cape couldn't understand a word. He was pretty sure he was getting threatened in Russian—he wasn't positive about the Russian, but the threats were clear. He could read the subtitles in Marik's eyes.

The gun was a small automatic from a manufacturer unfamiliar to Cape. But the trigger was where it was supposed to be, and there didn't seem to be any external safety, and that was good enough for him. He dragged Marik to his feet and spun him around. Cape saw people running across the grass, some pointing in their direction. Their struggle had brought them to the edge of the water, and Cape could hear waves gently lapping the sand behind him, an oddly peaceful sound under the circumstances. Marik narrowed his eyes as Cape forced the pistol under his chin.

"I think you dropped this," said Cape evenly. "Maybe if you tell me who you work for, I won't give you an emergency tracheotomy."

Blood rimmed Marik's mouth like a goatee. He spat out every word.

"Ya nechevo ne znayu."

Cape decided to see if Marik spoke any English. The cops would arrive any minute. Very deliberately he pulled the hammer back on the automatic until it locked, watching Marik's eyes go wide with the *click*.

"I'm not a cop," Cape said slowly. "That means I don't play by cop rules. Understand?"

Marik's face twisted in rage and he coughed violently, the gun sliding sideways under his chin, its barrel slick with his blood. Cape tried to pull Marik closer but lost his grip as his left side burned with a sudden cramp, as though someone dragged a soldering iron across his rib cage. Cape struggled to stay on his feet as Marik jerked to the left, but a spray of blood spattered his face, blinding him. As he dropped to his knees, Cape heard a cracking sound in the distance, the sound of wet kindling starting to catch fire. He tried to keep the gun extended as he wiped his eyes frantically with his left hand, but when his vision cleared, he saw the wet sand between his feet and knew it was his own blood.

18

ANGELO WAS SICK OF being everybody's bitch.

He walked down the hallway shaking his head. The whole problem with the movie business was that no one person was ever in charge, but *everyone* thought they should be in charge. Adam-fucking-Berman wants to make a blockbuster movie, prove to everyone in Hollywood he's as good as they are. Grace—that holier-than-thou bitch—she thinks she's in charge of the movie, that she's got everyone over a barrel. And they both think Angelo should solve their fucking problems. And who takes the risks? Who feels the heat?

Take a wild guess.

It won't be that way forever. Patience will win out over arrogance. Let them think I'm their monkey-boy for now, but one day I'll be in charge.

As he neared the giant doorway, Angelo brought himself back to reality. Forced a mild expression on his face before pushing the button.

"Hello, Angelo," said the voice from the intercom.

Angelo took a deep breath as he entered the office.

"Another hard day?" asked Harry Berman from his plasma screen on the wall. Today he was broadcasting from a hotel room—it looked like a business hotel you'd find in any city, nondescript, the blinds pulled shut.

"A challenging day," said Angelo.

"If I understand the situation, things have become complicated," said Harry mildly. "Drugs?"

"There will be more negative publicity."

Harry laughed, his teeth a brilliant white. "There's no such thing as negative publicity. That's something my brother has never understood. People don't go see movies they haven't read about in the tabloids."

"Yes, sir," replied Angelo. "But the investigation—"

"Should proceed," said Harry solemnly. "We owe it to our investors. Our employees. And ourselves—to set things right."

"Yes, sir."

"Harry."

"Yes, Harry."

"The detective Grace hired—is he still on the case?"

Angelo hesitated. "I ... I'm not sure."

"Fly him out here," said Harry decisively. "Show him around. I'd like to meet him, be of any help I can."

"But Mr. Berman said ... that is, the other Mr. Berman ... Adam said—"

Harry frowned, a downward arc across the screen, slicing the room in half. The speakers vibrated when he spoke.

"Angelo!"

"Sir?"

"Do you remember our last conversation? About remembering who you work for?"

Angelo nodded at the screen.

"I'll invite him out, sir," he said. "But I honestly don't know if he can make it."

19

Cape let gravity knock him down and roll him into the surf.

The water was freezing. The salt bit into his side like acid, but Cape plowed through the shallows until he felt the bottom drop out. Bending at the waist, he kicked as hard as he could and dove. Somewhere along the way he lost the gun.

He broke the surface seconds later, gasping for air, then dove again before he could get his bearings. Cape spent a lot of time in the water but knew he didn't have the strength to cover any distance. He guessed his first dive took him barely ten feet away from the beach. When the pounding in his ears became unbearable, he surfaced again and tried to take a deep breath but gasped when he saw two eyes staring back at him.

A seal floated six feet away, smiling pleasantly at his aquatic visitor. Seals and sea lions were always swimming near this beach—it was one of the tourist attractions of the park—but it was still unnerving to have company.

"Are they gone?" Cape asked the seal hopefully.

The seal blinked once and disappeared, its tail breaking the water as it dove.

Cape saw he was only twenty yards from where he'd been standing. Some driftwood and a pile of black seaweed clung to the sand, but no sign of his assailant. Maybe a dozen people stood atop the retaining wall, pointing in his direction and shouting. Cape thought he heard sirens but wasn't sure. He felt lightheaded and was beginning to see spots. Time to get out of the water.

He raised his arm to start his stroke and almost screamed. A hot wave ran under his left arm and he felt a tearing along his ribs like Velcro. He forced himself ahead with his right arm, and by the fourth stroke he found a rhythm and closed his eyes, willing himself to remain conscious. His arms were lead weights. He thought of the seal and how effortlessly it had moved through the waves.

Where there's seals, there's soon to be sharks. Cape remembered the advice of an old surfing instructor and redoubled his efforts. While it was bad enough getting shot, being eaten on the same day would be more than he could handle. With the music from *Jaws* playing against the pounding of blood in his ears, Cape felt sand between his fingers and let himself sink, crawling the last ten feet to the beach. Coughing and spitting, he tried to stand, but vertigo dropped him back on his hands and knees next to the pile of seaweed he'd seen from the water.

Cape glanced down and swallowed hard, fighting the urge to retch. The pile of seaweed was Marik. Cape recognized him from his clothes, but his face was gone. The front and right side of the head torn away, jagged edges of his skull peeking out from the collar of his leather jacket.

Cape rolled onto his back and shut his eyes. The sound of approaching sirens mixed with the chatter of the tourists to create a white noise that filled his ears like the roar of a conch shell. The waves tugged at his legs, begging him to return to their embrace as Cape felt his body slip away.

Before he passed out, Cape saw an image of the seal swim across the backs of his eyelids, and he silently asked the sharks to leave them both alone. But he knew they wouldn't.

Everyone knows that sharks have a taste for blood.

20

"You want to run that by me again?"

Adam Berman sat behind his desk, his bloodshot eyes glaring at Angelo. It was almost two in the afternoon, and the drinks from lunch had worked their magic. The booze had seeped into his consciousness and uncovered his inner reptile. To Angelo he even looked like a snake, his tongue flitting between his lips as he sneered across the desk.

"The detective who was investigating Tom's death," repeated Angelo for the third time. "The one in the article."

"Yeah?"

"It seems he got shot."

"Did *we* shoot him?"

"No ... of course not."

"Then why the fuck do I give a shit if some private dick got shot?" Adam yelled. "Why is this entire news bulletin of any interest *what-so-fucking-ever* to me?"

"He was working for the studio," replied Angelo. "Investigating one of our producers, who might have been involved with drugs."

Adam sat up, blinking rapidly. "Drugs? You didn't say anything about drugs. What about drugs?"

Angelo swallowed and braced his feet, mentally adjusting the cup but keeping his hands at his sides.

"I, uh, mentioned that the first time—the police found drugs in Tom's apartment."

"Drugs?" Adam smashed his fist on the desk. "I can't stand anyone who uses drugs." He paused, reaching for the glass tumbler on his desk. Angelo noticed the ice was fresh, the drink amber. Probably bourbon.

"Fire him," muttered Adam.

"Who?"

"What do you mean who? Didn't you just say they found drugs in Tom's apartment?"

"Yes, but—"

"Then fire Tom, Goddammit," snapped Adam. "Today."

Angelo screwed up his face. "Tom's dead."

"Fire him anyway," said Adam, pounding the desk again. "What about the detective? Is he dead?"

"I ... I don't know, sir," replied Angelo. "Grace didn't say ... she was pretty upset. I'm sure the papers—"

"The papers?" screamed Adam, standing up. "The fucking papers know about this?"

"Well, it *is* a shooting ..."

"You're a vibrator with no batteries, you know that?" Adam scanned his desk for something to throw. "Fucking useless."

Angelo shifted his weight. "The investigation—"

"Has nothing to do with my movie!" shouted Adam, grabbing the receiver off the phone. "Make some calls, Angelo. *Fix this*—make this go away." He shook the phone like a club. "None of this shit matters. Only the schedule matters."

"I understand," said Angelo.

"Make it all go away."

"I'm on it."

"Or I'll make you go away, Angelo."

"Consider it gone, sir."

"The schedule is all that matters," shouted Adam, pounding the phone's receiver against its base. "The *schedule*." Again the phone came down, harder this time. "*The schedule!*" The phone shattered, bits of plastic flying across the floor.

Angelo sighed, relieved that today's object of frustration had been attached to a cord.

"Anything else?" he asked.

"Yeah," said Adam, sinking back in his chair and grabbing his drink. "Get me a new phone."

21

"THESE CHAIRS ARE AN embarrassment to the city."

The interrogation room only had two chairs, both made from cheap plastic and aluminum, and Cape sat in one of them. Vincent sat in the other, looking immaculate in a gray suit and cornflower blue tie. The table between them had been scarred by cigarettes before the state of California made it illegal to smoke in public buildings. Cape didn't smoke, but there was something about the room that made him long for a cigarette. A quiet despair seeped into the pale green walls.

"They're supposed to be uncomfortable," growled Beau. He was leaning against the wall behind Vincent. In the small confines of the room, his voice reverberated against the walls like an electric bass.

Vincent shifted uncomfortably in his seat and straightened his tie. "He's got a point, Beau. We could go somewhere and—"

Beau cut him off with a warning glance, then turned on Cape. "This room is discreet—me, I like discreet. Some people, on the other hand, like to cause a ruckus wherever they go."

"Ruckus?" Cape put a wounded expression on his face. "I'm not even sure I know what a ruckus is." He turned to Vincent, who shook his head noncommittally.

"You are a pain in my ass," said Beau. "Here I am, tryin' to conduct a proper investigation, and you go and get yourself shot in the middle of it, waste my valuable time."

"Nothing personal."

Beau shook his head sadly. "Now if you'd found a clue in the park, maybe drugs, or maybe a written confession from Jimmy Hoffa—that might have helped the investigation. But no, you had to find yourself a dead Russian."

"Was he Russian?"

"Seems that way," replied Vincent. He pulled a stack of black and white photographs from a manila envelope and pushed the one on the top toward Cape. It was an image of a man's hand, fingers curled in early-stage rigor mortis. On each knuckle was a curving black line, a symbol tattooed into the flesh.

Cape squinted at the photo. "That's the Cyrillic alphabet."

Beau clapped slowly, the sound echoing off the walls. "Send the boy to college and see what he comes home with? Lots of game show trivia, but no common sense."

Vincent took the photograph and returned it to his pile. "When we took the driving gloves off your dance partner at the beach, he had those on both hands."

"What's it say?"

Vincent shrugged. "We don't know yet. Had a guy on the force who knew Russian, but he left to become a school teacher when he didn't get a promotion."

"Budget cuts," said Beau.

"Well, who was he?"

Vincent shook his head. "An import."

"Import?"

"Prints didn't come up on any local or federal databases," explained Vincent. "I seriously doubt this was a first offense for this guy."

"No way," said Cape. "He's done this before."

"So we think he's fresh off the boat, imported for this kind of job."

"I'm flattered."

"You're lucky," said Beau. "Hadn't been for the dead Russian's spine, you'd be leaking on the carpet every time you took a drink."

Vincent nodded. "The first shot entered his back almost directly behind his heart but came in at an angle and ricocheted off his spine. That's why it grazed your ribs instead of going straight through both of you."

"How's your side?" asked Beau.

Cape raised his left arm and winced. "Hurts."

"Good."

Cape used his right arm to feel the bandages wrapped around his torso. "The doc said the bullet gouged the bone and bounced off, so it's more like a deep cut than a gunshot wound, but I'd rather have a hang nail."

Beau nodded for Vincent to continue his lecture.

"The second shot took the guy's head off."

Cape exhaled slowly. "I wasn't sure," he said. "I had his gun under his chin when the first shot hit me, so I thought—"

"We thought that, too," said Vincent. "But his gun hadn't been fired."

113

"Lucky for you," said Beau. "We found the gun in the water, maybe six feet from shore."

"Where was the shooter?"

"On the hill, looking down toward the beach. That's our best guess."

Cape nodded. "In the same car as the guy that came after me."

"Or a rooftop in the square," said Vincent. "Either location makes it easy to dump the rifle."

"You found the rifle?"

By way of answer, Vincent opened a brown cardboard box at his feet. Cape took the gun from Vincent and hefted it, guessing it weighed close to fifteen pounds. He had seen a lot of guns over the years, but this one was new to him. The lines of every gun said something about why it was made. Hunting rifles had clean barrels and stocks carved from burled wood that looked like it came from the forest where the game lived. Target pistols had custom grips and ergonomic curves so sleek they were practically works of art. The gun in Cape's hands consisted of hard, angular shapes that tapered toward the barrel, giving it a distinctly predatory look. It was a gun designed to shoot a man from a great distance. From so far away you'd never hear the shot that killed you.

"What is it?" He set the rifle on the table.

Vincent pulled a card from his pocket and read aloud. "A Dragunov SVD, according to one of the instructors on our shooting range."

"Never heard of it."

"It's a Soviet sniper rifle," said Vincent, glancing at the card. "Shoots a 7.62-millimeter cartridge that's different from the standard NATO cartridge, accurate up to one thousand meters."

"*Sheesh*," muttered Cape. He reached over to touch his left side. "Where do you get one?"

"Not at your local gun shop," said Beau.

"Why leave the rifle?" asked Cape. "Or why not, right?"

"Exactly," said Beau. "Drop the rifle and walk away. The rifle's compromised 'cause it's been shot, but it can't be traced, so why not trash it? Makes it easier to disappear into the crowd."

Cape opened his mouth to ask something else but caught himself. He looked from Vincent to Beau, his expression grave.

"The first guy was just a decoy—they trashed him just like the rifle."

"Sure looks that way," said Vincent. "Maybe they ship him over and give him a shot at you. If he takes you on the beach, then he gets a green card, a blonde with big tits, and a rent-free apartment in the Land of the Free. Or he gets a suitcase full of *rubles* and goes home, vanishing into thin air. But if he fucks up, which he did, then he's disposable."

"Nice."

"Either way, the guy behind the hit doesn't get his hands dirty."

Beau pushed himself off the wall and stretched. "Looks like you made yourself some new friends."

"Any idea who might want you dead?" asked Vincent.

Beau took a step forward. "Don't ask him *that*, Vinnie—it'll take too damn long."

"Hey," said Cape.

"First you got to consider all the people he's pissed off over the years," said Beau. "Clients, lawyers, cops—the list goes on and on. Then you got to look at the ex-girlfriends—could take forever. Hell, even I wish he were dead sometimes. Like today, for instance."

Vincent raised a hand for silence. "Any idea who would want to *kill* you?"

Cape told them about the visit from the Russians at his office.

Beau was incredulous. "You just now bringing that up?"

"You guys were doing all the talking."

"Withholding evidence," muttered Beau.

"Bullshit," said Cape. "You weren't even working on the movie thing beyond asking my client a few questions. You said yourself it was a waste of time."

"Compared to four homicides, it is," said Beau. He turned his attention to the rifle. "We got plenty of Russians in San Francisco, but not many bad ones. That's an East Coast problem."

"They say who they were working for?" asked Vincent.

Cape shook his head. "Not when they came to the office. But I'd just left the apartment where you found the drugs when I spotted the tail, which makes you wonder."

"They could have been on you all morning."

"Not a chance," said Cape. "You should have seen how these guys drove."

"The heroin," said Beau.

"Maybe," said Vincent cautiously.

"Which means it might have something to do with Frank Alessi," continued Beau. "Fat Frank has a hand in every drug deal in this town."

Vincent frowned. "But why follow Cape?"

"He can't very well follow you," said Cape. "And Frank doesn't like me much."

Beau nodded. "That's a fact."

Vincent raised his eyebrows.

"Frank and I *interacted*, you might say."

"You crossed him?" asked Vincent. "And you're still alive?"

Cape shook his head. "Actually, I inadvertently did Frank a favor, which is even worse. A prick like Frank would rather kill you than be in your debt."

"Seems pretty thin."

"Nothin' about Fat Frank is thin," said Beau.

"Maybe I'm on to something," said Cape, as much to himself as anyone in the room.

"Like what?" asked Vincent and Beau in unison.

"Haven't a clue," said Cape. "But clearly drugs are involved. What are you guys gonna do?"

Vincent shrugged. "We need probable cause."

"You told me there was a turf war going on," said Cape. "Isn't that reason enough to ask Frank a few questions?"

"Frank's a legitimate businessman," said Beau, his jaw working to keep a straight face. "Construction, import-export, restaurants. Large political contributor to both parties. A model citizen. Don't you read the papers—seems Frank's got nothin' to do with drugs or killin' people."

"That reminds me," said Cape. "I need a favor."

"You mean *another* favor," said Beau. "Forget it."

"Has the press done anything with the shooting?"

"Not the whole story, if that's what you mean," replied Vincent. "Tourists have been interviewed, and the radio's buzzing about a shooting in Ghirardelli Square, but the papers don't know who got killed, because we haven't told them jack shit. Frankly, we didn't know shit until about an hour ago."

"We still don't know shit," said Beau.

"Then I want you guys to do something for me."

"What?"

"I want you to kill me," said Cape.

Beau smiled broadly.

"With pleasure."

22

"YOU LOOK PRETTY GOOD for a dead man."

Grace stepped through shafts of sunlight, the canopy of trees overhead keeping most of the path in shadow. Her dark hair looked almost gray in the half-light, creating the illusion that Cape was seeing her as she would appear twenty years in the future. He wondered if the shadows let him age as gracefully.

"It must be the lighting."

They walked along a winding path, the air heavy with the scent of eucalyptus. The Presidio was probably the most beautiful naval base in the country, converted to a national park years ago when the Pentagon started closing bases to save money. The park ran from the Golden Gate Bridge to the cusp of downtown. It boasted a YMCA, a bowling alley, a post office, and historic homes available for rent, the former quarters of the naval officers who had served on the base. But it had no attractions worthy of the attention of anyone working in the drug business, organized crime, or any other felonious enterprise. Cape figured it was a reasonably safe place to meet, and he didn't want to go back to his office just yet—he wanted to keep moving.

The most recent addition to the Presidio was a state-of-the-art film and graphics facility built by George Lucas. The trees were so thick on either side of the path, Cape wouldn't have been surprised if an army of Wookies jumped out at any moment, Chewbacca in the lead.

"Too bad I left my lightsaber at home."

"Excuse me?"

"Never mind," said Cape. "Just thinking out loud."

Grace looked at him as she walked. "How did you manage to get yourself killed?"

"I was taken from the scene in an ambulance," replied Cape. "So was a guy in a body bag. The newspapers know what the cops tell them, and the cops were a little vague."

"And you have a friend at one of the papers."

"That doesn't hurt," said Cape. "Once one newspaper reports their version of the story, the others typically assume it's accurate. That's a dirty secret of the newspaper business—they're either understaffed or lazy. Fact-checking is a pain in the ass and often overlooked if a scoop is already lost. The stories were ambiguous."

"*Possible second fatality* is a suggestive phrase."

"That's the idea."

"What are you hoping to gain from your untimely demise?"

"Breathing room. I can't conduct an investigation if I'm spending all my time looking over my shoulder."

"Sorry I got you into this."

Cape laughed. "I'm not sure *what* you've gotten me into. That's the problem. But you're not responsible—the client never is—it was my decision to take the case."

"But you didn't know … I mean, I didn't know …"

Cape raised a hand gently and let it drop to his side.

"Your case was either pure imagination, total bullshit, or something bad enough that people would kill for it. It turned out to be the latter, which means trouble."

"You talk as if you get shot at every day."

"I try not to make a habit of it," said Cape. "But if I was afraid of guns I wouldn't be doing this."

"Why do you do this?"

Cape shrugged. "Because I can."

"That's not much of an answer."

Cape squinted as they emerged into a clearing. "I used to work for a newspaper. Then I worked for another. And another. After a while it was time to do something else."

Grace looked his way again. "You were a journalist?"

"A journalist is just a pretentious reporter," said Cape. "It's like your distinction between movies and films."

"Were you a good reporter?"

"Very."

Grace gave him an appraising look from head to toe. "You don't suffer from a lack of confidence, do you?"

"Only when I first step out of the shower."

Grace laughed.

"My first editor was an asshole," said Cape, "but he knew what he was doing. My second month on the job, he told me to get close to the Mexican gangs running the dope business—and try to avoid getting killed—in that order."

"He does sound like an asshole."

"Yeah," said Cape. "But I loved every minute of it."

"Why'd you leave?"

"You read the papers lately?"

"What do you mean?"

"If a story isn't about a celebrity, an athlete, or the paparazzi chasing them, you won't find it on the front page," said Cape. "After a while I started telling my friends I was a lawyer, politician, or advertising executive—somehow those seemed more respectable than being a reporter."

"But you weren't writing stuff like that."

"No," said Cape. "But the stories I wrote didn't make a difference, either. They might make for good reading, or get a politician to express *sorrow and outrage at the problems in our fair city*, but the city didn't change because of anything I wrote."

"Now you sound cynical."

"Not at all," replied Cape. "Read the headlines today, then go to the library and read the headlines from ten years ago. Five will get you ten the stories are the same. *Mayor cuts budget. Trouble in the Mideast. President promises tax reform.*"

"This is starting to get depressing."

"You're missing the point. I'm saying that I couldn't change those things—they were too big, too complex for one person to solve. So I decided to stop writing about other people's problems and start doing something about them. I just needed to *do something*."

"So you woke up one day and said, 'I'm going to be a private investigator'?"

"Actually, it never occurred to me," replied Cape. "Then one day I get a call from an old friend who says his sister has gone missing and the cops aren't buying his story."

"I know the feeling."

Cape let that sit for a minute before continuing. "I always had a knack for finding people. Over the years I'd learned where to look, what questions to ask, how to piss someone off just enough to get a reaction."

"You found her?"

"Yeah, I did," said Cape. "And it made a difference."

"Where was she?"

"With a very bad man," said Cape. "I got her back, he got hurt, and I got arrested."

"Arrested?" said Grace. "Why?"

"I think it had something to do with the bad man getting hurt," said Cape. "But in the end, she came home and he went to jail. And I knew what I wanted to be when I grew up."

"The risk doesn't bother you?"

"I used to be a war correspondent," replied Cape. "A real reporter gets into lots of scary situations, but he can't fight back. I'd rather be a participant than a spectator."

"Sounds like you've been doing this a long time."

Cape shrugged. "Long enough to know it doesn't do any good to wish you'd done something else."

Grace nodded absently, walking quietly along the path. Cape suspected she was thinking about her own choices. When she spoke again her tone had changed, as if changing the subject put a weight back on her shoulders.

"The studio wants you to come to New York."

Cape stopped walking. "They know I'm alive?"

"No—sorry—no, they don't. I didn't know myself when I called them. I was ... kind of upset."

"You're gonna make me blush," said Cape. "So what did they say?"

"I talked with Angelo, that unctuous asshole. He said Mr. Berman wanted to meet you, see if he could help."

"He said that before I was shot, or after?"

"Does it matter?"

"I don't know," said Cape. "It might."

"It was like we were having two different conversations. I was calling to tell them about the shooting, Angelo was calling me to see if you could come to New York."

"Which Mr. Berman?" asked Cape. "Adam or Harry?"

"Angelo didn't say, now that you mention it," replied Grace. "But it sounds more like something Harry would say. Adam isn't normally that, umm ... helpful."

Cape nodded. "I'd like to drop in on the folks in New York unannounced, if it's all the same with you."

"Sure," said Grace. "But you don't think the studio has anything to do with the shooting? I thought you said there might be a connection between the drugs in Tom's apartment and a local drug dealer?"

"There probably is, and I'm going to check that out. But Tom was working for the studio when he got killed. And we still don't know he didn't jump."

Grace turned, her nostrils flaring. "He didn't jump."

Cape held up both hands. "The point is we don't know what Tom was into, or how those drugs got into his room, or why someone tried to kill me on the beach."

"I'm your client and you're telling me you don't know anything," said Grace. "What are your rates again?"

"Funny," said Cape. "You want me to start earning my fee, then you'll let me ask your bosses some questions."

"Even if they're not involved?"

"They might know something without knowing they know it. That's sort of how this works."

Grace took a deep breath. "Just—"

Cape cut her off. "Tom was working for Empire when he got killed."

"So?"

"Now I'm working for Empire, and someone tried to kill me."

"A lot of people work for Empire," replied Grace, defensively. "What are you getting at?"

"You work for Empire."

"You think someone wants to kill *me*?" Now she sounded more indignant than alarmed. "Why?"

"I don't, really," said Cape. "So far the heat has been entirely on me, but you were close to Tom, and now you're connected to me. So I'd be remiss not to mention the possibility."

"*Remiss?*"

"I did really well on my SATs."

"I'll bet."

Cape chose his next words very carefully.

"I don't think you should be worried," he said. "But you can always call off the investigation."

"I'm not ready to fire you yet." Grace forced a smile. "The only thing I'm afraid of is what you might find out about Tom."

Cape thought that if he'd been Tom, he couldn't ask for a better answer.

"I'll probably fly to New York sometime tomorrow," he said.

"I know there's a flight out later today."

"There's someone I have to visit first."

"What does he do?" asked Grace. "Another reporter? A cop? You seem to know some interesting people."

"*She*—my friend's a she."

Grace coughed. "Sorry, guess that's none of my business."

Cape laughed.

"What's so funny?"

"She's not that kind of friend," said Cape. "In fact, she doesn't really like men. Not that way, anyhow."

Grace gave Cape a quizzical expression. "So what does she do?"

"She kills people," he said. "With her hands."

23

WHEN SALLY WAS FIVE her parents died in a car accident on the outskirts of Tokyo. They were both killed instantly in a head-on collision with a truck driven by a *yakuza*, a member of the Japanese mob. Sally's father had been a colonel in the U.S. Army, a special investigator looking into yakuza weapons smuggling. There were rumors the car accident had been an assassination.

Sally's mom was Japanese and beautiful. You could see her in the shape of Sally's green eyes and the tone of her complexion, the luster of her black hair. Her dad was American of Irish descent and gave Sally his freckles and his laugh, a raucous bark only heard on rare occasions.

Sally had no other relatives, so when her nanny Li Mei adopted her, there was no one to object. Li Mei had left her home in Hong Kong for Japan many years before, for reasons she kept to herself, but she felt it was best to return to old family and friends. Upon arriving in Hong Kong, the first thing she did was enroll Sally in school. It was a private and very exclusive school, yet there was no tuition. In fact, the school paid Li Mei handsomely in exchange for Sally's attendance.

The school was run by the Triads, whose absolute control of organized crime in Asia was under constant threat. That was the reason for founding the school, to protect their interests.

By the time she was twelve, Sally could speak English, Japanese, and Chinese with no discernible accent. She could swear in all three like a sailor, since her classes emphasized colloquial sayings and street slang as much as formal speech. And, like most children, Sally knew basic arithmetic.

Sally also knew how to make poison from common household plants. She could hit a man in the eye with a throwing knife from almost thirty feet away, or crush his windpipe with two fingers and a sudden jab to the throat. She could disguise herself as any age, gender, or nationality, or become invisible, blending into the shadows like a wraith.

Sally was an excellent student. The men who ran the Triads watched her progress very closely. Then one day, in return for her loyalty, they decided to betray Sally. No one ever said life in the Triads was fair.

They never lived long enough to regret their mistake.

Sally left her past on the far side of an ocean and moved to San Francisco. As far as anyone knew, she was a martial arts instructor who lived modestly in a converted loft above a grocery in the heart of Chinatown. She kept to herself, but a few people knew who she had been and what she was capable of doing. One of them was Cape.

As he trudged up three flights to her loft, Cape tried to keep his breathing shallow. The stairs were killing him. The bandages wrapped around his ribs were too tight, rubbing against the wound. With each step he felt the scar being carved deeper into his skin. Amazing how one little gunshot wound could make you feel your age.

The sliding wooden door was already open. Stepping inside, Cape called out Sally's name, scanning the vast open space.

The right wall was covered entirely in mirrors with a bar at waist height, giving the first impression of a dance studio. That image was shattered by the facing wall, filled with racks holding a dizzying variety of training weapons—wooden swords, bamboo poles, throwing stars, sparring pads for hands and feet.

In the center of the room, three heavy bags were suspended from the exposed beams overhead. Above those were nylon ropes arranged in a complicated web, used for climbing and balance training. Cape glanced into the rafters and saw her, but only because he knew where to look.

Sally was directly above him, hanging upside down from one of the ropes, watching Cape with a disgusted look on her face. She shook her head sadly.

"Pitiful."

"What?" asked Cape defensively.

"You were a sitting duck."

"You're the one in the vulnerable position."

"Really?" Sally looked as relaxed upside down as most people do sitting on a couch.

"Absolutely. The door was unlocked, and you're hanging upside down. Unarmed."

"I knew it was you."

"What if it wasn't?"

"Had it been someone else, I would have been somewhere else."

"You sound like a fortune cookie," replied Cape. "How did you know it was me?"

"Your footsteps—no two sets are alike. You're favoring your left side, by the way."

"Suppose I was a foot impersonator?"

Sally barked out a laugh. "Suppose you were?"

"Well, I could have a gun."

"You do have a gun," replied Sally. "It's in a holster in the small of your back, under your jacket."

Cape frowned. "I need a new tailor."

Sally wrinkled her nose. "Guns."

"I'm aware of your views on firearms. Those of us lacking your talents need—"

"To compensate?"

"Precisely."

"Is that why *men* always carry guns?"

"If it weren't for guns we'd be scratching ourselves all the time."

"Men do that anyway."

"But my original point remains, that you were vulnerable."

Sally snorted. "So shoot me."

"That's a helluva dare."

"No, I insist," said Sally. "I want you to shoot me."

"It might make a mess."

"I have a woman that cleans every Saturday."

"It would be awfully loud in this enclosed space."

"Trust me," said Sally, swinging slowly back and forth.

Cape shrugged, then drew his gun as quickly as he could. He didn't intend to pull the trigger but thought he might prove a point. The gun had barely cleared the leather holster when he felt the knife at his throat. He hadn't looked down as he drew, but he did blink, and in that instant Sally had disappeared. As he felt the cold *tanto* blade press against his neck, Cape realized he never even heard her hit the floor.

"*Your quarry is never where you think it is,*" said Sally, standing on her toes to whisper in his ear. "*So strike where it will be next.*"

Cape lowered his gun. "Was that Confucius?"

"No, a teacher I had in Hong Kong."

"*I don't skate to where the puck is,*" replied Cape. "*I skate to where the puck is going.*"

"Who said that?"

"Wayne Gretzky, the hockey player."

Sally nodded. "He would have done well at my school."

She took a step back so Cape could turn and face her. The knife had vanished somewhere within folds of black cotton wrapped around her diminutive body. Just over five feet tall, she looked about as dangerous as a dandelion.

"Was that the lesson for the day, *sensei*?" asked Cape, bowing. "What do I owe you?"

"No charge for remedial students." Sally returned the bow.

They moved to a small alcove off the main room, where a traditional Japanese tea sat ready. They both sat on tatami mats, Sally looking infinitely more comfortable than Cape. He told her about his visit from the Russians and his fun at the beach. When he was finished, Sally frowned.

"The Russian mob."

"I'm pretty sure it's not the Russian tourism council," said Cape.

"You must be a detective."

"You've dealt with them before, I take it."

Sally sipped some of her tea. "Once, in Hong Kong. They're crude, but thorough."

"Thorough."

Sally nodded. "Very."

"Swell." Cape touched his side.

"What does your client have to say about all this?"

"Grace says she doesn't know what's going on. Right now I'm inclined to believe her."

"Grace? Your client's a *she*?"

Cape sighed.

Sally looked at him and shook her head. "Are you trying to help her, or save her?"

Cape held up his hand in warning. "I already got an earful from Beau and Linda."

"They're your friends—you should listen to them."

"I've learned from my mistakes," said Cape in a tired voice. "I am a changed man."

Sally snorted. "Men don't change," she said. "And your taste in women is atrocious."

"We just have different tastes," replied Cape. "Any other advice? Want to lecture me on the proper technique for cunnilingus?"

Sally snorted again. "There is no *technique*, you testosterone-soaked buffoon. There is only *desire*. If you enjoy it, then she'll enjoy it."

"You know, this has been a really great visit. First you establish that you can kick my ass, now you're lecturing me on bedroom etiquette. You sure know how to make a man feel welcome. Are you going to kick me in the nuts on my way out?"

Sally laughed and held her hands up.

"I forget sometimes how sensitive you are."

"Only during the weeks when people are trying to kill me."

Sally's expression changed. "Murder is rarely personal for people like this—they just want you out of the way."

"I think I made it personal when they came to my office."

"Want to know what I think?"

"Always."

"I'd get out of town until you know what was going on."

"Way ahead of you," replied Cape. "I'm taking the red-eye to New York."

"Want company?"

Cape nodded. "That would be great."

"You need a place to stay until the flight?" asked Sally. "I don't have any classes today."

Cape shook his head. "I have one more stop to make before heading to the airport."

Sally raised her eyebrows.

"I'm going to visit the Sloth," said Cape.

"You've got some strange friends," said Sally. She set down her tea and walked silently back to the large room, where she jumped into the air, grabbed a rope, and disappeared. Cape shook his head and smiled.

"I'll take them any way I can get them," he said.

24

CAPE THOUGHT LINDA'S HAIR seemed happy to see him, but he couldn't say the same for Linda.

She was standing at the bottom of the steps leading to the Sloth's house, a small Victorian directly across from Golden Gate Park. Her hands were on her hips, which was never a good sign. "You're late," she said sternly as he walked up the driveway.

Cape glanced at his wrist and realized he wasn't wearing a watch. This was clearly an argument he could not win.

"You're right," he said a little too quickly. "I'm an inconsiderate asshole. Anything else?" Linda's hair swayed back and forth, which Cape chose to interpret as acceptance of his apology. Her frown, however, said he wasn't out of the woods yet. "You've probably got plenty of other things to do, and I should have more respect for the value of your time," he added.

Linda's eyes narrowed.

"I have brought dishonor to the institution of friendship," intoned Cape solemnly, his hand over his heart, "and I swear that from this day—"

Linda's right hand shot out in warning as her hair moved into fighting position.

"Enough," she said. "Another forced platitude and I might gag."

"So I'm forgiven?"

"No, but I'm exhausted," she replied. "Let's go inside."

One step over the threshold made it clear that someone unusual lived in the house. The large living room was directly off the front entrance, overlooked by an open kitchen that sat behind a short counter. Despite the size of the room, the furniture did not fill the space in any traditional, decorative fashion. Instead, small islands of chairs and tables were arranged by function. A small couch and chairs were clustered tightly around a television, VCR, and DVD player, everything within easy reach. A few feet away a chair, reading lamp, and desk were surrounded by a semi-circle of bookshelves. Half a dozen such groupings dotted the carpet, each a small shrine to a very specific activity, each within a few feet of the next. And in the center of them all was mission control.

An elaborate array of four plasma screens perched above a large curving desk, below which sat four servers, each the size of a small refrigerator and capable of storing untold amounts of data. Cables of every color snaked their way through a hole cut into the center of the floor. Arranged between the monitors was a plethora of peripheral devices, most of them unavailable from your local computer store. Cape thought he recognized one or two from the bridge of the Starship *Enterprise*, but Captain Kirk was nowhere in sight. Instead, sitting behind the desk with a bland expression on his face, was the Sloth.

When he was a child, the Sloth was diagnosed with a rare neurological disorder that put his world in slow motion. It could take him an hour to walk across the room, almost five minutes to finish a sentence. The doctors said there was nothing they could do. He moved within his own time frame. The other kids were unkind, as kids always are, and gave him a nickname after the slowest-moving mammal on the planet. But the Sloth didn't care—or no one could tell if he did.

Years later, the Sloth came into contact with his first computer, and the machine revealed that his physical curse came with a hidden blessing. While his body moved like a glacier, his mind could travel faster and farther than a beam of light. The Sloth saw patterns in data streams invisible to anyone else. He could hear music in numbers and equations that baffled mathematicians for years. He was, quite simply, a genius in the truest sense of the word.

As Cape stepped closer, the Sloth looked up from his keyboard and smiled, an expression that would have looked pained on anyone else. The pale eyes were watery behind glasses, but the warmth in his gaze was unmistakable. It had been the Sloth's sister that Cape found on his first investigation, an incident that forever changed the trajectory of both men's lives. Cape started working with the Sloth while still a reporter, and Linda worked so closely with him that Cape never saw the Sloth without Linda at his side—interpreting for him, doing field work, or simply keeping him company.

His keyboard was a liquid-crystal pad set into the table. As Cape watched, its surface rippled with light. Words and symbols scrolled past, fleeting glimpses of thoughts that were literally at the Sloth's fingertips. The keyboard was activated by touch, the sensitivity so high you could trigger it by exhaling. For the Sloth, it required a little more effort than that. As his hand twitched spasmodically across the surface, words appeared in glowing rows on the screens in front of Cape.

I FOUND SOMETHING.

"What do you mean, you found something? I just called this morning." Cape turned from the Sloth to Linda. Talking to them together was almost like communicating with a single person, half the conversation verbal and the other half subtitles.

"While you kept us waiting," replied Linda, "we were hard at work." Her hair nodded in agreement.

Cape said nothing as more words flashed onto the screen.

DIDN'T FIND MUCH … TOO EARLY.

The Sloth's hand moved sideways, conjuring a new set of words on the next screen.

EMPIRE PICTURES. FOR SALE.

"How can you know that?" asked Cape.

"It's called reverse trend analysis," said Linda. "Sort of a quantitative approach to rumor mongering."

"In English, please," said Cape.

Linda huffed. "You know how the news is always describing the latest trends. *Bell-bottoms make a comeback. All-starch diet the new craze—pretzels the key to longevity.* Fashion, cars, whatever?"

"Sure."

"Well, they don't just pitch trends arbitrarily based on some editor's opinion," explained Linda. "They track them—or, in most cases—they pay some consultant who tracks them."

"How?"

"That's what's interesting. The most common method involves measuring column inches in newspapers and magazines across the country. That's the amount of space given to a particular story."

"Got it," said Cape. "So if short skirts are getting progressively more space in the newspaper's fashion section, then the trend analysts say there's a good chance you'll be seeing a lot of short skirts next season."

"Right." Linda nodded. "You add up all the space given to a specific topic in each publication you're tracking, then sort it by subject matter. More space over time means a trend."

"Sounds tedious."

"It used to be," agreed Linda. "That's why consultants charged ridiculous fees to wade through all those papers with a ruler, adding things up. But now that everything's online, all you need are the right software filters."

Cape looked over at the Sloth. "And I imagine you've written your own."

Linda walked over to stand directly behind the Sloth. "Sloth wrote a program this morning that scanned for any mentions of Empire across two hundred different publications currently online. He also scanned for mentions of the top ten media companies and expanded that search to five hundred publications."

"Over what period of time?"

"The past six months," replied Linda.

"That's got to be an insane amount of reading," said Cape. "Or filtering."

"Not really," said Linda, her hair bobbing with excitement. "Because there's another filter to screen for stories related to Empire's business model—words like 'film critics,' 'art films,' 'asteroid'—that sort of thing. Then Sloth added a final filter to track the smallest articles related to the topic."

"Smallest?" asked Cape. "I thought you were looking for the largest."

Linda shook her head. "That's for trends—we're looking for rumors. Sloth reasoned that a rumor would get the least amount of space, because the editor would have little to go on—other than one source, and that might be unsubstantiated. A small mention in the back of *Variety* or *The New York Times*, for example."

"Then what?"

"We looked for recurring mentions, but always on a small scale," said Linda. "Under the assumption that a series of small articles might constitute a leak about an actual event. It hasn't been substantiated, or announced, so it's still only a rumor."

"So it gets printed in a few different publications, but never gets a lot of space," said Cape.

"That's the theory, anyway."

"OK," he said. "What did you find?"

"Multiple mentions over the past two months that a major media company was looking to buy another movie studio," said Linda. "The last two specifically describe the acquisition as a mid-sized studio capable of producing both small films with critical appeal and commercially viable movies—they need the balance to hedge the purchase price against changes in the marketplace."

"That could fit Empire's profile," Cape said. "But which media company are we talking about?"

"I'll give you a hint," said Linda, putting her hands on top of her head and waving them back and forth like ears. "Think of a massive entertainment conglomerate."

"What are you supposed to be?" asked Cape. "The Easter Bunny?"

Linda dropped her hands. "*A mouse.* I'm talking theme parks, cartoons ... ring a bell?"

"Oh, *that* media company," said Cape. "Didn't they buy a studio last year?"

"The year before, and they said at the time it was their first major acquisition in the film industry. Their first, not their last."

Cape frowned. "They don't strike me as the kind of company that would be too happy about negative publicity."

"You mean like drug smuggling on the set of one of their movies?"

"Yeah," said Cape. "Could screw up the whole deal and maybe cost the Berman brothers a lot of money."

The Sloth's right hand jumped like a frog.

SOUNDS LIKE A MOTIVE.

"As good as any," said Cape. "What's your confidence level?"

HARD TO SAY ... EDUCATED GUESS
UNTIL I CAN ACCESS THEIR FILES DIRECTLY.

"You can do that?"

The Sloth smiled slowly, his mouth a little lopsided on the left, as if that side were struggling to catch up.

"Is it legal?"

The Sloth blinked, as if the concept of legality were new to him.

"Forget I asked," said Cape. "Just let me know what you find."

He turned to Linda, then back to the frail genius next to him. "And thanks."

The screen lit up again, words dissolving and forming anew.

THE GIRL.

"Who?" asked Cape. "My client?"

IS IT PERSONAL?

Cape gave Linda a warning glance. "For her, or me? She knew the murder victim, if that's what you mean."

Sloth made no reply, and the words sat unblinking on the screen for several seconds until they changed again.

DON'T GET HURT.

Cape smiled and squeezed the Sloth's shoulder. "Thanks, old friend. Anything else?"

It seemed to Cape that a playful smile appeared briefly at the corner of the Sloth's mouth, then disappeared. He turned his head slowly, one degree at a time, glancing over at Linda. The words changed again.

BUY A WATCH.

Cape looked over at Linda, who was smiling broadly.

"That's next on my list," said Cape as he headed for the door. "Going to the airport now—after all, I don't want to be late for my plane."

25

"WE COULD ALWAYS CANCEL our arrangement."

The Major smiled and held the receiver at arm's length to protect his hearing. When the shouting stopped, he brought it closer and fanned the flames he'd just lit.

"I'm sure it is minor investment for you," he said slowly. "We can work together another time." His arm uncoiled like a spring before the rebuttal screamed down the line.

As he talked on the phone, the Major watched Ursa through the glass window of the office, pacing around the empty warehouse. Even next to his giant companion, the shipping containers looked big, each one eight feet square and capable of holding half a ton of laboratory equipment. Everyday shipments were made to hospitals all across the country, sensitive measuring devices and lab equipment packed in custom foam sized to fit the containers. The Major marveled at the precision of the operation, so different from the anarchy of his current venture.

"You sound committed," said the Major soothingly. "Commitment is all I ask from business associates. We must share risk if you expect to share reward." This time he kept the phone pressed to his ear, listening carefully for the grudging response. When it came, he rapped on the office window and signaled Ursa to join him. He took out a handkerchief and wiped his prints off of the phone, then cradled the receiver gently.

"Get the car," he said to Ursa. "I want to go shopping."

26

CAPE LIKED FLYING ABOUT as much as getting shot. Maybe less.

He and Sally caught the last flight on JetBlue from Oakland to JFK. The plane was full, but even Cape had to admit the flight was a smooth one. Sally pointed out that he was safer in a plane than crossing the street or, in his case, strolling on the beach at Ghirardelli Square.

"I know that," said Cape. "Doesn't mean I have to like it."

"You hate situations you can't control," replied Sally. "Like turbulence."

"Or aging aircraft."

"This plane's brand new," said Sally. "This airline's practically brand new."

"Financially strapped airlines are a problem," suggested Cape. "The first thing they cut is maintenance."

"This airline's making money. You told me so yourself when we bought the tickets."

Cape said nothing, glancing out the window to make sure the wing was still connected to the fuselage.

"I've never known anyone who so actively courts danger but wants it to happen completely on his terms," said Sally.

Cape turned away from the window. "I suppose you think that's contradictory."

"I think it's very Western," replied Sally. "You want to choose how and when things occur. But you can't choose ... all you can do is *prepare*."

"Are you prepared?"

"Always."

Cape looked out the window again.

"Face it," said Sally. "You won't be comfortable until they let you fly the plane."

"You think I should take flying lessons?"

"I think you should go to sleep," said Sally, closing her eyes.

Knowing sleep was beyond his grasp, Cape took out his notebook and turned to a clean sheet of paper. Down the center of the page he started to write the names and descriptions of all the people involved in the case so far. After he'd written a description of the guy at the beach, he scanned the list to see if he'd overlooked anyone. Slowly, almost reluctantly, he added Grace to the list.

By the time the plane started its descent into JFK, the page looked like a child's drawing—lines, circles, and boxes connecting the names. Many had been erased and redrawn as Cape tried to establish links between various people and events. He squinted at the paper, hoping to see a pattern emerge, but his eyes were tired and all he could see was a jumbled mess.

"I see you've solved the case," said Sally, stretching herself awake.

"Absolutely. It was Colonel Mustard in the park with an AK-47."

"I thought he favored the candlestick."

"Times change."

"So tell me again why we're about to land in New York," said Sally. "You really think the studio is involved?"

Cape shook his head. "No, I don't. Why would they fuck with their own production?"

"So?"

"I think the Russians have something to do with the drugs, and the movie happens to be in the middle of it. I think the movie provided some sort of cover for moving the drugs, but whether Tom—the dead producer—acted alone or worked with someone else from the studio, I couldn't tell you. I asked the Sloth to dig into Tom's finances before I left. If he finds a money trail, we can follow it back to the source."

"Then isn't this trip pretty much a waste of time? I get that you want to talk with the brothers running the studio, but you could do that over the phone."

"True."

"And even if they know something," continued Sally, "I doubt they'll want you to know."

"You forget how persuasive I can be."

"You forget they're the ones paying you."

"Also true," said Cape, shrugging. "But I can't think of anything else to push against, and I needed to get out of San Francisco for a couple of days."

"So we're hiding?"

"I prefer to call it laying low," replied Cape. "Aren't you the one who told me to keep a low profile?"

"Yeah, but I know you—you're like a dog with a bone. There must be something else to this trip."

Cape smiled. "You must be a detective."

"Not me," said Sally. "I'm just the girl from the escort service."

"I'm meeting a cop."

"What cop?"

"Guy named Michael Corelli—Beau hooked me up."

"NYPD?"

Cape nodded. "Their Organized Crime Unit—OCU if you prefer acronyms. In Corelli's case, that's mostly involved *La Cosa Nostra*, the nice old men sitting in the supper clubs watching *The Sopranos* on DVD."

"Corelli's an Italian name."

"Yeah," said Cape. "Beau says Corelli has a chip on his shoulder about the whole thing, takes it very personally. When he was growing up, his dad had to pay extortion money to keep his store open. Some of the guys collecting the money were his friends' fathers. Corelli decided to chase the mob before he was old enough to ride a bike."

"You think he might know something about our Russian friends?"

"Not specifically, but he's bound to know a helluva lot more about the Russian mob than I do."

"We don't know they're with any mob."

"Gotta start somewhere," said Cape. "Someone tries to kill you with a sniper rifle, it's usually not their first offense. And I could use a few pointers."

"Like how to say *hello* in Russian?"

"Or *please don't shoot me*."

"How about *fuck off or I'll kill you*?" asked Sally. "I think I'd like to know that one."

"If it comes to that, I don't think you'll need a translator."

Cape felt his ears pop and normal gravity return. The flight had landed on time. He looked at his writing pad one last time before stuffing it into his bag, frowning at the illegible scribbles and overlapping lines and boxes. He took a deep breath and blew out his cheeks.

"What a mess," he said.

27

SOMEWHERE DEEP IN HER subconscious, Grace was struggling to choose between crying or masturbating.

She stared at the ceiling and watched the reflected light from her alarm clock, her hands resting lightly on her abdomen. A moment ago she'd been thinking about Tom, his crooked smile and gentle touch, the wounded expression on his face when she'd told him it was over. The sweetness of the man even after she'd pushed him away, his undying support of her at every turn. Only now, over the past few days, had she realized that he must have loved her.

Grace felt the tears welling up as she faced the awful truth that she never felt the same way he did, and she never would. She wanted to give him that, at least, a confession of love to his ghost and his memory, but no matter how much she wished it had been true, the feeling wasn't there. Her feelings ran deep, but not deep enough.

She closed her eyes, then blinked them dry, letting her thoughts drift. From Tom to the movie. From giant asteroids to Empire Studios. Harry and Adam, the cast and crew. To the detective she'd hired impulsively, a man she'd just met but trusted as if she'd known him forever.

Must be those eyes, she thought, laughing at herself. She was a sucker for blue eyes, and his had that touch of gray near the center. She wondered how old he was, decided he was probably her age. The eyes made him look older, but the rest of him looked about right. The sandy hair would hide the occasional white strands, so that was no help. Did it matter?

She let her right hand slip across her waist as she took a deep breath and closed her eyes. She lay like that for a minute, her fingers barely moving, when suddenly a car engine reverberated through the walls of her bedroom. Her eyes snapped open as her hand moved from under the covers to reach for the bedside lamp.

Sleep isn't coming tonight, she thought miserably. *And neither am I.*

Swinging her legs over the side of the bed, Grace padded to the bathroom as the sound of the car Dopplered down the street. She briefly wondered who was out for a drive at four in the morning but quickly turned her attention to the shower. Once under the stream of hot water, the sounds from the street disappeared.

She thought about her day, which would begin in just under three hours, and all the work still to be done. Sitting on her desk were stacks of binders, ledgers, and production notes moved from Tom's apartment to hers. Tom was meticulous about production details, schedules, and budgets. Naturally she'd talked with his assistant producers and some of the crew about what they'd planned to do next, but his notes were critical. She had to start getting up to speed on his half of the production, something she couldn't put off any longer.

Grace rolled her neck under the pulsing spray as she visualized the black binders waiting in the next room. She shuddered and turned the faucet as hot as it would go as she realized she was afraid to open the notebooks. Suddenly the drugs found in Tom's apartment flashed into her mind, a secret life hidden inside canisters of film. A secret she didn't want to know.

But those were just drugs. Surprising, definitely. Confusing, certainly. Something that needed to be explained, but nothing to be afraid of. The drugs were a mystery, not a written record of events. Circumstantial evidence but not a written confession.

Grace didn't want to open the notebooks because she knew, deep in her gut, that that was where the ugly truth lay waiting.

28

CAPE WAS WORRIED THAT they wouldn't let him check into the hotel without first getting a Botox injection.

The people moving through the lobby came together as one seething mass of beautiful bodies and perfect hair, loosely connected by furtive glances at the giant mirror on the lobby wall. Everyone was young and excruciatingly attractive. The pair behind the registration desk—a young man and woman—were even more striking than their guests. Cape wondered if the hotel's employment application had minimum requirements for cheekbone development.

The Soho Grand sat at the fringe of everything hip and trendy, its austere design popular with models, photographers, and advertising executives—anyone self-conscious or pretentious enough to put fashion before comfort. But it had the perfect location. Empire Studios was only a few blocks away, so Cape and Sally decided to embrace the madness.

Just off the lobby was an enormous bar curving around a cavernous space filled with geometrically challenging tables and impossibly high stools, all accented by halogen lights just dim enough to guarantee eye strain. Cape spotted Corelli instantly. He stood out like a carbuncle.

Cape stepped into the bar as Sally continued toward the elevators. Corelli stood and extended his hand. Around five-ten, black hair cut short and peppered with gray. The lines around his brown eyes multiplied when he smiled. He wore black shoes, gray slacks, and a white dress shirt with the sleeves rolled up, revealing a faded tattoo of a scorpion on his right forearm. Cape guessed the tattoo was probably older than most of the guests at the hotel.

"Guess I stand out around here as much as you do," Cape said as they shook hands.

"Beau wired me a photo," said Corelli, his voice rich with Brooklyn undertones. "Said you were uglier in person."

"An honest cop," said Cape. "So rare these days."

"He also told me you should be dead."

Cape nodded. "For the time being, anyway."

"He asked if I wanted to place a bet on whether or not you'd survive this case. I bet against you—hope you don't mind, but Russians are involved."

"Two cops betting on my life expectancy? I'm flattered."

"Don't take it personally," said Corelli. "We only bet on people we like."

"Thanks for meeting me." Cape took a seat on one of the ergonomically challenged stools. "Beau said he knew you from the service."

Corelli nodded. "Semper Fi."

"And that you saved his life," said Cape.

"He mention that he saved mine first?"

Cape shook his head. "He left that out."

"He would," said Corelli. "What's your story? Beau told me he lost his badge once, but you got it back."

Cape gave him a noncommittal shrug. "It was stuck between the cushions of his couch."

"That's not how I heard it." Corelli smiled. "But I can see why he likes you." A woman in her early twenties brushed past their table, wearing a miniskirt cut short enough to pass for a belt. Corelli almost got whiplash as she passed by. "This place is surreal."

Cape flagged down a waitress dressed demurely in a skintight purple jumpsuit. "Not my normal scene, either." Cape was feeling the flight and ordered coffee. Corelli was off-duty and went for a Bud.

"I saw you talking to that Asian number in the lobby," said Corelli. "You know her?"

"Old friend."

"Want to introduce me?"

"Stay away from her," suggested Cape. "She'll tear your heart out."

Corelli laughed. "Don't they all."

"I meant it literally."

Corelli half smiled but let it go, realizing he'd missed something.

"So Beau tells me you made some new friends," he said.

Cape nodded. "I don't know how many. Two for sure. There were three, but ..." He let his voice trail off.

"Dead guy on the beach," said Corelli. "He had Cyrillic letters on his fingers?"

"Yeah."

"You're dealing with the *mafiya*," said Corelli, putting extra emphasis on the *y*.

"The Russian mob."

"Yeah," nodded Corelli. "Charming bunch of guys."

Their drinks arrived and Cape charged it to his room. "What can you tell me?"

"Thanks," said Corelli, raising his beer. "I can tell you a lot of stories, you tell me when to stop. They're everywhere, but it's hard to get a handle on the organization itself."

"The feds must be all over them."

Corelli's mouth twisted into a cynical grin. "You'd think so, wouldn't you? Know what happened when *La Cosa Nostra* first came over from Sicily?"

"The politicians went into denial?"

"You must know something about mob history."

Cape shook his head. "No, but I know something about politicians."

Corelli nodded his approval. "In the sixties, J. Edgar Hoover was too busy worrying about Communism to do anything about the mob."

"J. Edgar also had to worry about what dress to wear on the weekends," said Cape, "and finding shoes to match."

"True, but it was years before anyone in the government even acknowledged the existence of organized crime. By then it was too late. The Mafia controlled the docks, the labor unions, and most of the garment industry—and those were the legitimate enterprises."

"You saying the government didn't learn from its mistakes?" said Cape. "I'm shocked."

"Some things never change," said Corelli. "The Russian mob was treated the same when it first appeared in this country. In the seventies, Russian gangsters started coming over in force, but it was another ten years before the FBI assigned a single agent to the problem. *Ten years.*"

"How'd they get into the country?"

"A lot of them are Russian Jews by birth. Back home they probably didn't give a rat's ass about being Jewish—their only religion was money—but their heritage proved mighty useful when it came to immigration."

"Asylum?"

Corelli nodded. "Don't get me wrong—a lot of Russians emigrating in the seventies and eighties were legitimate dissidents, sponsored by U.S. citizens. They were good people who had to either get out or go to jail."

"But not all of them."

"Some were fresh out of the *gulag* and on the verge of going back. Instead they found religion, claimed persecution, and came in under the radar. And after the first wave got a foothold in the U.S., they sponsored their scumbag friends and relatives back home."

"What about *perestroika*?" asked Cape. "The fall of Communism. That must have changed things."

"Yeah, it opened the floodgates. Easier to leave Russia, travel abroad, come back home, or change your citizenship. Even better, it meant millions of dollars in foreign aid pouring into Russia, every cent flowing through the fingers of the *mafiya*."

"How?"

"These guys built the black markets in Russia," said Corelli. "They were the only economy Russia had, so they already controlled 90 percent of the banks. I read an FBI report that estimated almost *six hundred billion* in foreign aid was stolen during the nineties."

Cape whistled. "Naïve question, but didn't the Russian government notice?"

Corelli laughed. "That's the best part—the old guard was so determined to control the money, even after the collapse of the Communist Party, they turned to the KGB."

"A brand you can trust."

"Exactly. Government officials told the organization formerly known as the KGB to work with the *mafiya* to siphon off money from the now-private banks and give the government direct access to the funds."

"Nice."

"It gets even better," said Corelli, pulling his stool closer. Nothing made a cop happier than finding a bureaucracy worse than the one he had to deal with on a daily basis. "The KGB got in bed with the *mafiya* and helped them steal all the money. They turned the loosely organized collection of gangsters and thugs into a well-funded, multinational crime organization."

"That's the spirit of capitalism for you."

"So much for the Cold War, huh?"

"No shit."

"So that's your history lesson for the day," said Corelli. "Any questions?"

"How big is the organization?"

"Let's put it this way," said Corelli. "New York's Russian émigré community numbers about three hundred thousand—that includes law-abiding citizens as well as thick-necked goons. But in Brighton Beach alone, there are almost *five thousand* Russian criminals. That's why they call it Little Odessa."

"Brooklyn."

"My borough," nodded Corelli. "Different neighborhood from where I grew up, but still Brooklyn."

Cape raised one eyebrow. "Five thousand?"

"More than the five families of *La Cosa Nostra* combined," said Corelli. "How about that?"

"Surprised you don't hear more about them."

"You will—*The Sopranos* still sell a lot of DVDs, but the feds actually made headway against the Mafia after Giuliani, since they put Gotti away. After a series of RICO indictments against mob bosses in Miami a few years back, Russians stepped in to take their place. Now half of Miami is under the control of the Russian mob, when before they were only minor players."

"Where else are they?"

"Pretty much everywhere, but only about seventeen cities with any strength."

"Only?"

"There'll be more," said Corelli. "Don't doubt it for a second."

"How about San Francisco?"

"The *Lyubertskaya* crime family has a growing presence on the West coast."

"Why haven't I heard of them before?" asked Cape. "Why hasn't Beau?"

"He probably has, but just doesn't know it. The Russians partner when they can't dominate. They stay in the shadows unless they're running things."

Cape sat up straighter. "Partner?"

"They strike up alliances," said Corelli. "In the case of San Francisco, that's the Italians and Chinese. The Russians will cut deals with them, offer to supply muscle, get to know the city."

"And then?"

"If there's a chance to expand their operation by fucking over one of their business partners, they don't hesitate."

Cape nodded but said nothing. He was out of his depth and knew it. He needed a way in, something that could reduce the scope of the hunt down to a single, tangible target.

"What are they into?" he asked. "Drugs, unions, what?"

"That's the big difference between the Italians and the Russians," said Corelli. "The Italians have a rigid organizational structure, with turf clearly assigned to different captains."

"*Capos.*"

"You must watch *The Sopranos*, too," said Corelli. "They specialize in certain types of criminal activity—mostly unions, gambling, and extortion. But the *mafiya*, the Russians, they'll get into anything that turns a dime."

"Anything."

"The usual stuff—drugs, extortion, gambling—muscle businesses with no finesse involved. But the Russian mob has also been implicated in arms smuggling, Wall Street investment scandals, gasoline tax evasion—even rigging hockey games."

"The NHL?" Cape raised his eyebrows in disbelief. "I knew the league had problems..."

"Believe it," said Corelli. "It was a cash cow for the *mafiya* for a while. A lot of the best players came from former Soviet countries, and the mob squeezed every one for a percentage of their salary. They threaten the players, and if that doesn't work, they threaten their families."

"That supposed to cheer me up?"

Corelli leaned forward and put his hand on Cape's arm. When he spoke, his voice was as flat as his eyes. He sounded like a cop who had seen too much and finally lost his sense of humor, as black as it might be. "Let me be clear about something. These guys are animals. The Italians might threaten to kill you, and in most cases they'll mean it."

Cape met his gaze. "But the Russians …"

"They'll kill your whole family," said Corelli. "They go after cops, journalists, judges. They don't give a fuck. The ones behind bars threaten people from their jail cells. They laugh at our judicial system. I guess after you've been in the *gulag,* you don't scare too easy."

Cape nodded. "Thanks for the warning."

Corelli leaned back, his face softening. "That's about all I know."

"One more question."

"Shoot."

"You mentioned drugs. What drugs are we talking about?"

"Let's see," said Corelli, his tongue moved around the inside of his cheek searching for a memory. "On the import side, they've done business with the Colombians for years—that's all cocaine, mostly smuggled by the Russians into Eastern Europe. On the export side, they move a lot of Turkish heroin."

"Why Turkish?"

"Just happens to be where it comes from," said Corelli. "Turks smuggle most of the heroin moving through Eastern Europe, including the stuff from Pakistan and Afghanistan. According to the government, those drugs fund terrorists."

"I thought that was oil."

"You and me both," replied Corelli. "But when it comes to heroin, you can tell it's Turkish by checking the morphine content—higher than average, sometimes double. The Russians buy it wholesale, then ship it to the States and other drug-addled Western countries."

"Beau always talks about drugs coming into the U.S. along the West coast from Asia."

"He's talking about the Triads."

Cape thought of Sally. "Another fun group of people I wouldn't want to mess with."

Corelli nodded. "Triads pretty much control all the drugs in Asia. The Russians might buy from them and distribute in other countries, but they don't move any heroin themselves into San Francisco or L.A."

Cape shook his head to clear it, a wasted effort. He tried again. Corelli watched him with a sympathetic eye.

"You're just groping around in the dark, aren't you?"

"You've discovered my secret investigative technique," Cape said as he reached for his coffee. "Now I'll have to kill you."

"You have a plan?"

"Not really," said Cape. "You have a suggestion?"

"I think you should go to a plastic surgeon, change your name, and lay low for a while."

"Thanks for the vote of confidence."

"I like you," said Corelli. "I just don't like the odds."

"Me neither," admitted Cape. "One more question?"

Corelli shrugged and took a swig. "I'm off-duty, like I said."

"I know the organization behind the crime, thanks to you, but I need to know the people behind it."

"You want a handle on the guys who tried to kill you." Corelli watched Cape carefully, not liking where this was going.

Cape nodded. "Or someone who knows them."

Corelli sighed. "If you're asking for what I think you are, then I'm gonna win that bet with Beau."

"I won't take it personally."

Corelli looked at him for a full minute, then sighed again.

"You want to meet someone in the *mafiya*."

"That would be nice."

Corelli laughed despite himself.

"I'll see what I can do."

29

"I won't be dead forever."

"That's too bad."

Sally was in the lotus position on the floor of her hotel room, looking far more comfortable than Cape felt. He was sitting on a narrow, high-backed leather chair that must have been designed by an art director with an impossibly small ass. Cape shifted in the chair and managed to replicate the discomfort on his other cheek.

"So I'm going to visit the Berman brothers at Empire this afternoon," he said.

"Need a date?"

"Nah," replied Cape, shifting again. "I'll do better on my own at the studio. But if Corelli comes through for us with a name, I'll need you to suit up."

"So I guess I have some time to kill."

Cape gave Sally a deadpan stare. "In your case, I'd say that's a poor choice of words."

Sally smiled. "I don't freelance anymore," she said. "How are you going to get into Empire's offices?"

"It's a surprise," said Cape, standing. He hobbled toward the door, both his legs asleep. "See you tonight."

After leaving the hotel and walking south a few blocks, Cape turned east until he hit Canal Street, where he found a vintage clothing store. After buying what he needed, he changed in their dressing room. At a hardware store two blocks away, he purchased a metal tool chest and a pair of cutting pliers. He paid cash at both places—no point leaving a credit trail until he was officially back among the living.

Empire was located on the edge of the meatpacking district in a gray five-story building at least a hundred years old. The neighborhood still held slaughterhouses on the west side, but most of the old warehouses were converted into expensive lofts and swanky offices. Yet despite the high rents, there was still enough blood in the streets to give the air a metallic taste when the wind came off the harbor.

The idea for gaining access to Empire Studios unannounced came from listening to Grace describe Adam Berman's fondness for breaking things. Cape figured someone had to come and fix them.

Walking into Empire's lobby was like stepping into a time machine. After passing through a century-old façade, you entered modern Hollywood, a visual onslaught of light and noise. The wall behind the reception desk was dominated by a large flat-screen showing a continuous loop of previews for Empire's films, new and old. On either side of the desk were dwarf palm trees, looking much taller than their fifteen-foot height in the enclosed space. Behind the desk was a woman who at one time had been beautiful, before her piercing compulsion got out of hand.

Cape winced involuntarily as she smiled, each eyebrow ringed with four silver hoops, her lower lip encircled by a gold ring, and her nose pierced with a diamond stud. Cape couldn't count the number of rods and loops in her ears, but he managed to spot not one but two gold balls protruding from her tongue.

"Wek-kum to Em-pah," she said, struggling with the *l* and *r* for obvious reasons. "Can I he-ep you?"

Cape smiled, keeping his tongue to himself.

"Here to fix Mr. Berman's phone," he said, holding up his toolbox. In the worn blue coveralls, he was the walking image of a repairman.

"Again?" said the human pin cushion.

Cape nodded. "Third time this week, I believe."

"OK, I have to call," she said, the last word sounding like "caw."

Cape shook his head, a worried look on his face. "Call who, though? Mr. Berman's phone is broken."

"Sek-ur-ity," she replied.

Cape shrugged and leaned against the desk. "I guess he can wait."

The girl hesitated, the phone halfway to her ear. Her eyes dilated with fear at the prospect of making Mr. Berman wait for anything.

"Fifth floor," she said, suddenly enunciating clearly in her rush to get the words out. "Take a right when you step out of the elevator."

By the time the elevator reached the top floor, Cape had taken off the coveralls and stuffed them into the toolbox. There were only two offices on the fifth floor, one at each end of the hall. Cape turned right. At the door, he slipped the cutting pliers into his pants pocket and set the toolbox on the ground before turning the handle.

Adam Berman was sitting behind his desk, flipping through a stack of paper secured with a large paper clip. Probably a script. Cape hadn't known whether Adam was the fat brother or the tall one, but even from across the room it was obvious.

"So you're the short, fat one," said Cape pleasantly.

Adam looked up, startled, obviously not used to people showing up in his office unannounced. "What did you say?"

"I said I'm here to fix your phone," said Cape, stepping over to the desk.

Adam glanced at the phone, then back at Cape, annoyed. "Somebody already did that," he said. "This phone's not broken."

Cape pulled out the pliers and carefully cut the cord running from the back of the phone.

"It is now."

Adam opened and closed his mouth like a guppy, his eyes wide in disbelief.

"Who the fuck are you?"

Cape set the pliers down and pushed his sleeves back dramatically, stepping back from the desk.

"OK, Mr. Berman," he said, spreading his arms wide, "here's the pitch."

"Oh, fuck," muttered Berman. "Just what I need—some nut-job screenwriter tryin' to pitch a movie. I'll give you points for having big nuts—sneaking in here—but if you don't turn around in one minute and get the fuck out, I'll make sure you *never* work in the movie business."

"Here's the story," continued Cape, undaunted. "A big time producer commits suicide in the middle of a movie by—now get this—jumping off the Golden Gate Bridge. Only he didn't commit suicide—*he was murdered!* So the movie studio hires a hot-shot private detective to get to the bottom of things. I'm thinking George Clooney to play the detective. Or maybe a younger Bruce Willis—like his early days on *Moonlighting*. Or maybe Brad Pitt with the same attitude he had in *Ocean's Eleven*, only looking older..."

Adam's eyes narrowed as he sat up in his chair.

"You're that detective Grace hired."

"How'd you guess?" Cape dropped his hands. "You think I look like Brad Pitt?"

"I think you look fired," said Adam, his face red. "They told me you were dead."

"That's what they said about Elvis." Cape took one of the seats in front of the desk.

Adam sat up even straighter, incredulous that Cape sat down without permission. Unconsciously he reached for the tumbler on his desk.

"Did I say you were fired?"

Cape nodded.

"Then what the fuck are you still doing here?"

Cape shrugged. "Well, I have another client," he said simply. "Who wants me to work on the same case."

"Who?" demanded Adam, leaning forward.

"Normally I don't discuss—"

"*Who?*" yelled Adam, veins bulging in his neck.

"Your brother," said Cape, watching for a reaction. If Grace was right and the brothers barely spoke anymore, he had some leverage. If she was wrong, he'd be finished before he got started.

Adam blinked, his mouth opening and closing. He was apoplectic. It was a full minute before the words came out, and then only in a strangled whisper.

"You're … a … dead … man."

Cape reached out and took the tumbler from Adam's hand, then stood up and walked over to the sideboard. Holding the glass up to the light he caught a golden residue along the bottom of the glass and guessed bourbon. Pouring a new drink he set it down in front of Adam, who reflexively wrapped his fingers around the glass.

"Relax, Adam," said Cape reassuringly. "I'm already dead, remember? Let's talk about something else."

Adam glanced at the broken phone, then at the door behind Cape. There was no escape. His eyes reluctantly came back to the detective. He swallowed half the drink in one gulp. "I got nothin' to say to you," he said slowly, "except *stay away from my business.* That means you can investigate whatever the fuck you want, but don't mess around with my production, or my schedule, or my producers. I don't care how many bodies pile up, as long as they don't prevent me from shooting."

"Such a compassionate position," said Cape. "I'm sure the press would—"

"That's another thing," spat Adam, pulling on the drink again. "Since you showed up, the press has been on me like flies on shit."

"You worried bad publicity might ruin the sale?"

Adam's eyes opened wide, then narrowed again quickly. He finished the drink.

"What sale?"

"What a sense of humor you have," said Cape. "The sale of Empire Studios, of course."

"Who told you about that?" demanded Adam.

Cape hummed a familiar tune before answering. "It's a small world, after all," he said cheerily.

"Jesus." Adam put the empty glass down heavily. He slouched in his chair and exhaled as if he were a balloon slowly deflating.

Cape deftly took the glass and returned to the sideboard. Adam watched him, mute, his eyes half-lidded and red. When Cape put the full glass back in Adam's hand he sat up a little straighter, blinking. He took a loud sip and coughed. Cape let him sit there for a while before saying anything.

"Look, Mr. Berman," Cape said gently. "I'm really not trying to fuck anything up for you. That's not my intent, anyway." Adam relaxed physically, but the hostility in his eyes remained. Cape forged ahead. "And I don't really give a shit if you and your brother want to sell the company."

Adam started to say something, then hesitated. His stare shifted from Cape to the glass in his hand.

Cape had been a detective long enough to know what it meant when someone broke eye contact. "Does your brother know you're planning on selling the company?"

Adam shook his head as if to clear it. He breathed deeply through his nose, then exhaled loudly. When he spoke, his voice had regained some of its earlier tenor, only now it resonated with forced charm instead of hostility. His slur had evaporated with his drink.

"I don't believe this hypothetical sale you're talking about has anything to do with your investigation," he said. "Do *you*?"

170

Cape smiled, the picture of reason. "I honestly don't know. But if you *were* trying to sell the company, I don't think you'd want a prospective buyer to discover that one of your producers was smuggling drugs...do *you*?"

Adam raised his right hand but caught himself before it became an angry gesture. Instead the hand fluttered dismissively. "Drugs," he said. "I *abhor* drugs."

"So you're saying Tom was acting alone?"

"Tom?"

"Your producer," said Cape. "The one who fell off the bridge."

"Tom," nodded Adam. "A real tragedy."

"He worked for you a long time."

"Did he?"

"According to Grace."

At the sound of her name, Adam's eyes hardened, but he smiled expansively.

"Grace is a helluva producer," he said warmly. "But she's a bit, well, *close* to the situation, if you get my meaning?"

"Because she and Tom were involved?" asked Cape bluntly, letting Adam know gossip wouldn't distract him. Letting him know it wasn't news.

Adam laughed coarsely. "OK, so you *are* a detective."

"Cut the bullshit, Adam. What's the deal with the sale?"

Adam moved back in his chair, then came forward again as he talked.

"I love my brother," he said deliberately, looking Cape in the eye, "but he's a pretentious windbag. He thinks we're making art."

"What are you making?"

171

"Me?" said Adam. "I'm in the movie business—I have perfected the art of putting asses in seats. That's the only *art* I give a shit about."

"Fill the theaters," said Cape. "Big box office."

"Fuckin-A," said Adam, pounding his fist on the desk. "You want *haute couture*, go see a play. You want simple and friendly, stay at home and watch television. Movies should be *events*. Movies should be *big*—big screen, big stars, big opening weekend, big box office. Big—big—*BIG!*"

"That's a lot of bigs."

"When it comes to movies," replied Adam, "it can't be big enough. Whoever said size doesn't matter never worked in the movie business."

"And your brother doesn't agree?"

"You can take all the statues and awards my brother collects for his films and sell them at a garage sale, for all I care."

Cape noticed the statues and trophies scattered around the room. One wall was dominated by wooden shelves set behind glass, each cluster of silver and gold idols accented by a plaque with the title and year of the corresponding film. Maybe Adam meant what he said, or maybe someone else put the statues in here. Cape scanned the plaques and didn't see a single award for self-awareness.

"You're saying critics and award shows don't matter to the studios?" he asked.

Adam's mouth twisted with disdain. "The real dick-measuring contest between the studios is over how much their movies grossed by the end of the year. Who's got the most cash to throw at the next picture. *That's* how you get the big stars. *That's* how you get to make more movies. It's a numbers game, plain and simple."

"And you want to win."

"We have won." Adam pounded the desk again. "We've proven we can compete with those Hollywood cocksuckers."

"So why sell?"

Adam nodded to himself, rocking a little in his chair as if to build momentum. The reticence he'd shown only minutes before had evaporated in the heat of the discussion. He was on a rant, and there was no stopping him.

"Movies cost money," he explained. "*Big* movies cost *big* money."

"OK."

"You know how much money?"

"Big money?" offered Cape.

"Exactly," said Adam, nodding. "*Big money*. That asteroid movie we're making cost almost two hundred million dollars, and that's *before* marketing and distribution costs. The special effects alone cost almost fifty million—it cost almost ten million just to destroy San Francisco."

Cape raised his eyebrows. "You're destroying San Francisco?"

"Sure," said Adam, waving his hand. "No big deal—the guys at Industrial Light & Magic are doing the computer graphics. It's only ten seconds of screen time, but it's critical to the story, so you gotta pay. In the last movie we destroyed Paris—it was great."

Cape remembered the scene—gargoyles on Notre Dame gazing down upon an apocalyptic wasteland. "I forgot you destroyed Paris."

"Absolutely," said Adam, grinning. "Pissed off the French, let me tell you. After we released the film internationally, the *frogs* started a letter-writing campaign to get the movie banned. 'Course the publicity drove the Germans and the English to the theaters in droves. I heard the audiences cheered when the asteroid toasted the *Champs Élysées*. We broke a London record for box office receipts—it was great."

"You were talking about costs," prompted Cape, "and the sale."

"Right," said Adam. "So like I said, movies are expensive. To get this one made, I had to beg, borrow, and steal."

"In that order?"

Adam narrowed his eyes, then gave Cape a thin smile.

"Funny guy," he said.

"So how'd you get the money?"

"That's the point," said Adam. "Every time you make a movie it's a gamble, and the stakes are huge. The movie's a hit, everybody gets rich. It's a bomb, then we're talkin' a lot of cash right down the drain, not to mention the reputations of a lot of people who take themselves very seriously."

"Not sure you answered my question," said Cape pleasantly.

"Relax," said Adam. "Because it's a gamble, and there are only so many people out there with that kind of cash, it's different for every movie. That's a big part of my job."

"Raising money."

"Finding investors to back the production costs."

"Where do you find them?"

"Anywhere I can," said Adam simply. "Under a rock, if I have to. Sometimes it's a rich eccentric who wants a taste of Hollywood, other times it's a big corporation looking for product placement in the film. We've even fronted the money ourselves, or split costs with another studio."

"Sounds complicated," said Cape sympathetically.

"It's a pain in the ass," said Adam fervently. "And that, you nosy son of a bitch, is why I want to sell the company."

Despite the language, Adam's tone was comparatively civil. Cape realized this had become a business conversation for him, not something personal. Adam Berman was on a soapbox, representing himself in the court of public opinion. Cape had just heard the rough draft of the press release. He marveled at the ability to move seamlessly from one mood to the next, light to dark and back again, with almost no physical warning signs. Looking at the half-empty glass in Berman's hand, he concluded it wasn't just the booze. This guy was right out of central casting for a Hollywood stereotype—the bombastic type-A movie executive. Adam was so lost in the role that he'd forgotten how normal people behaved.

Cape decided it was time to reel him back in. "So if you sell, then someone else can pick up the tab. You get to focus on making movies again."

Adam snapped his fingers and pointed, his eyes bright. "Bingo. The big-ass media company gets the prestige of owning a premier movie studio, and we get the big corporate checkbook to fund production of the next asteroid movie, or whatever we decide to shoot after that."

"So you want me to be discreet."

"I want you to go away," said Adam, "but obviously that's not gonna happen, not if my dear brother wants you around. Shit, I can't even get you outta my office."

Cape shrugged. "Inertia."

"Maybe it's better that you're looking into this instead of the cops. Maybe that abrasive *bit*—" He caught himself, barely. "Maybe Grace was right about that."

"The cops *are* looking into this."

"That's what worries me," said Adam, rubbing his chin. "They'll bumble around, the way cops do, and fuck up my schedule. Unless you figure something out first—then maybe they'll lose interest, go back to eating donuts."

"Does that mean you're not going to fire me?"

Adam shook his head, suddenly magnanimous. "You've got *chutzpah*," he said. "I could use some of that around here. And besides, we're a family business—you're one of us, I guess."

"Gosh," said Cape, knowing the sarcasm wouldn't register.

"You Jewish?" asked Adam. "Me and Harry, we're Jews. Not that it makes any difference, but it's always nice to work with another member of the tribe, you know what I'm saying?"

"I'm circumcised."

"Close enough!" Adam slapped his hand on the desk. "Welcome to the Empire family."

Cape stood up. "Thanks, Mr. Berman," he said, backing slowly away from the desk. He figured it was better to leave on a high note. "I won't let you down."

Adam nodded absently as he fondled the empty tumbler in his hand and stared vacantly at his desk.

Cape was at the door. "Anything else you need?"

Adam's head swiveled sideways. He frowned as he stared at his desk, as if trying to remember something. When he glanced at Cape, his eyes looked glazed once again.

"Yeah," he said. "Get somebody up here to fix my phone, will you?"

30

Angelo wondered if a pierced tongue really felt better during oral sex.

Strolling through the lobby with the cup of corporate coffee he'd bought on the corner, he pushed his sunglasses onto his head so he could make eye contact with the receptionist as he crossed to the elevators. He figured one more week of meaningful eye contact and she'd agree to blow him in his office.

"Heh-whoa, *An-juh-woh*," she said warmly, light glinting off the metal in her face. Jesus, but those had to hurt going in, and what did she do at an airport? Must be a strip search every time.

"Hey, Celene," said Angelo, dropping his voice an octave to signal his virility. "What's goin' on?"

"Not much," she replied, smiling broadly at having said something that didn't sound like a tongue twister. Angelo construed her expression as pure lust. "That phone guy is here."

Angelo stopped in mid-stride. "What phone guy?"

"To fix *Mistuh Buh-man's* phone," said Celene tentatively.

"I got that phone fixed yesterday," Angelo said to himself as much as anyone. Then, turning back to the receptionist, he asked, "What did the guy look like?"

Celene smiled hopefully. "Kinda cute."

Angelo scowled. "And security took him up?"

Celene blanched, the metal pins in her eyebrows, nose, and lips vibrating with anxiety. Before she could say anything, Angelo snapped.

"You're fucking kidding me. You didn't call security?"

Celene looked at her bank of phones, willing them to start ringing.

"He's up there now, with no escort?"

Celene looked up and shrugged. "He *th-thed* the ph-phone was broken."

Angelo stared at her for a full minute with open disdain until he felt cold sweat trickle down his back, his imagination running wild over who might be wandering around upstairs. Suddenly that blowjob seemed impossibly far away.

Without another word, Angelo turned and sprinted for the elevators.

31

THE LIGHTED BUTTON ON the intercom stared at Cape like an unblinking eye, daring him to make the first move.

Cape had left Adam Berman alone with his empty glass, then walked the length of the hallway, hesitating only briefly at the elevator. Even though he'd been embraced as the newest member of the Empire family, he doubted Adam would remember having said that, let alone admit it. Cape estimated he'd been in the building at least twenty minutes, if not thirty. He was pushing his luck if he wanted to avoid a confrontation with security.

With a final look over his shoulder, he pushed the button.

Nothing happened. No buzzer or chimes sounded from the other side of the door. He hoped to get himself inside as he did with Adam, without an invitation. He tried the door handle, but it was locked. Leaning closer to the intercom, Cape pushed the button again, speaking clearly into the microphone.

"Avon calling."

Silence. Cape stood for several seconds, wondering if he should have claimed to be the Fuller Brush Man, but worried he'd be dating himself. He was considering *aluminum siding* as his next play when he heard the click of an electric door latch.

Harry Berman smiled placidly from his screen. Cape took a short step backward, trying to put the face in some kind of perspective. Despite Grace's descriptions, the first encounter with the floating visage was unnerving. The gigantic eyes blinked as Harry quietly regarded his visitor, giving Cape the queasy sensation the wall was shaking in an earthquake

"Have a seat, detective," said Harry, the bass from the speakers reverberating through Cape's chest.

Cape scanned the room as he pulled up a chair some distance from the screen. One wall was all windows, though the blinds were drawn, obscuring what Cape imagined was a view of New York Harbor, if his bearings were right. The other walls were bare, paneled in an expensive-looking dark wood, with the exception of the wall facing Cape, which was moving again.

Harry's enormous head swiveled left and right as he followed Cape's visual tour of the office. The motion made Cape dizzy. He was glad to be sitting down.

"Pretty spartan, I suppose," said Harry pleasantly. "I'm not there to spruce it up."

"Where are you?" asked Cape, studying the scene behind Harry's giant head. Sailboats bobbed in choppy waters off a rugged coast, the horizon bleeding away on either side.

"Someplace safe," replied Harry. "Someplace nice."

"Safe from what?" asked Cape, careful to look at the camera above the screen. "Or should I say whom?"

Harry smiled, but his eyes looked infinitely sad. "Do you know much about sociophobia, Mr. Weathers?"

Cape shook his head. "Not really," he replied. "Fear of social situations, interpersonal contact—is that right?"

"In most cases, yes," nodded Harry. Cape was getting used to the motion. It was like being at sea, onboard a fishing boat. Once you adjusted to the scale and the motion, your stomach settled down.

"But not in your case?" asked Cape.

"My case is a bit more ... *extreme*, I suppose."

"You seem perfectly comfortable to me," said Cape, trying to sound sincere.

"Oh, I am," said Harry, smiling. "But if you were to come here—or I there, well ..." His voice trailed off, echoing around the room.

"Uncomfortable."

"Paralyzed," corrected Harry. "Absolutely rigid with anxiety. Unable to speak."

"Must be hard for someone in the movie business."

"It was devastating," nodded Harry. Cape resisted the urge to nod with him, the force of the motion so compelling. "But I'd already established my reputation in the industry by that time, and I was always well connected. I'm not the first media mogul to run his empire over the phone. The whole damn industry is just a bunch of people yakking on cell phones."

"So it hasn't stopped you from running Empire?"

Harry shook his head. "Quite the contrary," he replied. "It has given me ... perspective. I can look at things from a distance, both literally and figuratively."

"I thought you might be hiding from someone," said Cape. "Someone in particular."

"You have someone in mind?"

Cape shrugged. "I was hoping you'd tell me. Maybe I could help you find them before they found you."

"No one is looking for me," said Harry emphatically. "And no one can find me."

Cape studied the coastline again as Harry broke eye contact. Something about the water, the way the view seemed too big for the window. The sense you were up high, not in a beach house. He switched his gaze back to the camera. "Surely your presence has been missed."

Harry's eyes narrowed, then grew wide again as the smile returned. "You're talking about my brother, aren't you, Mr. Weathers? Or should I call you Cape?"

"Cape's fine."

"An unusual name," said Harry jovially. "Is it a family name, or is it short for something?"

"*Capable*—my parents wanted to instill confidence at an early age."

Harry chuckled, the sound like kettle drums in the confines of the office.

"How refreshing to meet someone with a sense of humor."

"You're the first person to notice," said Cape. "And you're right, I was asking about your brother. It seems he's running the show these days."

Harry nodded. "It does seem that way, doesn't it? But surely in your profession, you must know that things aren't always as they seem."

Cape shrugged. "You haven't made a movie in a while."

"True," said Harry. "My circumstances have removed me from the day-to-day joys of production, but there are other matters that demand my attention. The studio's relationships with certain actors, critics, distributors, and theater owners, for example. I spend hours on the phone each day maintaining those contacts."

"Adam has certainly kept busy in your, um, absence," said Cape. "He's been stacking one movie after another, each one bigger than the last."

"Ours is a collaborative venture," replied Harry. "My brother brings ambition, and I bring craft. Together we've proven that Hollywood can exist outside of Los Angeles."

"Is that why you started Empire? To prove something?"

Harry chuckled again. "You are direct, aren't you?" he said amiably. "I like that, I must say. Yes, I suppose that's true. My brother was blacklisted in Hollywood, did you know that?"

"No, I didn't."

"Indeed." Harry nodded until a giant hand appeared briefly and stroked his chin. "He was working for one of the big studios—it doesn't matter which one—they're all the same. He was moving up quickly. Reading scripts, getting a hand in development. He was attached to several major projects."

"What happened?"

"He slept with a co-worker, another young producer."

"So?" asked Cape. "Doesn't that happen all he time in Hollywood?"

"Of course it does, but this young producer was engaged to the head of the studio."

"Oops."

"You have a talent for understatement, Cape," replied Harry. "My brother fucked the wrong woman, and we got fucked in return."

"We?"

"The studio chief went after both of us," explained Harry. "It was personal, and he was very powerful. You know the expression *you'll never work in this town again?*"

"He meant it."

"Hollywood is a small town," said Harry. "He knew we were brothers, and he decided to burn the whole family. I was working at another studio and already had two small, critically acclaimed movies under my belt. I had good relationships with some actors. I was going someplace, but it wasn't meant to be—one indiscretion later and we were on the street. Goodbye Hollywood, hello New York City."

Cape searched Harry's projected face for any signs of remorse or anger, but found none. "Given it was your brother Adam who left his fly open, you seem pretty gracious about the whole thing."

Harry frowned momentarily, then looked at Cape with a somber expression.

"I love my brother, but he's a child. An impetuous boy who has dedicated his life to winning a game he doesn't understand. He is brilliant, in his own way, but he needs adult supervision."

"You're saying you're still in charge," suggested Cape. "And not out of touch."

The wall rose up again as Harry smiled, then settled.

"Are you referring to the *sale* of Empire Studios, detective?"

"Am I?"

"How discreet of you to not simply come out and say it."

"So you know about it?"

Harry laughed, loudly this time. Cape unconsciously gripped the arms of the chair.

"Know about it?" asked Harry. "Why, Cape—*I arranged it.*"

Cape looked closely at the foot-wide eyes on the screen and nodded in understanding. "You have all the industry contacts."

"My brother doesn't spend much time in theme parks," said Harry. "He's afraid of mice."

"Why sell?"

"Didn't Adam explain that to you? For the money, of course."

"But control of the studio. Your films—"

"Are my legacy," said Harry. "I don't care if anyone goes to see my movies on opening weekend—I want to know people will be watching my movies ten, or even a hundred, years from now."

Cape remained silent, waiting for the punch line.

"But even I have to admit that artistic vision won't pay the rent," continued Harry. "And even for my so-called *small* films, the rent is considerable. Now that our studio can attract top talent, the quality of our films has gone up considerably."

"And so have the budgets."

"A small film costs over ten million dollars," said Harry. "And that assumes all the actors take a pay cut, because they want to make the film, maybe win an award. The big movies—my brother's cartoon creations—cost a fortune. They used to generate enough money to carry us through the next production, but finding individual investors to back each individual movie has become … untenable."

"So you made the call to let the big entertainment companies know that Empire was on the block."

"Of course, but don't tell Adam. He's more productive when he thinks he's in charge. After he started getting calls, he acted like it was his idea."

"Why didn't you tell him yourself?"

Harry sighed, causing Cape to lean back in his chair as the wall appeared to expand outward. "My brother and I don't speak."

"Why? You seem to agree on the sale."

"We agree on almost everything, when it comes to business," said Harry. "It's art that pushed us apart. My brother has a chip on his shoulder that won't go away. He's obsessed with size, with money. He believes that I think he's a hack, with no artistic sensibilities. And I suppose he's right."

"You're brothers."

"That only makes it worse," said Harry. "Sibling rivalry on a colossal scale. It's why we worked so well together at the start— boyhood competition applied to the movie business. But when we started measuring our success differently, when the critics and the press started to favor my films over his movies, then the underlying tension became too great. A couple of years ago, it came to a head. That's when I lost my brother—to the greed of Hollywood."

"But you both want the money from the sale."

Harry shook his head. "For different reasons, Cape. Very different reasons. The infusion of capital will free us both to pursue our own interests, without being dependent on this symbiotic relationship between his movies and mine. I won't look to him for cash ever again, and he won't be under the shadow of my films with the critics."

"You're going to split Empire into two different companies," said Cape. "And you need someone to fund your separation from your brother."

"Right now we're Siamese twins who have grown to hate each other, joined at the hip. The buyer of our studio is the surgeon, and their money is the scalpel." Harry moved his head sideways to reveal fog on the horizon. The sailboats had vanished and the water looked choppy.

"You want Adam to think he's the one driving the deal."

Harry nodded. "I don't know if he'd scrap the deal altogether, but he'd certainly mess it up, if only out of spite. He couldn't stand knowing he was the beneficiary of my contacts, my influence. He'd try to cut a deal with another company, just to prove he could go it alone—costing us months, if not years of progress."

"My lips are sealed."

"I'm taking that for granted, detective."

"But why tell me in the first place?"

"I have a feeling you'd find out eventually," replied Harry. "You seem, well … tenacious."

"Stubborn, at any rate." Cape shifted in his seat, waiting for the next time Harry pulled back from the screen. *Fog on the water.* Cape had seen that view before, driving in a car.

"I believe in being forthright," said Harry. "You can tell when you're speaking to a man of character, even if you're looking at him through a camera lens."

"Speaking of which," said Cape. "How did you know who I was? I never introduced myself."

The giant eyes blinked, revealing nothing. "You're not the only resourceful one involved in this case, detective. I do my homework.

And to be honest, I don't get many visitors." The eyes shifted toward the door, then back to Cape.

Cape took the hint. "But you're probably overdue for a visit from Angelo."

Harry smiled again. "Another man who does his homework. How excellent. Don't worry about Angelo. He's just a little over-protective. Sometimes forgets who he works for."

"Must be tough, between you and your brother."

"Poor Angelo must bear the brunt of our rather dysfunctional relationship. I suppose it's made him conflicted. I think sometimes it's easier for Angelo to work for himself than either Adam or me."

"I'm not worried about him, but I don't have much time," said Cape. "And I doubt he'll do anything but waste mine, even if you and your brother are the ones paying me. It would be easier on everyone, especially Angelo, if we didn't cross paths."

Harry chuckled again. "You certainly sound *capable*. I look forward to seeing your progress with the investigation."

"So do I." Cape stood and started toward the door. "Thanks for your time, Mr. Berman."

"Harry," boomed the friendly voice. "I was always just Harry."

"Well, Harry," said Cape, turning back to face the camera. "I was just wondering…"

"Yes?"

"Are you in San Francisco?"

Cape threw it out with no preamble, studying the screen for a reaction. A look to the left, a glance upward. The pupils contracting. *Nothing.* Harry gave him the poker stare again, the eyes blinking slowly.

"Because," Cape continued, "that view behind you, it looks like Sea Cliff, a swanky neighborhood on the north side of San Francisco. Multimillion dollar homes up on a cliff overlooking the ocean. Popular with celebrities, pro athletes, maybe guys who own movie studios. You don't get fog on the water like that anywhere on the East Coast, and out west you really only see it in northern California."

Harry smiled gently. "Glad you're on the case, detective."

Cape could take a hint. The interview was over. He turned and stepped into the hallway, making sure the door latched behind him before walking briskly to the elevator. He was glancing toward Adam Berman's office when the door burst open and Angelo stepped into the hallway and pointed at Cape, his mouth open in alarm.

Cape knew it was Angelo. No self-respecting security guard would wear a suit like that, and he fit Grace's description to a T.

"You!" Angelo shouted. "What were you doing with Mr. Berman?"

A gentle *ping* announced the arrival of the elevator. As the doors opened, Cape stepped in and turned to face Angelo, who was storming down the hall.

"You'd better go see Harry right away, Angelo—I think he's pissed," said Cape as the doors began to close. "He was so red in the face that I had to adjust both the color *and* the contrast on his big screen, but it didn't seem to help."

Angelo reached the elevator doors too late to stop them from closing. Cape glimpsed one glowering eye through the narrowing gap between the doors as Angelo pounded his fist against the metal, his face turning colors you couldn't get on any TV, no matter how big the screen.

32

"I COULD SHOOT YOU now, if you want."

Corelli was waiting in the lobby bar when Cape returned to the hotel. He'd secured a small table near the entrance, on the fringe of a crowd that eddied around the bar with surging sexual energy and a bad case of congenital hipness. Cape felt his eyes would start watering any minute from all the pheromones in the air.

"Thanks anyway," said Cape. "I'm already dead, remember?"

"I never met anyone in such a hurry to go from being dead to getting killed," said Corelli. "Thought I'd save you the trouble of getting whacked by someone you don't know."

"That's really thoughtful, but I'll pass. I take it you found me a gangster?"

Corelli nodded. "If anyone knows the guys you're up against, it'd be him."

"And he's willing to talk?"

"Not exactly."

"What does that mean?"

"It means I don't know."

"You haven't talked to him?"

"Won't talk to cops," said Corelli. "Doesn't trust 'em."

"Why see me?"

"Because you'll see him first."

"Is this a riddle?"

Corelli scowled. "I can't introduce you, but I can tell you where to find him. The rest is up to you."

Cape nodded. "Fair enough."

Corelli studied Cape before continuing. "I want you to understand you'll be on your own."

Cape nodded. "You're saying you don't have jurisdiction."

"I'm saying no one does," said Corelli, "except the Russians. The guy I'm going to tell you about is in Brighton Beach."

"Brooklyn," said Cape. "You mentioned that."

"A scenic seaside community of hard-working immigrants, if you want me to quote from the guidebook."

"Sounds lovely."

"It is," said Corelli, "especially this time of year. And most of the people out there are gems. But it's also a major hub for the *mafiya*, so badges don't mean much in that neighborhood."

"That's OK—I don't wear one."

"I know," said Corelli. "With your attitude toward authority, I'm not surprised."

"You've been talking with my third grade teacher, haven't you?"

"Just wanted you to understand the environment, smart-ass."

"They came at me in broad daylight in San Francisco, Corelli," said Cape. "It can't be any worse out here."

"Good point. I guess you're fucked either way."

"So who am I looking for?" asked Cape.

Corelli hunched his shoulders and leaned forward, his elbows on the table, the caricature of someone about to whisper a secret.

"The guy you're looking for is called the Pole."

"He's Polish?" said Cape more loudly than he intended. "I thought the *mafiya* wasn't an equal opportunity employer."

Corelli shook his head impatiently. "He's called *the Pole*, but he's Russian. From Odessa originally—real name's Sergei Kovovich. Tough son of a bitch. Been shot ten times, twice with a shotgun, and survived three bombings. Of all the old bosses in the Russian *mafiya*, he came the closest to running the whole thing himself."

"So why do they call him the Pole?"

"It's one of those gangster nicknames," replied Corelli. "Probably got it inside—it's short for magnetic pole, 'cause the guy's magnetic."

"He's *what*?"

"He's got so much lead and steel buckshot in his body, the doctors couldn't get it all out," replied Corelli. "They say the lead is slowly killing him from blood poisoning, but they've been saying that for years. But the shrapnel and bullet fragments have rubbed against each other for so long, they've become magnetized."

"You're serious."

Corelli nodded. "Get too close to this guy and your watch will stop."

"I don't wear a watch," said Cape, remembering his last exchange with Linda and the Sloth.

"Just as well."

"You said he came the closest to uniting the mob," said Cape. "Why past tense?"

"He's retired," said Corelli. "Guess he got tired of getting shot. All the other bosses were jealous of his power, so after a while they took turns trying to take him out. It became almost a rite of passage as people rose higher in the organization. The last attack killed his wife. So the Pole got them together and divvied up his holdings on the condition they leave him alone."

"Did they?"

"He's still alive," answered Corelli, "and nobody's made any moves against him, at least as far as we've seen."

"Sounds dubious."

"I checked with some guys at the Bureau, and they swear he's low profile."

"But he stayed in Brighton Beach."

Corelli shrugged. "It's home."

"Why not go back to Russia?"

"The guy spent fifteen years in the *gulag*," replied Corelli. "I don't think he misses the mother country."

Both men were quiet for a minute. Cape asked, "If he's retired, why not approach someone more current?"

"Two reasons," said Corelli. "The first: someone currently in the game won't talk to anyone they don't do business with—they'll just shoot first, then hide your body before you can even introduce yourself. So unless you're willing to go undercover and go into business with these guys, you're an outsider. And if I'm not mistaken, you don't have that kind of time."

"Reason number two?"

"There's a difference between retired and out of touch," said Corelli. "The feds I spoke with swear the Pole knows *everybody*. He's an icon to younger gangsters. They come by and pay their respects, ask his advice—that sort of shit. So if anyone knows your friends in San Francisco, it's him."

"So what's the risk?"

"He may be retired, but he's still an important guy. That means protection. I don't know who, or how many. But he's not going to be alone, even if it looks that way."

Cape nodded. "Where do I find him?"

Corelli pushed a crumpled piece of paper across the table.

"Drew you a map," he said, "you being a tourist. Take the F-train at the station near the Brooklyn Bridge and go all the way to Brighton Beach. There's a small park next to the boardwalk. The Pole plays chess there every morning while he eats breakfast."

"Who's he play with?"

"Himself, mostly," answered Corelli. "Every once in a while someone joins him for a game, but the rest of the time he sits there quietly, moving pieces on both sides."

Cape took the map and put it in his pocket. "Thanks, Corelli." He stood, extending his hand. Corelli's grip was firm, his eyes serious despite his smile.

"This guy may not be that talkative."

"I know."

"So don't hesitate to walk away. Don't press him."

"Sure."

"We'll find another guy."

"You always this overprotective?" asked Cape. "You must have little kids at home."

Corelli laughed. "A four-year-old and one on the way."

Cape nodded. "Thanks again."

"Remember, he won't be alone."

"That's OK," said Cape. "Neither will I."

33

If you want to change your perspective, just look at the ocean.

Harry Berman always believed water was healing. It was almost spiritual. That's why he owned several waterfront properties around the world. And this particular view of the ocean really was extraordinary, especially when the fog rolled in.

Are you in San Francisco? Harry didn't laugh much these days, but the detective's question was so blunt it was comical. Hiring the detective hadn't been Harry's idea—that credit went to Grace—but there was no denying the man's determination. He might be getting paid by the studio, but he worked for himself. For the truth. He was clearly an anachronism, a stubborn fool who probably watched too many Humphrey Bogart movies growing up.

But didn't we all?

The ocean surged as whitecaps danced across the water, but the view didn't really change. Its impact was the same no matter what time of day it was, as constant as the sea itself. Much like Harry's power, undiminished despite his being physically absent from the studio. If anything, being gone had only enhanced his mystique. He reappeared whenever he was needed, and he could be anywhere at the speed of light. On a television screen, a computer, a phone. Reaching across the digital landscape to bring order to chaos. To take the reins from his schizophrenic brother.

But if it all turned to shit, Harry would just disappear. Even Adam wouldn't be able to find him.

Having that detective on the payroll was probably making Adam nervous. Anything or anyone Adam couldn't control was considered a problem, a cancer. A threat. But Harry had known men like the detective over the years. Even the smartest of them had more courage than brains. A man like that would succeed or die trying.

Harry wasn't going to bet which one was more likely. He never liked to gamble and wasn't about to start now. Life was too short. Besides, he had the ocean to keep him entertained.

The detective was Adam's problem now.

34

CAPE DECIDED TO CONDUCT the rest of his investigation from the shower.

He felt the stress of the past few days slowly dissipate as the water cascaded over him. If he could convince the hotel to install a waterproof phone, and if the hot water didn't run out, then he'd never have to leave. And since he didn't look anything like Janet Leigh and Anthony Perkins was dead, he figured he'd be safe in the shower.

After what seemed like a long time, he felt the temperature begin to falter and heard a distant banging in the pipes. Either that or it was the hotel manager pounding on the door, demanding that he stop wasting all the hot water. Grudgingly and against his better judgment, Cape stepped from the shower back into reality.

He examined his side in the mirror as he wrapped a towel around his waist. A livid red tract ran along his left side, halfway up his ribs. Tender to the touch but more stiff than painful. Throwing another towel around his shoulders, Cape walked into the bedroom and lay down, reaching for the television remote. Selecting the menu option, he scrolled through the pay-per-view movies offered by the hotel.

The first three were action films based on successful comic books. The next two were adapted from best-selling spy novels. The next was based on a popular television program from the seventies that Cape thought was stupid when he was a kid. The next four featured popular young actors or pop stars appearing in remakes of famous films from the fifties. "Franchises," said Cape morosely, switching the remote to regular television. "Nothing but franchises."

Cape flipped through the channels, too exhausted to focus on anything in particular. He jumped from reality TV to the news, though he had trouble telling them apart. As his mind shut down and his thumb kept twitching, he worked his way toward the outer reaches of cable. A woman with a turban and a grossly exaggerated Jamaican accent promised to reveal secrets of a successful love life. Cape was staring at the phone number flashing across the screen, thinking he should write it down, when he fell asleep with the remote still clutched in his hand.

The dream came in a rush, an onslaught of images with no build-up or story line, a jumble of random anxieties set to music. Busby Berkeley trapped in a tequila nightmare.

Cape was facing Tom, the airborne producer, who looked as he appeared in the police photographs—skin purple, bloated, and split from the impact and exposure to salt water. There were no whites to his eyes—they were completely black as he stared at Cape accusingly.

Cape was about to say something in his defense when Tom clapped his hands together, and suddenly they were surrounded. All the people Cape had met over the past few days circled them, clapping their hands and stomping their feet. Grace, Adam and Harry

Berman, even Ursa stood cheering. Tom crouched and crossed his arms over his chest, and Cape noticed for the first time that Tom was wearing a fur hat and a sash belt, just like a Cossack from an old movie. Tom kicked and jumped as the crowd pounded out a rhythm. Behind him, the night sky was filled with asteroids and colored planets, shooting stars bringing light and fireworks to the celebration.

Tom produced a sword out of thin air, a curved blade with a golden pommel. He was spinning now, the sword flashing in brilliant arcs as Tom kicked and danced across the floor toward Cape.

Cape tried to move his arms but couldn't, vaguely aware he was dreaming but unable to do anything about it. All he could do was stand there and watch as Tom spun closer, anger and betrayal reflected in his black eyes.

With a final flourish, Tom leapt into the air, the gleaming blade moving like a scythe. Cape felt the steel cut through his neck as his head separated from his body and flew into space, sailing over the crowd like a rogue asteroid. From a great height, Cape watched as his headless body collapsed to the floor. The cheers and shouts from the crowd were deafening. The last thing he saw, as his head disappeared into the night sky, was Grace moving his body aside and taking his place at the center of the circle.

Cape sat up with a start, hand at his neck. He tilted his head back and forth to make sure it was securely in place. The hotel room was dark except for flashing lights from the television. The Jamaican woman was back, this time promising to predict his future.

"I already know," muttered Cape. "I'll get beheaded by an angry Cossack and turned into a rogue asteroid." He grabbed the remote and turned off the television. "And one day my head will plummet back to Earth, destroying either Paris or San Francisco."

He stood and stretched, looking at the clock. No way he was going back to sleep. He rummaged through his bag until he found the phone number Grace had given him. It wasn't this late in San Francisco.

The phone rang eight times before a connection was made. Cape heard voices in the background and remembered that Grace had mentioned it was a cell phone. It was another minute before she came on the line.

"It's Grace."

"If someone invites you to a Russian folk dance," said Cape, "don't go."

Grace recognized his voice. "Where are you?"

"Still in New York," said Cape. "Where are you?"

"ILM," said Grace, adding, "Industrial Light & Magic."

"George Lucas's place," said Cape. "Special effects."

"Right. We're using cutting-edge graphics on this picture."

"You want to call me back?"

"No," said Grace hurriedly, "I'm glad you called ... I was think-ing ... wondering how you were doing." Cape heard the sound of a door closing, then white noise in the background instead of voices.

"You wouldn't believe what the guys here can do," said Grace excitedly.

"Have you destroyed San Francisco yet? I was hoping to clean out my apartment before you did."

"How did you know about that?" demanded Grace. "That's sup-posed to be kept under wraps. We're not even featuring that scene in the movie trailer."

"Adam Berman told me."

"You talked with him?" Grace's tone suggested she was either impressed or worried. "And he told you about San Francisco? He must have been in a good mood."

"He was, right after his bad mood—and right before his other bad mood."

"That's usually the way it is with Adam—I think the term is bipolar."

"He's nuts," said Cape.

"You're not the first person to make that observation," said Grace. "What else did he tell you?"

"That he loves his brother."

Grace laughed abruptly. "He's got a strange way of showing it."

"That's what I was thinking," replied Cape. "What have you been up to?"

"Back into production ... which feels good," said Grace. "I finish up here tomorrow, then we start shooting again at the end of the week. By then I want to have all the numbers straightened out, which is a pain in the ass."

"What numbers?"

"The ones I inherited from Tom," said Grace. "The film budget, including all the breakdowns."

"What do you mean by straightened out?"

"I just have to get up to speed on where all the money came from, and where it's going."

"Isn't that why you have a budget?"

"When you start production you've estimated every cost, but once you begin filming, everything changes. You save money during the film transfer, then you move it to cover the overage in editing. You shoot more days than you expected because of bad weather, then you've got to find the money somewhere else. By the time you're done it's a completely different set of numbers. Tom was handling all of that."

"So you have to understand where Tom spent money and how much you have left?"

"Pretty much," said Grace. "Plus, Adam wants me to adjust the points."

"Points?"

"Sorry," said Grace. "Percentage points—the money the film makes that's given to certain people if it's a hit."

"Profit sharing," said Cape.

"Something like that, although the way the points get assigned in Hollywood is complicated. Some people don't get any, others get a percentage of the gross receipts at the box office, while others get a percentage of the net profits, if there are any."

"I take it your stature on the film has something to do with what you get."

"Exactly. It's very, well, political."

"So what does Adam want you to do?"

Grace hesitated, as if she'd backed herself into a conversation she'd rather drop. Cape let the silence linger.

"Adam wants me to change the allocations because of Tom's death."

Cape sat up straighter on the bed. "Is that legal?"

"I didn't think so at first," said Grace, "so I told him to go fuck himself. And besides, it's a shitty thing to do, since Tom's daughter deserves to get his share of the profits."

Cape didn't say anything. She was right—it was a shitty thing to do—but he didn't want to derail her explanation, which was sounding more like a motive with every breath.

"So Adam faxed me the contracts for the film, and right there in the fine print nobody read—including me—it says that, in the event someone leaves the picture during production, for any reason, then he or she will be paid for their time on the set but forfeit all their points associated with the final release of the film."

Cape waited another minute before saying anything. "So you're saying that because Tom got killed, the rest of you will make more money?"

"Uh-huh," Grace said quietly. "That's about the size of it. The way the contracts are written, it's the same as if he walked off the set."

Cape was wide awake now, the dream long forgotten. "How much more money?"

"That's part of what I'm supposed to figure out," replied Grace. "Tom was the senior producer, so he got more points than I did. Most will go to Adam and Harry, split equally between them, and the director gets a big chunk. Frankly, it will ultimately depend on how we do at the box office."

"Say the movie does better than the last asteroid film," suggested Cape.

"Millions," replied Grace without hesitation. "We could be talking millions."

Cape stared out the window of his hotel, watching the red taillights of the taxis chase each other around lower Manhattan.

"What happens if you get killed?" he asked.

"You're not on that ag—"

Cape cut her off. "What happens?"

"Same thing," replied Grace. "The money goes to Adam and Harry. Most of it, anyway. The same is true if I walk off the set."

"Right up until the final day of production?"

Cape heard Grace take a deep breath and let it out. "As far as I can tell. I'd need a lawyer to look at the contracts. I have a guy in L.A."

"Call him."

"Way ahead of you."

"How could he—or you—have missed this?"

"We've made four movies with Empire," said Grace, sounding very tired. "Everyone just assumed it was their standard contract, same as the last one."

Cape didn't respond. He stared out the window, letting his eyes drift out of focus as the cars painted colored lines up and down the street.

"Nice business, huh?" Grace's voice was tinny and weak over the wireless connection.

Cape turned away from the window. "When will you understand the rest of the film's budget?"

"Maybe a day or two," said Grace. "I need time to go through the books, and right now I'm too busy destroying San Francisco. Why?"

"Don't know," replied Cape. "Money is a damn good motive—so I'd like to know where the money's going and, if possible, where it came from."

Grace was quiet for a moment as the weight of the conversation landed on her. "When will you be back?"

"Good question," said Cape. "Guess it all depends on whether or not I get killed again."

35

"WE'RE TALKING TODAY," SAID Cape. "Not killing."

Sally frowned. "Doesn't that depend on how the conversation goes?"

They were walking down the steps to the subway. It was late morning and the air was cool, but they could feel the temperature and humidity rise as they made their way into the station. When they reached the platform, Cape leaned against a steel girder while they waited for the train. Sally stood facing him, eyes scanning the crowd as they talked.

"I just want to talk to this guy," said Cape. "Get to know each other."

"That's the problem."

"What?"

"Most people who get to know you eventually want to kill you."

"I'll keep the conversation short."

When the train arrived, Sally and Cape got on separately, sitting opposite each other in the same car. Cape looked briefly at the map

Corelli had drawn while Sally studied a guidebook she'd bought at the hotel gift shop. *A Walking Tour of New York's Five Boroughs.* She opened the fold-out map for Brooklyn as Cape glanced idly at their fellow passengers.

Half an hour and a few stops later they were on foot again, Sally heading north and Cape going East. As she walked up the street, Sally casually tossed the guidebook into a garbage can. Cape walked slowly—the park was only half a mile away.

The neighborhood had character. Brownstones and small wood houses shared blocks with aging brick apartment buildings. Shops of all kinds peppered the streets, most looking family-owned, or at least independent from the big chains. Unlike most of Manhattan and almost all of San Francisco, this felt like a real neighborhood, not another colony in the Starbucks Empire.

Most of the people seemed elderly, and few made eye contact as he passed. A block from the park he noticed a group of teenage boys standing outside a drugstore, smoking and tracking his progress.

The park was really an open square. Other than a small patch of grass at its center, the square was cobblestone, dotted with wooden benches and small, square tables made of concrete. The tables had four cement chairs flanking them, sprouting from the ground like toadstools. Maple trees had been planted between the tables, spaced about ten feet apart. Their wide branches and thick leaves filtered the sun and cast a dappled light across the stones.

The far side of the square abutted the old boardwalk, and beyond that lay the Atlantic Ocean. According to the guidebook, it was only a three-mile stroll along the boardwalk to Coney Island. A row of four narrow buildings with windows overlooking the park on one side and the ocean on the other stood watch over the entire scene. Cape assumed they were condominiums.

The square was almost empty this early in the day. On the north side, two old ladies sat talking and feeding pigeons. While one gesticulated broadly as she talked, the other methodically nodded and tore pieces of bread from a large roll and threw them at the birds milling at their feet. When the first woman finished her rant, she lowered her hands and took the bread, giving her friend a chance to wave her hands and respond. This ritual continued, each one taking a turn feeding the birds while the other dramatically acted out her opinion.

Near the center of the square, a middle-aged man sat reading the paper and smoking by himself, wearing a long black coat with the collar turned up against the breeze. He looked up when Cape crossed the perimeter of the square but returned promptly to his reading, seemingly uninterested in anything other than the sports page.

The Pole was almost directly in front of Cape only twenty feet away. It wasn't hard to pick him out. He was sitting at the third table from the edge of the square with a large chessboard in front of him. To his right was a folding card table that straddled the built-in cement stool. On it was a bowl, silverware, a glass, a pitcher of water, a bucket of ice, and a bottle of vodka.

Cape stepped around the table so his shadow fell across the chess board. When the outline of his head reached the center of the board, he stood quietly and studied the position of the pieces. The old man seated before him didn't even bother to look up.

It was a full minute before Cape broke the silence.

"Rook to queen four."

The Pole might have been a statue. For all Cape knew, the old man hadn't heard him or, more likely, didn't choose to acknowledge the interruption. Sixty seconds can be a very long time. Cape stood immobile as another minute passed before the Pole slowly reached across the table and moved the white castle to its new position. Without looking up, he gestured at the stool across from him. Cape sat down.

Another two minutes passed before the Pole moved the black queen sideways, threatening Cape's bishop on the diagonal. Before the man's arm returned to his side Cape noticed the raised flesh on the back of the hand, two gnarled lumps that looked like extra knuckles.

Cape took his time, eyes on the board and not his opponent. When he moved one of his pawns, he felt the man across from him change his posture subtly. The pawn was quickly captured, but Cape moved his bishop to safety. Almost an hour later, eight black pieces sat alongside the board opposite six white pieces the Pole had captured. It was Cape's move.

Very deliberately he reached toward his queen, hesitated, then lifted a knight and swung it forward and to the left. "Check," he said, looking across the table. The Pole nodded to himself, looking at the board, and then raised his head slowly.

The man was striking. He was also younger than Cape expected. Perhaps late fifties, but the handsome young man he must have been was still clearly visible in every feature. His thick hair was gray with streaks of black, matching the pattern of his full beard. Both cheekbones and forehead were high, framing blue eyes so pale they were almost translucent. Cape had been to Alaska once and seen that exact shade reflected in a glacier—the color of ice older than humanity and colder than the grave.

On the left side of the Pole's face, partially hidden by his beard, was another sizable lump, a plateau surrounded by deep pockmarks of scar tissue. He wore a gray sweater with an open collar, and Cape noticed similar scars at the top of his chest.

The Pole smiled by way of greeting and Cape caught himself before he flinched. The teeth along the top of his mouth were perfect, but the bottom row was a ragged ravine. In the brief instant before the smiled disappeared, Cape was reminded of shark's teeth. It was as if the teeth had been knocked out, one at a time, and set back in place at haphazard angles. No doubt a favorite pastime in the *gulag*.

"Check," said the Pole in a rich voice, the Russian accent barely discernible. "But not mate."

Cape smiled without showing his teeth. Beyond one or two mishaps at the orthodontist, he couldn't compete on that level. "Not yet."

The Pole smiled and nodded, this time not showing his teeth either. He reached over to the card table and grabbed a pack of cigarettes. Cape didn't recognize the brand but saw they were unfiltered. He also noticed the spoon on the tray begin to wobble as the Pole's hand passed over it. When it came time to reach for the lighter, the Pole merely opened his hand. The metal Zippo jumped two inches into his waiting grasp.

The Pole caught the surprise in Cape's face and smiled again.

"You are not a policeman," he said. "They never come alone."

Cape said nothing, watching as the Pole pried the lighter free with his other hand.

"And you are not FBI," the Pole said definitively.

"How do you know?"

"They don't know how to play chess."

Cape smiled. He knew one or two feds that might take exception to the remark, but he kept his mouth shut.

"And you are not a reporter."

Cape raised an eyebrow in question.

The Pole shrugged. "Many years ago, in Russia, it was said that I had one killed." He shrugged again. "Now they leave me alone. Rumors are useful that way."

Cape took one of his business cards and set it down in the center of the board.

"I'm not interested in you," said Cape very deliberately. "I'm interested in what you might know."

The Pole took a drag on his cigarette and exhaled, squinting through the smoke.

"Where did you learn to play chess?"

"My mother."

"Me also!" said the Pole, nodding his approval. "Your father—you did not play with him?"

"Some," said Cape. "When he wasn't working. You?"

The Pole shook his head. "I never knew my father. He was killed in *gulag* when I was boy." He practically spat the word *gulag* across the table.

"That must have been rough."

The Pole shrugged again. "It was Soviet Union," he said. "But chess—a great game. An important game. You can endure much, if you know chess."

"I never thought of it that way," said Cape.

The Pole nodded. "You know the term *babushka*?"

"Grandmother, isn't it?"

"Correct."

"I think that's about the only Russian word I know."

"Everyone knows *babushka*," said the Pole. "It also means old woman, but only someone special. It is a term of great affection."

Cape waited, wondering where this was going.

"I had a babushka," said the Pole, his eyes turning inward. "Not my real grandmother, but a lovely old woman. Very kind. Once a month, my mother would take me to visit her. She lived far outside Moscow, to the north."

The Pole smiled at some private memory before continuing. "Before we would go inside my babushka's house, my mother would always tell me to beat the old woman at chess."

"Did you?"

The Pole frowned. "No, though I knew that I could—she could play chess, but not very well. I let her win."

"She was your babushka," said Cape simply.

"*Da*," said the Pole. "You understand."

Cape shrugged. "We all have kind hearts when we're kids."

The Pole showed his teeth. "That was the lesson my mother wanted me to learn." He took another drag on his cigarette. "To harden my heart, so I could see things without emotion. She knew the way of the world."

Cape said nothing as the smoke from the cigarette coiled listlessly in the air between them.

"Then one day, my mother sat me down in the kitchen. She said my father was not coming home from *gulag*." The Pole stamped

212

out his cigarette and continued. "I was just a boy, but old enough to understand that he had been murdered by the State."

Cape watched the Pole's eyes regain their focus, the glacial blue hard and clear.

"The next day we went to visit my babushka," continued the Pole. "We played ten games of chess, and I beat her every time. I never lost at chess again."

Cape nodded his understanding. "Your mother wanted to protect you from getting hurt."

"She wanted me to see things clearly," replied the Pole, "so I could survive."

"Looks like you have."

The Pole held his gnarled right hand in front of his face and looked deliberately at the raised flesh. He was dying slowly, but still alive. Still in the game.

"Come back tomorrow," he said, "and we will finish our match."

Cape gestured toward the remaining pieces. "That gives you more time to study the board."

The Pole grinned. "Don't ever forget, it is *my* board."

"See you tomorrow," said Cape.

"*Da zavtra.*"

Cape was two blocks from the subway when Sally fell into place beside him, appearing out of a side street.

"That was boring."

"I like boring," said Cape. "When it's boring, no one gets hurt."

"He had a bodyguard—middle-aged guy in the long coat."

"Saw him," said Cape. "No one spends that much time with the sports section, even in this town. And he was a little studied in his boredom with the surroundings. Was he packing?"

Sally nodded. "Submachine gun with a folding stock. Saw it when he shifted in his seat—he must have hemorrhoids from sitting all day."

"I didn't see you," commented Cape.

"Neither did he. That's the idea, remember?"

"I meant it as a compliment."

Sally stopped walking long enough to curtsy.

"Did you learn anything?"

"Not yet," replied Cape. "We have to come back tomorrow."

"So he can have you checked out."

"I assume so."

"You trust him?"

"Absolutely not," replied Cape, "but I like him."

"See how you feel after tomorrow," said Sally.

"Deal."

36

"WOULD YOU LIKE TO eat one of your testicles?"

Angelo didn't respond, hoping it was a rhetorical question. He stood with his back to the door of Adam Berman's office, his hands in a defensive position over his crotch, while Adam paced back and forth behind his desk.

"You fucked up, Angelo, letting that guy in here."

"I know."

"I could cut your balls off," said Adam with conviction.

"You mentioned that, Mr. Berman."

"Did I?" asked Adam, halting momentarily. When he resumed pacing, he added, "Well, then, I guess I meant it."

"You are a man of your word, Mr. Berman."

"Stop kissing my ass and do something right for a change. Did we get the adjusted numbers from Grace yet?"

Angelo hesitated. "No … no, we haven't."

"Fuck," said Adam. "What's taking so long? I want actual costs to date against the budget, new distribution of points, revised estimate of marketing costs, all that shit. It's just fucking math, for chrissakes."

"I don't think she agrees with—"

"She doesn't have to agree," snapped Adam, stopping to point a stubby finger at Angelo. "She just has to run the numbers."

"Actually," said Angelo hesitantly. "She *does* have to agree."

Adam squinted at him. "What are you talking about?"

"The clause," said Angelo, "in the contracts."

"What clause?" demanded Adam. "There are so many fucking clauses in these movie contracts that even I can't remember them, and my name's on all of 'em."

"The contracts were written to allocate a share of the gross receipts to every principal member of the production team," said Angelo. "The amount given to each person varies by seniority and contribution to the film, *after* all costs incurred are deducted from the total."

"Why do you think I want to see the new numbers? I want to know how much is already spent."

"But these contracts stipulated that those amounts could be reallocated if anyone left the team during production, even in the event of death."

"Tell me something I don't know," said Adam testily. "So what clause are you so worried about?"

"Re-allocating percentages in the middle of production isn't unheard of, but it is a bit unusual," explained Angelo.

"So?"

"So the lawyers added a clause that says *all remaining parties must agree to any changes* during production. If all parties don't agree, then the percentages remain as they were. In this case, that means Tom's estate would get his share after the movie opens."

Adam was staring at Angelo. "The lawyers?" he asked, incredulous. "The lawyers? What lawyers?"

"The lawyers," said Angelo simply. "Our lawyers, the director's lawyer. Grace's lawyer. All the lawyers."

"I fuckin' hate lawyers," mumbled Adam. "They've ruined the movie business."

Angelo was pretty sure Adam had a law degree, but it seemed an inopportune time to mention it.

"Does Grace know about the clause?" Adam asked.

"I don't think so," replied Angelo. "It wasn't in the fax we sent of the contracts she asked for—it was an addendum, so we, well... we just didn't send it. Unless she asks her lawyer to go through the contracts, she'll just be working under the assumptions you gave her on the phone."

Adam nodded, pacing again.

"So she figures out the budget—how much we've spent, how much we have left for production, then sends us a copy of the revised budget and the new allocations."

"Right."

"Then she's culpable in the whole thing, right?"

"How do you mean?" Angelo shifted uncomfortably from one foot to the other.

"She sends us a new budget, then she's putting in writing that she's OK with the new numbers," said Adam. "So if anyone's lawyer gets in a huff, we hang the whole thing on Grace. Why would she rework the numbers if she didn't agree, right? And while the lawyers go at it, we hold on to the money. The interest alone should pay some legal bills."

"But she'll say she never knew about the clause."

"Her word against ours," replied Adam. "Inadmissible."

He's starting to sound like a lawyer, thought Angelo. "But what about the investors?"

Adam blinked, frowning. "What about 'em?"

"If she's got Tom's budget, she'll see how the cash flow has been stop-and-go instead of simply drawing on money already in the bank. That's not how we normally do business."

"We've been a little strapped for cash," said Adam belligerently. "Or hadn't you noticed?"

Angelo forged ahead, emboldened by the lack of projectiles this far into their conversation. "Then won't the investors want to ask the producer how their money is being spent? You said the money guys were pretty hands-on. And won't Grace naturally want to know where the money's coming from?"

Adam sat down heavily, reaching for the glass on his desk. It was half full—or half empty, depending on how you looked at it. From Angelo's perspective it looked like it might hurt if it hit him in the balls, so he stepped sideways to position himself behind a floor lamp.

"Maybe she won't ask," suggested Adam in a tired voice, setting the glass down without taking a sip.

"You're probably right, Mr. Berman." Angelo tried to sound positive—maybe the glass was half full. "Maybe she won't ask."

37

"ROBIN HOOD WOULD BE impressed."

Cape leaned against the wall of Sally's hotel room as she methodically removed items from a black duffel bag. Two curved pieces of wood emerged from a zippered pocket, followed by a coil of string that looked like fishing line. Last came a thick center section wrapped in wire. By themselves the pieces looked like wooden sculpture, or parts to an arcane musical instrument. But when Sally laid all the pieces together on the bed, it was obvious what was being assembled.

The bow was four feet long, bending sharply from the center and curving back in the opposite direction at the tips. Each section was made from dark wood that had been meticulously shaped but not polished, so the bow seemed to absorb rather than reflect light. The sections were joined together by thin shafts of metal that glinted dully in the light from the window. When all the pieces had fused into a single deadly shape, Sally stood the bow upright and pulled the string taut, her forearm rippling from the strain.

"Robin Hood," she said. "Another great warrior who preferred the company of his own gender."

"What are you implying?" asked Cape. "Is this another lesbian conspiracy theory?"

"I'm just saying that he spent an awful lot of time with those Merry Men."

"What about Maid Marion?"

"A cross-dresser," said Sally definitively. "Very common in those days."

Cape raised his eyebrows skeptically.

"And what about the tights?" demanded Sally.

Cape frowned. "I'm just glad Errol Flynn isn't around to hear this."

"Who?"

"Errol Flynn!" said Cape in disbelief. "He played Robin Hood in the MGM classic opposite Basil Rathbone, who played the dastardly Sheriff of Nottingham."

"Dastardly?"

Cape nodded. "Dastardly. He had the evil-looking mustache and everything."

Sally looked at him with a blank expression.

"Basil Rathbone!" said Cape insistently. "Probably most famous for being the *definitive* Sherlock Holmes, both on the radio and in the movies."

Sally shook her head. "I'm not a movie buff like you, and I definitely don't watch Western movies."

"These weren't Westerns."

"I meant West—as in America." Sally rolled her eyes. "As in *not* Asia, where I grew up. Besides, I didn't go to the movies much. Too busy at school."

"Studying archery?"

"Among other things."

Cape gestured toward the bow. "How good are you with that thing?"

Sally gave him a look. "In feudal Japan, ninjas had to train for *a full year* with a bow—just a bow—before they were given a single arrow. To perfect their draw on the string."

"How long before you were given an arrow?"

"Six months," said Sally, shrugging. "Standards have really fallen off in the last four hundred years."

Fully assembled, the bow covered the width of the bed. "Isn't that kind of conspicuous?"

"I'll carry it broken down." Sally began sliding arrows from a compartment in the bottom of her bag. They were shorter than Cape expected, the shafts matte black. Hunting arrows, the tips flared and razor sharp. He wondered what other surprises lay hidden in this inconspicuous bag Sally checked onto the plane. Maybe a gattling gun, broken down to resemble a blow dryer.

"How long does it take you to put it together?" asked Cape. "In case we're in a hurry."

Sally cocked one eyebrow and looked at the bow, as if doing a series of mental calculations. "From the bag?"

"No, already on you."

Sally shrugged. "About ten seconds."

"Ten seconds?" Cape raised his eyebrows. "Not bad."

221

Sally held up a hand as if she'd forgotten something. "Am I blindfolded?"

"No," said Cape. "That scenario hadn't occurred to me."

"Then six seconds," she said. "But I'll already have it assembled."

"How?"

"I'll put it together when I'm in position. Before you get there."

"You never told me where you were last time."

"One of the trees."

"In the square?"

"Yup."

"How'd you get past the women on the bench?"

"They were distracted," replied Sally. "The pigeons were much more engaging than a short woman in tights."

Cape shook his head in disbelief. "That's not much cover."

"That's why I want the bow," replied Sally. "I don't like the layout of that park. It's impossible to get close without being spotted."

"I'm sure that's why our Russian friend goes there to play chess."

"You ready?"

Cape pulled up his shirt to reveal a Heckler & Koch USP jammed into his waistband, a compact 9-millimeter with a ten-shot capacity. Sally had taught him a few tricks for hiding unsavory items in his checked luggage. Cape had a carry permit for the gun in California, but carrying in New York could land him behind bars. He figured it was a necessary risk.

"Think it will come to that?" asked Sally.

"Corelli said we'd be on our own," said Cape. "But I'd rather play chess."

He let the tail of his shirt drop into place. Sally slipped the pieces of the bow into her bag. Ten minutes later they were on the subway headed to Brighton Beach.

38

Beau looked at Vincent, who looked disgusted.

It was almost like looking in a mirror, except Vincent was short, white, and dressed immaculately. But if he grew a foot, went from pine to mahogany, and traded in his pleated slacks for a pair of jeans, he and Beau would look exactly the same. Twin cops who needed a break.

"So what have we got?" asked Beau.

"Bupkus."

"He a suspect?"

Vincent cackled. "I wish." They sat at the dive bar across from the courthouse, where they'd just testified in another case. A real case with evidence, suspects, the whole nine. Not a circle jerk. Beau was throwing back coffee while Vincent stuck with mineral water. They were still on duty and sleep was a distant memory.

"How about this," said Beau. "We work backwards."

"We tried that."

"Let's try again."

Vincent groaned but didn't say anything.

"Pretzel Pete got killed by Freddie Wang's boys."

"Agreed," said Vincent, "but we'll never prove it. The tongs never give up anything."

"Agreed. And Cecil got stuffed in the slide at the zoo by Frank Alessi's goons."

"No doubt," said Vincent. "Frank has an overdeveloped sense of drama."

"But we'll never prove it," continued Beau.

Vincent looked sullen. "Frank's off limits."

"Respectable businessman," said Beau. "Big contributor to the mayor's election campaign."

"Fuck me."

Beau shifted in his seat. "Unless we nab one of Frank's guys on something else and get them to turn."

"Like who?"

"Was thinking of Gummy."

"The guy with no front teeth?" said Vincent. "He's a moron."

"Crystal meth will do that to you," said Beau. "Used to have a fine set of molars till he ground 'em down. And he used to be high up in the organization."

"I'm surprised they keep him around at all."

"He's somebody's nephew," said Beau. "But he might know something. He hears things, now and again."

"So do all schizophrenics."

"You got a better idea?"

"Go back to your list," said Vincent. "So who killed Otto?"

Beau shrugged. "You forgot about the dead Russian."

Vincent groaned again. "They're connected." It was a statement, not a question.

"Have to be," said Beau. "Drugs are involved, and the timing's too close."

"I don't know any Russians," said Vincent.

"Me neither."

"So maybe we talk to Gummy."

Beau nodded. "Maybe we do."

39

The Pole was at his usual table, studying the board and smoking. The bodyguard was earnestly pouring over the sports page a few tables away. When Cape's shadow crossed the board, the Pole flashed his stalagmite grin.

"*Esli druk akazalsa vdruk,*" he said pleasantly. "*If a friend appears suddenly.*"

"So we're friends." Cape sat down.

"*I ne druk, i ne vrak, a tak,*" the Pole replied. "*Well, not a friend, not an enemy.*"

"You're quoting someone."

The Pole nodded. "Vladimir Vysotsky—you know him?"

Cape shook his head.

"Vysotsky was great poet, great songwriter." The Pole paused to drag deeply on his cigarette. "His work was banned by the Soviets. You would like him—too bad you don't speak Russian."

"Maybe I'll learn," said Cape. "So you've decided we're not adversaries?"

"Ah, but we are," said the Pole, gesturing at the chess board. "It is the nature of men, eh? But here at this table, we can *talk* like friends."

Cape studied the Pole for a minute before answering. "You had me checked out."

"Of course."

"And?"

"You have not lied to me," said the Pole, adding, "yet."

"Which means I can be trusted?"

"It means you are smart." A flash of jagged teeth, a gesture at the board. "Your move." Cape studied the positions carefully before moving a bishop halfway across the board. "You are playing more aggressively than yesterday," observed the Pole.

"Sometimes the best defense is a good offense."

The Pole nodded. "And you have been on the defensive, eh?" He plucked a grape from the table to his right. The knife and spoon wobbled and clinked together as his hand passed over them. "Grape?"

"No, thanks." Cape shook his head. "I've been under attack since I started this investigation."

"And what is it you are investigating?"

"I'm not sure," said Cape. "I thought I was investigating a murder, then drugs, and now I think it's something else entirely."

"Something else." The Pole's pale eyes were bright with curiosity.

"Something I haven't seen yet."

The Pole pressed his lips together to hide his predator's grin. "Perhaps something you have seen, but do not recognize."

Cape looked up from the board. "You know the men who tried to kill me."

The Pole inhaled deeply on his cigarette and exhaled slowly, squinting at Cape through bluish smoke. "Even before the Soviets, it was hard to be Russian—the common man was always treated like a peasant. In the time of czars, back to the reign of Peter the Great, many Russians were sent to prison camps."

"As criminals?"

"What is criminal?" asked the Pole rhetorically. "Is feeding your family criminal? Or protecting your neighbor?"

Cape didn't sat anything. The point was clear.

"So these men that were branded thieves by the State—they banded together. They became *vory v zakone*."

Cape cocked an eyebrow.

"You would say *thieves-in-law*," explained the Pole. "But we call ourselves *vory*."

"We?"

The Pole plucked another grape. "There are plenty of old men who play chess. I am sure there are even one or two in San Francisco." He poured two glasses of vodka and handed one to Cape. "You came to me for a reason."

It was too early for anything but coffee, but Cape threw the drink back and felt his nostrils clear as the alcohol evaporated. A whole-wheat breakfast. The Pole nodded his approval. "*Na zdorov'ya.*"

"You were telling me a story about thieves."

The Pole set his glass down. "Vory are like brothers, bound together by a strict code of honor."

"Honor among thieves," said Cape without sarcasm.

The Pole nodded vigorously. "It is not unheard of, even outside Russia."

"So what's the code?"

"To be a *vor*, you must honor a way of life," said the Pole proudly. "There is much to the code, but at its core is a promise to resist the oppression of the State. We do not pay taxes and never cooperate with police."

Cape realized he'd rather not pay taxes and, according to Beau, rarely cooperated with the police. He thought he was a closet libertarian but now wondered if he was really a *vor* at heart.

"In a corrupt state, becoming criminal is an act of defiance," continued the Pole. "Is this not the history of America?"

"There's a big difference between throwing tea in the harbor and running extortion rackets."

The Pole waved his hand dismissively in a sweeping arc, causing his lighter to skitter across the tray. "Specific crimes do not matter. What matters is the act itself."

Cape kept his mouth shut.

"In many towns, these men became the law, creating their own courts where common men and women could seek justice."

"Or revenge?"

The Pole smiled at the question, the razor teeth glistening. "What is justice, if not revenge?"

"These criminals—these men. They became the *mafiya*?"

"*Mafiya* to some," nodded the Pole. "To others, *Organizatsiya*. Names do not matter."

"Some names do matter," said Cape.

The Pole's eyes flashed mischievously. "You speak of the men you are after—or the men who are after you."

"The Major and Ursa. Maybe others—those are the names I'm interested in."

"I know these men," said the Pole, his tone matter-of-fact. "But they are not part of the *Organizatsiya*. They are mere gangsters."

Cape frowned. "No offense, but what's the difference?"

"Once they were *mafiya*," said the Pole. "The Major was KGB."

"He mentioned that."

"The KGB—very important after fall of the Soviets. It was KGB that took money from state banks, working with the *vory*."

"That's quite a scam."

"Russians lack opportunity, but not ambition," replied the Pole. "Before the KGB was involved, we were very powerful in Russia and a few other countries, but not very organized. Not like the Italians or Chinese."

"I know about the Triads."

"Very dangerous," said the Pole. "Because they are all connected. A dragon with many heads, but still only one dragon. So when the *vory* agreed to work with KGB and use their connections in other countries—their spies—*mafiya* became bigger and more powerful. But the brotherhood lost its soul in the bargain."

"So the Major was on your side?"

"Never *my* side," spat the Pole. "A true *vor* does not associate with Soviet scum—he was an instrument of the State. I would never trust a man like that."

"But he worked with the *mafiya*."

The Pole refilled their glasses. "Until he broke the law."

Cape almost laughed but caught himself. "Isn't that the point?"

"The *human law*," said the Pole. "The *vor* way of life. He stole from other *mafiya*. Killed important members of the Russian mob."

"That must happen often," said Cape. "Turf wars, that sort of—"

"Not like this," said the Pole, cutting him off. "The Major stole indiscriminately. He betrayed the brotherhood."

"So why isn't he dead, if you guys are so big on revenge?" asked Cape. "Hasn't anyone tried to kill him?"

"Many tried," said the Pole in a tone that suggested he might have been one of them. "But some Russians … some of us are not so easy to kill." He raised his lumpy fist and tapped his chest where metal shot hid beneath his flesh.

"So that's why you agreed to talk to me."

The Pole nodded. "To cooperate with police or FBI—that is not the way. To even talk of these things is to become a *musar*."

"A rat?"

The Pole raised his eyebrows. "You said you could not speak Russian."

"I got the meaning," replied Cape. "I think every culture has its own rats."

The Pole nodded. "But you, my friend, are just someone I am playing chess with."

Cape raised his glass. "Here's to chess … and talking about mutual friends."

The Pole took a drink and smiled.

"So what's the Major doing in San Francisco?" asked Cape.

"This I do not know. He should not be in this country."

"What do you mean?"

"I know he has tried to come to the United States before but was not allowed. His name appeared on one of your government's watch lists."

"We have a lot of those."

"He is known to Interpol as a dangerous criminal. That is true of many criminals already in this country, of course, but the Major was stopped at least twice. This I know for certain."

"So he found a way around the system," said Cape. "He's persistent."

"He is dangerous, because he has no honor. The man who tried to kill you in the park—he had Cyrillic writing on his hands?"

"You read that in the paper?"

The Pole didn't answer. Cape didn't press it, saying, "Yeah, he did, but I don't know what it said."

"It meant he was part of a Russian mob, before working for the Major."

"Why change loyalties?"

"The *vory* are not what they once were," said the Pole sadly. "Many who call themselves *mafiya* are just *baklany*—punks. They will do anything for money—or debt, the lack of money. It is usually one or the other in Russia."

"Any idea what the Major is doing here?" asked Cape. "Or why he would want to kill me?"

The Pole took a new cigarette from his pack and reached out his hand to perform the levitation trick with his lighter. "The Major craves power. In that way he is not unlike other criminals, or other men for that matter. Remember, as KGB he had great power, but much of what he did was invisible. Known only to the State and its victims."

"So?"

The Pole stared thoughtfully at the board for a moment. "I think he wants to be famous."

"A famous criminal, like you."

The Pole frowned. "I am just an old man who plays chess in the park."

"You're not that old."

"No, the Major wants to be like John Gotti—or better yet, like Robert De Niro."

"You're kidding."

"All Russian gangsters love *The Godfather*," said the Pole. "It is funny, no? Big criminals in real life, watching movies to learn how to act."

Cape checked his bullshit meter. "You're serious."

"I have seen it in Russia, and also here," replied the Pole. "Grown men. Killers. Sitting around a television hanging on every word. *The Godfather. Goodfellas.* These movies are like religion to gangsters."

"What kind of movies did you watch?"

The Pole shrugged. "I prefer chess." He slid one of his pawns two paces forward, a move that cleared one of his bishops to threaten Cape's queen.

Cape blinked, trying to concentrate on the board while absorbing everything he'd just heard. He moved his knight forward, blocking the Pole's bishop. There didn't seem to be any other move open to him.

The Pole chuckled softly. "Is that your position, my friend? Are you the errant knight, trying to save your queen?"

"You're not talking about the chess game, are you?" Cape met his gaze.

The Pole smiled. "Am I not?"

"Unless you have a better idea, I have to see this through."

The Pole nodded. "It is time to finish the game." Stubbing out his cigarette, he reached for his bishop.

The board exploded as the air around them tore itself apart. A sharp crack from the cobblestones to their right, chess pieces flying like shrapnel. Cape grabbed the Pole by his collar and yanked hard to the right, rolling them underneath the stone table. Twisting his head around to look upside down across the square, he saw the Pole's bodyguard standing with a submachine gun braced against his shoulder. He was aiming at the condominiums overlooking the park when a sharp *whump* stole the air around them. The bodyguard spun around, gun skidding across the stones. Straining his neck to look around their table, Cape caught a glimpse of the bodyguard face down, blood pooling rapidly around his torso.

There was a rapid series of *twangs*, bass notes from Sally's bow. Cape released his grip on the Pole and rolled under the nearest table, pulling his gun as he came to a crouch. He stayed under the cement umbrella until he thought he heard the distant squeal of tires, but at this point didn't really trust his own senses. He held his position, watching the Pole laying under his own table, face down. After no more than a minute he saw Sally's legs approaching.

"Gone," she said as Cape stood. He walked over to the Pole, who had rolled onto his back and seemed unharmed. Cape grabbed his arm and helped him stand. The Pole looked from Cape to Sally, scanning her from head to toe. He looked at the bow in her hands and shook his head in wonder. He seemed unconcerned about his bodyguard.

Cape studied the four buildings straddling the boardwalk and spotted one of Sally's arrows in the wall next to a first story window.

Because the condominiums sat above the boardwalk, the shooter had plenty of height to get an angle on the square.

"Ground floor," said Cape. "Smart."

Sally nodded. "Easy run to the street and a waiting car. Not enough time for me to follow them."

"Don't worry about it."

"Couldn't see the reflection from the scope until the first shot," she said disgustedly. "The sniper must have used a cover and stood back from the window—we're dealing with a pro."

Cape nodded. "But you got a shot off."

"Three," said Sally. "Two went through the window."

"You think you got a piece of him?"

"I hope so," Sally replied, nostrils flaring. "But I doubt it."

Cape turned to face the Pole, who was staring at him with a bemused expression.

"You risked your life," said the Pole.

"I was just using you for cover."

"For an American, you are not a very good liar."

"Maybe using you as a shield would be smart," said Cape. "Just in case you were behind this."

The Pole smiled broadly to give the full view of his ragged grin. "If I were behind this, then you would be dead, my friend."

"I've already been dead once this week," said Cape. "And I'm getting tired of it."

"Then you must stop these men."

Cape studied the icy stare of the Russian's pale eyes. "You're saying I'm going to have to kill them."

"I am not telling you what to do," said the Pole. "I am telling you I would rather play chess with you than go to your funeral."

They heard sirens in the distance.

"What are you going to do?" asked Cape.

The Pole looked over at his bodyguard, the pool of blood shimmering in the noonday sun. For a moment the Pole looked angry, then sadness settled over his features before he regained his chilly façade. "I am going to buy a new chess board."

"We never finished our game," said Cape.

"True," said the Pole. "And I believe it is your move."

40

"You're lucky I haven't arrested you."

Corelli scowled across the table at Cape, who was struggling to look contrite as he bit into a ham and egg sandwich. The coffee shop was two blocks from the hotel. He and Sally had checked out immediately, and she was already on her way to the airport. Cape hoped to make the same flight but knew he was pushing his luck. An hour from now he might be behind bars.

"I could take you in for questioning."

"You mentioned that," said Cape.

"But you don't know anything about a homicide in Brighton Beach."

"Not if you bring me in for questioning."

Corelli gave him a cop stare for a full minute before exhaling. Grabbing his own sandwich, he took a ferocious bite.

"You're an asshole," he said with his mouth full.

"Beau didn't mention that?" said Cape. "Besides, I called you, remember?"

Corelli almost spat. "Like you had a lot of choice."

"I was never there," said Cape. "I don't know any Russian gangsters. I was just walking by when this nice old man asked me if I wanted to play a game of chess. I abhor guns. There were no dead bodies in the square when I was there. My dog ate my homework..."

"Enough!" Corelli held up his hand. "I get the point. You sure you're not a lawyer?"

"Not me," said Cape. "I'm one of the good guys."

"That remains to be seen," replied Corelli. "Talk to me."

Cape took him through it, from the beginning. When he finished talking, his sandwich was still warm, but Corelli's had long since vanished. Cape had left out only one important detail, and that was Sally.

"The cops on the scene identified the stiff as part of the Russian mob," said Corelli. "Now I have to play nice with Brooklyn homicide. So fuck-you-very-much for ruining my afternoon."

"I tried to keep it friendly."

"I tried to quit smoking," snapped Corelli, "but it didn't do any good."

"I was just an innocent bystander."

"Bullshit," said Corelli. "Innocent bystanders get killed—that's why they're called *innocent* bystanders. In my line of work, nobody's innocent unless they're dead. You, my friend, are what we call an *instigator*."

"I didn't instigate anything except a game of chess."

Corelli started to huff but let it go. Instead he shook his head and almost laughed.

"You think it's the same dickheads who tried to shoot you in San Francisco?"

"That'd be my guess," said Cape. "I don't know too many snipers."

"You're telling me the Pole's clean? I got guys looking for him right now."

"You're wasting your time."

"That's what I get paid for," replied Corelli. "I'm a cop, remember?"

"Do you think the Pole would kill his own bodyguard?" asked Cape.

"In a heartbeat," said Corelli emphatically. "If he thought it would get him something."

"Like what?'

"Do you trust him?' asked Corelli.

Cape considered the question. "Yeah," he said slowly. "I think I do."

"Maybe that's what he wanted."

Cape didn't know what to say to that. Corelli made a sound like he was coughing up a hairball but threw back some coffee before the Heimlich became necessary.

"The Brooklyn cops said there was an arrow stuck in the side of a building, right next to a window overlooking the park."

"That's where the shooter was."

"Of course that's where the shooter was," said Corelli. "I want to know where the fucking arrow came from."

"Maybe a sporting goods store?"

Corelli stared at him. "You're unbelievable."

"Just doing my civic duty." Before Corelli could respond, Cape jumped in again, saying, "Mind if I ask you a question?"

"A favor or a question?" said Corelli. "'Cause you used up all your favors already."

"A stupid question ... Why me?"

Corelli gave a humorless chuckle. "Getting tired of being in the crosshairs?"

"You want to change places?"

"Not a chance," said Corelli. "Your question's not that stupid, but the answer's simple—you were supposed to drop the case."

"But if the Major and his pet rock hadn't stopped by my office in the first place, this case probably would have dwindled and died on the vine. The cops had already written it off."

"That's not how it works in Russia," said Corelli. "Remember, the Major is ex-Soviet, ex-KGB, ex-*mafiya*."

"That's a lot of *x*s."

"Those guys ran the Soviet Union with absolute authority. They told you to do something, then you did it, no questions asked. They were the law. People who resisted disappeared, lost their families, or wound up in the *gulag*. Someone from the Russian mob warns you off a case, you drop it like a hot potato, even if you're a cop."

"This isn't Russia."

"Tell that to the Major next time you see him."

"But—"

Corelli cut him off with a raised palm. "Let me ask you as question—what would happen to the case if you got killed?"

Cape started to answer but caught himself as the answer started to sink in. "The cops would investigate—," he began.

"For how long?"

"Beau wouldn't let it rest," said Cape assuredly.

"True," said Corelli. "But without the department behind him …"
He let his voice trail off.

Cape nodded reluctantly. "If the case got cold …"

"Which it would, because the Major would shit-can whatever he's into just long enough for the cops to move on."

"Then my client's story about her friend getting thrown off a bridge—"

"—is just a story with no one willing to investigate," said Corelli. "Remember, these guys don't care how messy things get, or who knows they're the bad guys. You go away, their problem goes away, period—because nobody in their right mind is gonna pick up where you left off."

"How could a guy like the Major get into the country if they have him on a watch list?"

"Easy," said Corelli. "He's not applying for citizenship, so all he needs is a visa to get into the country."

"Don't you have to apply for a visa? Supposedly the State Department has the Major on a watch list."

"Say he goes to the American embassy in Moscow and applies for a visa—they check their list and bounce him back. He just goes to another country where he is allowed to travel, like Latvia, and gets a clean passport."

"What do you mean by clean?"

"He fills out the new application without mentioning any criminal record," replied Corelli, "which is highly illegal under U.S. law, but no one in Latvia really gives a shit. So now that he's got a clean passport, he contacts some friends in the United States and asks them to write a letter to the American embassy in Latvia on his behalf."

"Saying what?"

"He's an important business associate, a major investor, or an all-around swell guy. The morons at the embassy get the letter, issue a thirty-day visa, and the Major flies into the country from Latvia."

"Just like that?"

Corelli nodded. "And once he's here, no one at the State Department is keeping tabs on him, so he can travel freely within the U.S."

"Astounding," muttered Cape.

"It's what the politicians call a loophole."

Cape didn't say anything. He was thinking about a loophole big enough for the Major and Ursa to slip through and realized that tracking them was going to be almost impossible. All his usual tricks and online searches for credit reports, last known address, driver's license applications, were all useless. The men hunting him couldn't be hunted.

Corelli must have guessed the line of thought, because he softened his tone. "They only found blood near the dead Russian. You get hurt?"

"I'm shaken, not stirred," said Cape. "But I'll live."

"That's too bad," replied Corelli, his voice regaining its usual gruffness. "I bet Beau you wouldn't leave Brooklyn alive."

"You could always place bets on San Francisco."

"Already have."

"Thanks, Corelli." Cape put money on the table, stood, and extended his hand. "I owe you."

"That's the understatement of the year." Corelli stood and shook hands. "Watch your back."

"If you're ever in San Francisco—"

"Don't worry, I won't look you up," said Corelli. "I'd like to make it to retirement."

41

THE TRIP TO THE airport was only slightly longer than a Russian novel.

Plenty of time to make a phone call. Cape dialed a number he knew by memory and was surprised when Beau answered on the third ring.

"You're at your desk?" said Cape, incredulous. "I thought the street was your office."

Beau snorted into the phone. "Since you left town, things been nice and quiet. Gives a hard-working public servant like myself a chance to catch up on all the bullshit paperwork I gotta do."

"My tax dollars at work."

"Amen," replied Beau. "But don't forget, you're the dickhead responsible for half the paperwork on my desk."

"Point taken."

"But that isn't why you called, is it?" demanded Beau, his thunderous voice sounding all-knowing over the phone. "I just talked to Corelli."

"Shit."

"Said you came to town and left a dead body for him to clean up."

"I don't know anything about that, Officer."

"You're a menace."

"My flight instincts took over."

"That's about the only instinct you don't have. What do you want?"

"Did you test the heroin you found in the dead producer's apartment?"

Cape heard Beau's breathing over the line. "How do you mean, tested? We gave it the old taste test, and it passed. Tasted like junk, looked like junk ... must be junk. It's not powdered sugar, if that's what you want to know."

"What about the lab?"

"Sure, we always send a sample down to the boys in the lab, find out what's in it. The report's probably somewhere on my desk." Cape heard papers shuffling in the background. He'd seen Beau's desk. "What are you going on about?"

"Corelli said something about Turkish heroin," said Cape. "How it's different from the junk you get from Asia."

"Yeah, he's right. So?"

"I want to know where the heroin in the dead guy's apartment came from."

"Why?" The rustling noise stopped as Beau turned his full attention to the phone.

"I might know who put it there."

"Who?"

"My Russian friends."

246

"You think the Russians are making a play for the local drug trade?"

"No, I don't."

"Then what?"

"Something bigger," said Cape. "A lot bigger."

42

"Gummy, don't run."

Vincent spoke the words softly, as if trying to coax a kitten down from a tree, but it was no use. Gummy spun on his heel and bolted, slamming face-first into Beau's chest, bouncing off, and falling on his ass. Vincent bent down and gingerly grabbed him under the arms to help him stand.

They were ten feet from the main drag on Broadway, standing in an alley called Romolo. Since it had a name, Romolo was technically a street, but it angled sharply up from Broadway and ran into a dead end less than half a block up the hill. It sure as hell looked like an alley. But hidden on the left side halfway up the alley was the Hotel Basque, marked only by a neon blue sign with the word *hotel*. And on the ground floor of the hotel was 15 Romolo, one of the more obscure haunts in a city known for its bars and restaurants. Somewhere between a dive bar and casual chic, it drew an eclectic crowd that included lawyers, advertising executives, grad students, and the occasional mobster with a crystal meth addiction, like Gummy. When he stepped outside for a smoke, Vincent and Beau were waiting.

Gummy looked from one to the other, his face drawn. He wore an expensive black suit, crumpled from head to toe as if he'd slept in it. His eyes were black and jumpy, his hair greasy and thinning, his hands shaky. He had the burn-victim complexion of a meth addict. The edges of his mouth were stretched and pitted, lips wrapped around bleeding gums. His front teeth, top and bottom, had been ground to jagged stumps.

"How's the habit treatin' you, Gummy?" Beau sounded genuinely concerned. He walked Gummy up the hill to the end of the alley.

Gummy shifted his weight from one foot to the other in a spastic dance, a fire walker who realized too late the coals beneath his feet burned like hell.

"I don't use ice no more," he said.

Vincent nodded sympathetically. "Got too expensive, huh?"

"M-m-money's not a problem," said Gummy. "I g-g-g-got connections."

"That's right," said Beau, as if he'd just remembered. "You're with Frank Alessi's crew."

Gummy started to respond but coughed phlegm onto Vincent's jacket instead. Beau covered a laugh by pretending to cough into his hand. He wouldn't have been surprised if Vincent took out his gun and shot Gummy right there.

"I don't know *shhhit*."

"That's not what you just said," Beau drawled amicably. "You said you were connected."

Vincent wiped gingerly at his lapel with a handkerchief. "That's why we wanted to talk to you, Gummy."

Gummy's eyes jumped out of his head like a Tex Avery cartoon. "I got f-f-friends in high places."

Beau looked over Gummy's head. "Vinnie, what does moving ice get you these days?"

Vincent folded and put away the handkerchief, frowning. "Minimum five-year stint, I think. State Assembly just extended it."

Gummy twitched, then went quiet for a second. "I don't deal."

"That's the problem," said Beau. "You don't deal with us, you deal with a jury. See, Gummy, I got connections, too, over at Narcotics. They tell me you tapped into your connections to start moving the shit you're using, so you could get it wholesale and make ends meet."

Vincent chimed in. "Depending on the quantity, the jury might go with two years in, three on probation."

Gummy's eyes started to water.

"How long you think you'd last inside?" asked Beau.

"I read somewhere that addicts can go into shock if they get cut off," said Vincent.

"Hard to get crank inside," said Beau sadly.

"Why'd a connected guy like you start using in the first place?" asked Vincent.

Gummy resumed his fire dancing. "Gotta keep my edge, you know? Th-the ice keeps you sharp. Guy my age needs an edge."

Beau nodded as if he understood, and he did. Even before he left Narcotics, crystal meth had become an epidemic. Confounding law enforcement was the drug's unexpected appeal to normally law-abiding citizens. Truckers used it to stay awake on long trips. Middle-aged men and women tried to regain the energy and vitality of their youth. The gay community wanted a drug they could call their own. Ice had something for everyone, a seismic jolt of euphoria delivered straight to the cerebral cortex. Nobody saw the dark side of the little white crystals until they'd spread from both coasts to the Midwest, from the cities to the suburbs. Addiction came without warning or remorse. Ice was a body snatcher that sucked you dry, leaving behind a walking corpse too drained to know it was already dead.

"Everybody needs an edge," said Beau. "But Frank doesn't deal in trash, Gummy. Even a fat fuck like Frank's got standards."

"Wh-what are you sayin'?"

"I'm saying it's one thing to get judged by a jury, but a whole 'nother thing to get judged by Frank. Ice is a street drug, Gummy. Low rent, high risk. Frank know about your little hobby?"

Gummy shuddered. If he had any teeth left, they would have started chattering. "He knows I'm using—*was* using. Said he'd get me help. I'm in a program—twelve steps."

"That's great," said Beau. "Which step you on?"

"I forget."

"Don't sweat it, Gummy. Twelve's a lot of steps to keep track of."

"N*nn*o shit."

Vincent leaned in close and almost whispered. "Frank doesn't know you're *dealing*, Gummy."

Gummy's head swiveled around. "You're not gonna tell him?"

"Not if you help us," said Beau mildly. "This ain't about you, Gummy."

"It's about the zoo," said Vinnie.

"You been to the zoo, Gummy?"

Gummy looked from Beau back to Vincent, his eyes suddenly clear. "No, not lately. Not since I was a kid."

Beau nodded. "Me and Vinnie, we were just there. Know what we found?"

Gummy looked at his shoes and nodded. "Cecil."

"*Yeah*," said Beau brightly. "You always were good with names."

Vincent nodded. "We need a name, Gummy."

"We just want the trigger man," said Beau soothingly. "Doesn't have to go past that."

"Frank'll never know," added Vincent. "About any of this."

Gummy's lips started twitching as he ground his ruined teeth together. When he spoke, his voice was almost calm, as if he'd come down from some terrible mountain and was gathering his strength for his next ascent into madness.

"I don't know anything, you understand?"

Beau caught the change in tone. "'Course not, Gummy. We're not even havin' this conversation."

"That's right," replied Gummy. "We're not. But if we were—if we were talkin', then I might tell you to look at a guy named Anthony."

"Anthony got a last name?" asked Vincent.

Gummy shook his head. "I just know him as Anthony. Guys call him Big Anthony sometimes, 'cause he's tall. But he's not that big for a hitter. More lanky, you know. Kinda looks like a bird."

"What kinda bird?"

"A hawk," said Gummy. "Guy looks like a hawk."

Vincent looked at Beau, who nodded. Laying his right arm around Gummy's shoulders, Beau flexed his bicep, pulling Gummy close and almost breaking his neck. It was a gesture that was simultaneously tender and terrifying. Gummy gasped as Beau whispered intently into his ear.

"You better find those twelve steps or I'll kill you myself," he said. "*Get off the shit, Gummy.*" Beau uncoiled his arm and stalked off down the hill.

Gummy watched the two detectives walk away. Once they were out of sight he sat down heavily on the pavement and frantically clutched at his pockets for a lighter.

Beau and Vincent didn't say anything until they'd rounded the corner at Columbus and passed two or three Italian restaurants. It was still early enough for North Beach to draw tourists. At the fourth awning Beau stopped suddenly and pushed through the door, grabbing two bar stools before Vincent caught up with him. By the time Vincent was sitting shoulder to shoulder with his partner, Beau had ordered two shots of tequila.

"We celebrating?" asked Vincent.

"No," said Beau. "I fuckin' hate tequila. This is punishment."

"We got a name."

Beau turned to face Vincent. "How do you feel about it?"

"The name?" said Vincent. "I think the name's probably good."

"Not what I meant," said Beau. "How do you feel about bracing Gummy?"

Vincent threw back the shot and winced. "Like a manipulative scumbag."

Beau nodded and ordered two more shots. "Don't mind scaring the tough guys, the ones that need to be taken down a notch. Kind of like being a badass cop every once in a while."

"But a guy like Gummy..." Vincent let his voice trail off.

"Yeah." Beau looked straight ahead, at his own reflection in the mirror behind the bar.

Vincent gestured at the bartender to hold off on a second shot. The first one was already working its magic, eating a hole in his empty stomach. "So what now?"

"That's easy," said Beau. "We go bird hunting."

43

"I THINK YOU KILLED him already."

The steel blades made a satisfying *thunk* as they struck the wooden board. Had it been a real man against the board instead of a silhouette, he would have been killed ten times over from throwing stars in his eyes, steel blades in his neck, and the spear protruding from his heart. Cape winced in sympathetic pain as metal darts with tails of brightly colored thread flew across the room and hit the board-man squarely in the crotch.

"I believe in being thorough," said Sally. Dressed in black from head to toe, she seemed to appear and disappear out of thin air as she walked through shafts of sunlight streaming into the loft from skylights overhead.

"Taking out your frustrations over the shooting in Brooklyn?"

"I'm out of practice," said Sally. "I should have nailed the bastard."

"Maybe you did."

"The cops didn't find a body," she replied. "At best he's got a punctured shoulder."

"But we didn't get killed," said Cape. "Given the odds, that's not bad."

"Not good enough," replied Sally. "If you kill the bad guys *now*, you don't have to worry about them causing trouble *later*."

"It never works like that in the movies."

"This isn't the movies," said Sally. "If it were, then I'd be a buxom blonde and you'd look like George Clooney."

"Not Brad Pitt?"

"I'm trying to give you a fighting chance."

"If we're in a movie, there should also be a love interest."

"Who's got the time?"

Cape smiled. "Beau considered asking you out until I convinced him you had a gender bias."

"I like Beau," said Sally. "It'd be a shame to have to hurt him."

"You could let him down easy."

"I meant physically."

She walked over to the board and started removing the metal darts, sliding each one into a hidden pocket in her sleeve. "You still want to talk to Freddie Wang?"

"Yeah," said Cape. "But I'm going to see Frank Alessi first. He speaks the language."

"So does Freddie, but not with *gwai loh* like you—unless he's in the mood."

"Let's see how it goes with Frank," said Cape. "See if I learn anything."

"You're sure you want to waste your time with those guys?"

"You want take-out drugs in this town, it's either Chinese or Italian."

"You're the detective," said Sally, pulling the spear from the board. "I'm just the circus act."

Cape nodded at the spear, which ended in a two-pronged curve like a can opener. "How old were you when you learned to throw that thing?"

Sally hefted the spear and sighted down the shaft. "Not until I was eight."

Cape wasn't sure what he was doing when he was eight, but he was pretty sure he had a rock in his hand. Maybe some gum, but definitely not a spear.

"Somebody followed us to Brighton Beach," said Sally. "Or somebody told the sniper we were coming."

Cape shook his head. "Corelli and the Pole were the only people who knew we were going back. No way Corelli sold us out, and I don't see the Pole wasting his own guy, despite what Corelli thinks. He lives by a code."

"I think it's called the penal code," said Sally. "He's a criminal."

Cape heard the Pole's voice in his head. *What is criminal?*

"We were followed," said Cape.

"The Pole also spoke of *the brotherhood*," said Sally. "What if he and the Major are—what did he call it?"

"Thieves-in-law," said Cape.

"Put him on the list," said Sally sternly.

"OK, he's on the list."

"Who else knew you were in New York?"

"After my visit to Empire, all the usual suspects," said Cape. "Adam, Harry, Angelo. The receptionist, if you want to do this by the book. Beau, of course."

"Aren't you forgetting someone?"

"Who?" asked Cape, then answered himself. "You mean Grace."

Sally nodded. "She knew before you left. Plenty of time to set something up."

"She's my client."

"Who gets rich from her buddy Tom taking the big fall off the bridge."

"So why start an investigation?"

"To divert suspicion, of course," said Sally. "Happens in the movies all the time."

"This isn't the movies."

"You can't have it both ways."

"You're paranoid."

"Aren't you?" asked Sally. "You're the one with a target on your back." She walked the length of the loft, keeping her back to Cape. When she reached the far wall, Cape realized he was standing between her and the practice board, just slightly to the right. Before he could say anything, Sally spun on her heel and hurled the spear one-handed. He could still feel it whistling past his ear when it hit the board.

The only noise in the loft came from the spear, bass and treble notes alternating as it wobbled back and forth. It penetrated deeper this time, having struck the exact spot on the board as the previous throw. Sally looked from the board to Cape and curtsied.

"For my next trick, I will make someone from the audience disappear. Anyone? *Anyone?*"

Cape held up his hands. "I can take a hint—you want to practice."

Sally bowed in acknowledgement. "Call me when you're ready to visit Freddie Wang."

"Count on it."

44

CAPE FELT THE ADRENALINE rush of impending violence.

He was loathe to admit it felt good, but it did. Cape had decided his visit to Frank Alessi should be unannounced. The approach had worked in New York, and Frank didn't like company. He also didn't like Cape, which compounded the problem. Besides, showing up uninvited gave Cape an excuse to punch something other than a wall.

Cape had studied martial arts when he was younger but always considered himself nonviolent, until as a reporter he was thrust into situations that required a choice. Most people have the luxury of driving through bad neighborhoods without taking their foot off the gas, past impending crimes that happen as soon as their car rounds the corner, or the moment the sun goes down or the bars close. But if you stay around and watch, you become part of it, whether you want to or not. Do you just keep watching and write about it later, or do you step in?

The first time Cape saw a pimp beat up one of his girls, the decision was made for him. Cape was picking shards of the pimp's broken teeth from between his own bloody knuckles before he even stopped to think. He just reacted, and in that visceral moment discovered his own capacity for violence. It would be years before he found his calling, but he knew then he wasn't really cut out for the newspaper business. He looked in the mirror that night and realized he'd rather have bruised knuckles than a writing callous.

Frank Alessi's building was on the corner of Broadway and Columbus Avenue, directly across from Big Al's, an infamous San Francisco landmark. While most adult bookstores were anonymous storefronts squeezed between strip clubs in the red light district, Big Al's proudly announced its presence with a twenty-foot-tall neon sign on the corner of two of the city's busiest streets. The sign was in the shape of a gangster, complete with Tommy gun and smoking cigar. Frank's office was at eye level with the neon mobster, and Cape often wondered if that was how Frank regarded himself, looming over San Francisco and larger than life.

And Frank was growing larger by the day, if his dinner order was any indication. The Italian restaurant next door took his order and gave it to Chuck, their delivery guy, as they did almost every night. Fifty dollars later, Chuck was headed home for the evening, and Cape was holding Frank's dinner. An extra ten bought Chuck's baseball cap, emblazoned with the restaurant's logo.

It had been almost a year since the last time Cape called on Frank, but he doubted much had changed. Frank was a creature of habit, and Cape had been watching the front door for the past two hours. He figured maybe four guys in the building—one downstairs at the front door, one in the upstairs hallway, and two inside the office with Frank. There were always two with Frank.

Cape wasn't worried about the last two, because he hoped to have Frank's undivided attention by then. Frank wasn't the type to do anything rash unless you posed a threat, but he also wasn't inclined to invite you inside just to make conversation. It was a bullshit test of Frank's—you get inside and he might listen.

Cape knocked and felt himself getting the once-over from the thug behind the door. An old-fashioned peephole, no camera, since Frank was both old-fashioned and cheap. Besides, he was supposedly a legitimate businessman with nothing to fear except a tax audit. Apparently the roundness of Cape's eyes, the red cap, and the paper bag with grease stains passed inspection, because he heard the lock turning.

The door opened out in accordance with city fire codes, so Cape grabbed the knob and yanked as hard as he could. The man behind the door lurched forward a step but then recovered, so Cape reversed direction and slammed the door back in his face. He heard a satisfying crunch as the wood collided with the man's nose, snapping his head back into the door frame. Cape grabbed the front of his shirt and pulled him into the street. The man landed face down, coughing and spitting.

Cape bent at the waist to retrieve the paper bag, stepped inside, and locked the door. The stairs were on the right, and he took them two at a time. He guessed maybe thirty seconds before pounding on the door commenced.

Shifting the bag to his left hand, he reached under his jacket and pulled the revolver. He'd brought the Ruger for intimidation value, and as he crested the landing he cocked the gun and swung to the left.

He was facing the entrance to a sitting room off the second-floor hallway, where a squat man with thinning hair sat watching television and smoking a cigarette. When he heard the click of the hammer, he snapped his head around, jaw open, and dropped his cigarette on the carpet. He blinked rapidly to make the hallucination vanish, a delivery guy with a revolver, about to blow his brains out.

"You might want to put that out," said Cape gently, "unless you want to get us in trouble with the fire department."

The man stared, uncomprehending.

"The cigarette," said Cape more firmly. "Pick it up and put it out."

Keeping his eyes on Cape, the man bent and pawed at the carpet until he snagged the wrong end of the smoldering butt, cursed, and yanked his hand away. The second time he looked down. He reached awkwardly across his body for the ashtray next to his chair.

Cape nodded. "Now assume the position. Face down, hands behind your head." He kept the gun up and added, "And please keep your mouth shut—if I have to shoot, we're both in trouble." Cape pulled two plastic cable ties tight around the man's wrists, added duct tape around the mouth, then pulled his wrists down and used two more cable ties to secure them to his belt. It wasn't handcuffs, but it would keep him rolling around the floor long enough for Cape to get to Frank. Cape turned the volume on the television slightly higher, then walked down the hallway.

Cape holstered the gun before reaching the double doors at the end of the hall. After a gentle knock, he turned the brass handle and stepped inside.

The office resembled a museum of antiquities that had been turned into a furniture showroom. An eighteenth-century couch with carved feet shaped like lion's claws shared floor space with leather-backed chairs from a New York brownstone circa 1900. Every item looked expensive but nothing matched. The end tables belonged in a different room, if not another era, and the various floor lamps were no more related than justice and the law. Dominating the room was an enormous teak desk, and behind the desk sat an enormous man.

Frank Alessi sat resplendent in a pale gray suit, cufflinks, and a white silk shirt open at the collar. The lack of a tie offered a clear view of multiple chins, fully revealed in all their blubberous splendor, when his head snapped back in surprise at Cape's entrance.

Behind Frank stood a tall man with black hair, a high forehead, and a hook nose. Cape was reminded of a hawk as the man swiveled his head toward the door.

"Hi Frank," said Cape, holding up the paper bag. "Your dinner's getting—"

Two arms as big as pythons encircled Cape before he could finish his sentence. He dropped the takeout bag and gasped as he was lifted off the ground and squeezed mercilessly, his assailant's chin digging into his spine. Judging by the distance to the floor, the man crushing the life out of him was as tall as a refrigerator.

The attack stopped as suddenly as it had occurred. Cape felt the pressure on his chest disappear and he dropped to the floor, wondering if he'd just been accosted by a feeble carnival giant trying to guess his weight. Then Cape heard his captor utter a single syllable.

"Ow."

Cape didn't hesitate. Without turning, he raised his right foot and drove the heel of his shoe into his attacker's instep. Another *Ow*, louder this time. Cape spun and threw a punch where the solar plexus should have been and almost broke his hand, but the Fridge rolled onto his heels and fell, ass first, onto the hardwood floor.

"*Ow—ow—oww!*" repeated the Fridge. The bodyguard rubbed his left wrist with his right hand and looked at Cape with a wounded expression, his close-cropped hair and large ears giving him an almost childlike appearance. He wasn't nearly as large as Ursa by half, but he sure as hell wasn't buying his clothes off the rack.

Cape leaned forward to help the clumsy giant stand when he heard the unmistakable *click* of a gun being cocked. He raised both hands in the air and slowly put them behind his head before turning around. The hawk-nosed man was aiming a Kimber .45 automatic at Cape's face. Frank Alessi started clapping, a smug look on his face.

"What a dipshit," said Frank in admiration. "You want it in the head or the gut?"

Cape looked the Hawk in the eye and very deliberately dropped his hands to his sides before responding. "You're not going to shoot me, Frank," he said evenly. "You're a pillar of civic responsibility." Cape slowly unbuttoned his shirt to reveal his bare chest, then redid the buttons. "No wire."

"Am I supposed to be impressed?"

"You're supposed to be glad to see me," said Cape in a hurt voice. "We're old friends."

Frank narrowed his eyes and chewed his lower lip, trying to remember precisely why he disliked Cape so much. "You fucked up one of my sofas," he said indignantly, then in afterthought, "And you killed one of my guys."

"He wasn't *your guy*, Frank," replied Cape. "He was selling you out to the competition."

"That wasn't your business."

"He tried to shoot me, and I shot back," said Cape. "That was my business." Then he pointedly added, "I did you a favor, Frank."

Frank opened and closed his mouth like a fish, so pissed he might be in Cape's debt that he forgot what he was going to say.

"Speaking of getting it in the gut," said Cape, "I think your bodyguard just ruined your dinner." He gestured at the paper bag, upside down and split open, pasta and meat sauce strewn across the floor like blood and guts.

Frank went red in the face as he jabbed a finger at Baby Huey. "You're supposed to crush him, not give him a hug—the fuck is your problem?"

The lumbering guard thrust out his lower lip and rubbed his wrist. "I think I got carpal tunnel."

Frank nearly came out of his chair. "You got *what*?"

The Hawk leaned forward and whispered, keeping the gun on Cape the whole time. Frank wheeled around in his chair, incredulous.

"What the hell are you talking about?"

The Hawk shrugged apologetically, answering in a subdued voice.

"It's a repetitive stress disorder."

The Fridge nodded, holding up his left arm for examination. "Comes from making the same motion again and again and again, like typing on a keyboard; or, in my case, hitting guys—I always hit 'em the same way."

The Hawk shrugged and nodded. "It can be quite painful if not treated properly."

Frank looked from one thug to the other, his mouth open.

"I don't fuckin' believe this."

Cape jumped in. "This could be serious," he said. "We're talking on-the-job injury, Frank. That means workman's comp, medical bills, physical therapy…"

Frank leveled a finger at Cape. "You shut the fuck up." The finger swiveled toward the Fridge. "And you get off your ass and get me another dinner before I shoot you—you fucking *my-wrist-hurts* pansy."

"I know a good lawyer if you need one," whispered Cape as he helped the Fridge stand. The big man nodded and smiled like a grateful child before heading down the hallway.

"*Cape-fuckin'-Weathers*," intoned Frank from behind his desk. "Tell me again why I don't drill you right now?"

"Because unlike you, Frank, I have friends," replied Cape in a tired voice, adding, "who happen to wear badges—"

"—who know you're here," said Frank with a disgusted look on his face.

Cape nodded. "And they're dying for an excuse to dig deeper into your business affairs."

"And you think that if they find you floating face-down in the Bay after talking to me, that could be considered probable cause."

"You know, Frank, I don't understand why everyone tells me you're stupid."

Frank's eyes bulged. "Maybe I can't kill you so easy," he said, "but I can hurt you some."

"I can get your heroin back for you," said Cape nonchalantly.

Frank sat forward, darting a backward glance at the Hawk.

"What heroin?"

"You notice I didn't ask if you wanted to *get your smack back*?" said Cape. "Not going for the obvious rhyme took a lot of restraint on my part."

Frank's temples seem to balloon outward. "What heroin?"

"The stuff you sold to the movie producer," replied Cape. "Tom Abrahams."

Frank stared as if waiting for the other shoe to drop. A full minute passed before he said anything.

"Who?"

"How do you like the movie business, Frank?" asked Cape.

Frank hunched his shoulders and put both hands on his desk.

"The fuck are you talking about?"

Cape studied Frank carefully before asking the next question.

"Been to the zoo lately, Frank?"

Frank's eyes went flat. "I never go to the zoo," he said. "Can't stand the smell."

Cape nodded as if accepting the answer at face value. "Shame about Otto," he said sympathetically. "You think his wife will close the deli?"

Frank did the fish routine again, mouth opening and closing before any sound emerged. "What do you know about Otto?" He gestured at the Hawk, who nodded and shifted the forty-five to aim at Cape's chest.

"Talk," said Frank.

Cape looked from the gun to Frank, then nonchalantly walked over to the sofa and sat down. When you played cards with Frank Alessi, you had to bluff on every hand. Frank was a rottweiler—you show fear and he'd eat you for lunch, but you look him in the eye and he just sat there with a dumb expression on his face, wondering which hand held the dog biscuit.

"I know you didn't kill Otto," said Cape.

Frank looked disappointed—no biscuit in that hand. "No shit, detective."

"But you think Freddie Wang did."

Frank jerked his head sideways. The Hawk lowered the gun.

"And how is this your business?" asked Frank.

"You think he's after your half of the drug business," continued Cape. "He already controls the supply, so why not take over distribution?"

"Stop jerkin' me off," said Frank. "You want money for information, say so; you know something, spit it out."

"I don't know shit, do you?"

"I got my theories."

"But you can't test them without getting close to Freddie," said Cape.

"Give it time."

"Bullshit," said Cape. "It would take an army to get close to Freddie, unless you can turn one of his guys."

Frank shifted in his seat impatiently.

"My business," he snapped. "Not yours. You through wasting my time?"

"I'm going to see Freddie," said Cape matter-of-factly.

Frank spoke without thinking. "I'll give you twenty grand to kill him."

The Hawk's eyes bulged with surprise. Cape forced a laugh and shook his head, wishing for Beau's sake he'd been wearing a wire. "I'm not in that line of work."

"You're a fucking hypocrite," spat Frank. "You shot one of ours."

"He shot first," said Cape. "There's a difference."

"I don't see it."

"Then buy a pair of glasses," said Cape. "I'll give him a message, if you want."

"What's this to you?" demanded Frank. "Why the fuck are you here?"

Cape thought for a minute before answering. "I think I've been investigating the wrong case."

"Wouldn't be surprised," muttered Frank. "Don't know why anyone would hire an asshole like you in the first place."

"Does that mean I can use you as a reference?"

"Fuck off."

"Good night, Frank," said Cape. "Thanks for telling me jack shit about next to nothing." He nodded at the Hawk before heading toward the door. The gun had never wavered the entire time.

"Wait a minute," said Frank.

Cape turned.

"You really gonna see Freddie?"

Cape nodded. "My next stop."

"Go ahead and give him a message."

Cape stood there quietly, waiting for Frank to gather his thoughts. It didn't take long.

"Tell him I said he should stay where he belongs," said Frank. "In Chinatown."

"Anything else?"

"Yeah," said Frank. "If he tries to cross Broadway, I'll kill him."

Cape let himself out. No one tried to stop him. A minute later he was crossing Broadway and heading into Chinatown.

45

"Freddie Wang is a tapeworm."

"Is that an actual job description?"

"Yes, it is."

Sally led Cape down a twisted alley he never knew existed somewhere near the heart of Chinatown, only a few blocks but a world away from the tourist trade on Grant Street. The kitchen entrance to Freddie Wang's restaurant was a few doors down. A cook was standing outside smoking, his face illuminated by the dim glow of a facing apartment window. As they got closer, Cape noticed the cook's white jacket bulged on his right side and realized he was packing, a door guard dressed like the kitchen help.

"I see him," said Sally calmly. "Not a problem."

Cape nodded and kept walking. "You were telling me where to apply to become an intestinal parasite."

"Freddie Wang is a tapeworm living off the Triads," said Sally.

"I thought he ran the tongs."

"He thinks he runs Chinatown, but he can't take a piss without asking permission. He's just another mail stop in the network."

"A bureaucrat," suggested Cape.

"Yeah," said Sally, "that's exactly what Freddie is—not a leader, not a soldier, but not a civilian, either. Just a criminal parasite who thinks he's in charge."

"Maybe he should run for Congress."

Sally snorted but didn't reply. They had reached their destination.

The mock cook straightened into a tough-guy pose and said something in Cantonese. His tone made it sound like a threat. He was just shy of six feet, a good foot taller than Sally and narrower in the shoulders and chest than Cape. But Freddie Wang had his back, so he clearly pictured himself as the Jolly Green Giant.

Sally smiled sweetly and replied in a low voice, the picture of a demure Asian woman. When the guard leaned closer, her right hand shot forward like a cobra and snaked its way down the front of his pants before he got the first sentence out. Sally twisted her right hand violently as her left caught him by the throat and cut off his air supply before he could scream. The guard's eyes bulged in a cartoon freeze-frame of intense pain then slammed shut like twin garage doors as he fainted at their feet.

Cape winced. "I'd hate to see you on a second date."

"I don't believe in foreplay," said Sally. "Follow me."

She led them past cooks who looked to be the real deal, scrambling around a kitchen too small for their frenzied activity. Every wall was lined with four-top stoves, and every burner had a metal pot spewing steam into the low ceiling. Cape's eyes started to water from all the spices, and his nose twitched like a rabbit's. He caught a whiff of something that made his mouth water, but the rest was an indecipherable mélange. In the center of the wide room was an island with a wooden counter, and six men crowded around hacking up chickens, ducks, and one or two critters Cape suspected were on the endangered species list.

The men watched them pass with a mix of idle curiosity and suspicion, but something in Sally's bearing told them this was a formal visit, not a raid. Either that or they recognized her for what she was and didn't want their dicks torn off.

They pushed through a swinging metal door into a different world, the cacophony of the kitchen replaced by the white noise of dinner guests. A barely heard recording buzzed from tiny speakers in the corners, the strumming of a lute accompanied by plaintive Chinese singing. The room had tables in the center and booths along the wall. Sally and Cape chose a booth that allowed one of them to face the kitchen and the other the front entrance.

The restaurant was on the ground floor of an ornate two-story building in the heart of Chinatown. Red columns encircled by golden dragons and tigers framed the front door. Two stone Chinese dogs sat on either side of the short stairway leading to the large dining room. It oozed authenticity, a dining experience worthy of a postcard. And while it catered to tourists during the day, it served a very different clientele late at night.

Cape and Sally arrived just after eleven o'clock, and the restaurant was almost empty. Not far from their booth was a small round table holding a middle-aged couple and their son. The boy was maybe eighteen and had his mother's blonde hair and his father's square nose and chin. He wore a sweatshirt with *University of Iowa* emblazoned across the front. His parents smiled at each other as the boy used his chopsticks to chase the last dumpling across the table.

"Watch this," said Sally. Cape glanced over and saw a waiter carefully place a fortune cookie in front of each family member, starting with the father.

The dad cracked open his fortune cookie. As he read the tiny slip of paper, his brow furrowed. He looked up at his wife. She'd just finished reading her fortune and looked distinctly uncomfortable as she met his gaze. The boy looked in consternation from one parent to the other, his broken cookie still on his plate.

The husband said something to the wife that Cape didn't quite catch, but her response was unmistakable.

"Bastard!" she cried. "I *knew* it."

Grabbing her son by the arm, she stormed out of the restaurant. The husband angrily threw his napkin on the table and ran after her.

Sally smiled mischievously. Cape stepped over to the table and read the small slip of paper the father had left behind.

Your wife is having an affair. Ask her about it!

Cape raised his eyebrows and grabbed the wife's fortune.

Your husband will accuse you of his own crimes.

The son's fortune was perhaps the most insidious.

Your parents' marriage is a sham!

"Harsh," muttered Cape. He returned to the booth. "I saw this trick last time I was here."

Sally nodded. "Freddie likes to clear the tourists out before the tongs arrive at midnight. He's developed some ingenious techniques for getting lingering diners to leave."

"But how do they get so specific?"

"The waiters are tasked with profiling the patrons, then a guy in the back writes custom fortunes. Over the years they've become pretty sophisticated."

"Obviously," said Cape. Dumplings had arrived while he'd been reading fortunes. Using a single chopstick, he skewered one and raised it toward his mouth.

"Don't eat that," said Sally casually.

Cape froze, then lowered the dumpling back to the plate. "We're not eating?"

Sally shook her head. "I know the cooks."

"But I'm starving."

"But your bowels still function properly—trust me. That's Freddie's next trick for getting rid of unwanted guests."

Cape looked at the dumpling as if it were a land mine and pushed the plate away.

Sally barked something in Cantonese at the waiter, who nodded briskly before disappearing into the kitchen. After several minutes he returned with two fortune cookies and set one in front of each of them in turn. Sally read hers first.

Come upstairs.

She passed the slip over to Cape, who handed his over to her.

You will be dead soon.

Sally raised her eyebrows.

"Get in line," Cape said in a tired voice. Sally smiled.

As they climbed the stairs, Sally spoke quickly in subdued tones. "Since I'm here, Freddie will probably do his Fidel Castro routine," she said. "He'll pretend not to understand English, so I'll translate—gives him more time to react to questions."

Cape nodded. "After we're done, can we eat?"

"Anywhere but here."

At the top of the stairs, a short hallway led to double doors secured with a circular bronze latch almost a foot across. On either side of the door stood a guard, twin Chinese with broad shoulders and expensively tailored suits. Cape knew they carried guns but couldn't see an outline or bulge under their jackets. He and Sally reached the door and the twins stepped forward to frisk Freddie's guests.

Cape held his arms in T-formation while the guard on the right went to work. "Who's your tailor?" The guard ignored him and moved his hands slowly along Cape's legs. The guard checking Sally was tentative at first until she barked something in Cantonese that sounded like a reprimand. The guard blushed as he kneeled and patted her down. After a few awkward seconds of professional groping, the twins stepped back and pulled open the doors.

The cloying smell of incense assailed them even before they crossed the threshold. Cape fought back the urge to sneeze.

The room was dark, the only illumination coming from a curved lamp perched on a desk. Thick carpeting—a deep red the color of blood. Drapes the same color covered most of the walls, making the room virtually soundproof. Cape glimpsed sculptures sitting on small tables in shadowed corners but couldn't discern any details. Even the shape and size of the room itself was uncertain in the smoky haze.

As they approached the desk, a gnarled hand appeared in the pool of light.

From where Cape was standing, the hand looked disembodied, Thing from *The Addam's Family* crawling across the desk to greet them. He started humming under his breath—*They're creepy and they're kooky*—until Sally gave him a dirty look.

Two straight-backed chairs sat empty but Sally remained standing. Cape stood to her left, following her lead. To Sally's right, a man emerged from the shadows and stood at parade rest next to her, hands clasped behind his back. He was heavy, his contours more suited to Sumo wrestling than the restaurant business. Sally did nothing to acknowledge his presence.

As Cape's eyes adjusted, the shadowy figure of Freddie Wang materialized behind the desk, his crooked fingers clutching a cigarette that glowed like a red eye in the darkness. To his right sat another man, and despite the dim light Cape saw he was younger, probably in his twenties, with a broad face and shiny black ponytail. He muttered something to Freddie, who leaned forward into the light.

Freddie Wang commanded your attention, a sepulchral vision from the pages of a Sax Rohmer novel. His left eye drooped, smaller and dim, but the right eye glowed malevolently like a black sun. It was the eye of a demon. He had as much hair growing out of his ears as he did on his head, where it was stringy and gray, falling loosely around the collar of his suit. A finishing touch of repulsion was a cluster of three black hairs sprouting from a large mole on his cheek.

Freddie's hand scuttled back into darkness. They say hands always reveal your true age, so Cape figured Freddie was at least a thousand years old.

Freddie turned his black eye on Sally and spoke rapidly in Chinese. She responded in a different dialect from her exchanges with the waiter and guard. The phrasing was still unintelligible but somehow more distinct. Cape guessed they'd switched to Mandarin.

Sally kept her eyes on Freddie but spoke to Cape. "Ask your questions."

Cape nodded at Freddie. "Frank Alessi thinks you're planning on taking over distribution of the heroin trade."

Sally started to repeat the statement in Chinese, but Freddie responded almost immediately, a guttural cough laced with anger. When he finished, Freddie leaned forward and spat into the ashtray. Sally spoke clearly and succinctly.

"Frank Alessi is a treacherous pig."

Cape kept his eyes on Freddie and not the ashtray. "Frank says you started a war when you killed Otto the butcher."

Freddie delivered his answer with machine-gun velocity.

"Frank Alessi is a *lying*, treacherous pig," repeated Sally carefully, "who accuses other men of his own crimes."

Cape thought of the fortune cookies downstairs and wondered if Freddie took a turn at writing them. He waited a few seconds before speaking again. "Frank's unhappy you cut him out of your dealings with the movie producer."

Freddie leaned back in his chair and mumbled something to the young man, who shook his head. Freddie looked at Sally but didn't say anything. Seconds ticked by, and Cape decided to keep talking. "He thinks the movie business could be very lucrative as a new means of distribution, so he doesn't understand why you'd be so greedy."

Freddie remained motionless until the word *greedy*, at which point he banged his fist on the desk and uttered another clipped reply.

"If I am the one who is greedy," said Sally, "then why is Frank unable to fit in his own clothes?"

"You killed the man at the bakery," Cape said matter-of-factly. "The one who looked like a pretzel."

Cape watched Freddie carefully and saw in his expression that he'd registered the deliberate change in phrasing. Cape hadn't invoked Frank with his last statement—he was representing himself. The young man with the ponytail picked up on it, too, and leaned forward into the light. He twisted his face into a calculated sneer and spoke evenly in perfect English.

"Father, why do you waste your time with this mongrel bitch and her round-eyed companion?"

The heavyset man next to Sally chuckled. The young ponytail smiled cruelly at her and the fat guard laughed again, his stomach shaking.

Sally's right hand shot out so fast Cape barely registered the movement except for the *smack* of her hand connecting with the fat man's Adam's apple. A violent cough as he clutched both hands to his neck and collapsed to his knees, wheezing. Nobody moved or spoke; Freddie and his son avoided eye contact as if someone had farted. Seconds ticked by. After a long minute of rasping agony, the Sumo fell heavily onto his face, unconscious.

Sally smiled sweetly at the young man behind Freddie and said something in Mandarin. His eyes grew wide and he scooted back in his chair, pulling himself into the shadows next to his father.

Freddie took a long drag on his cigarette and leaned forward, smoke swirling around his leering eye. "My son is young—has much to learn," he said in careful English, consonants bending awkwardly around neglected vowels. "But he has a point. Tell me, *little dragon*, why do you associate with this *gwai loh*?" He pointed at Cape with a crooked finger.

Sally nodded in acknowledgment of the question and held Freddie's gaze a long time before answering, also in English.

"Because he keeps his word," she said evenly. "*He understands honor.*" Then she added something in Cantonese before breaking eye contact with Freddie.

Freddie blinked and sat back as if Sally had slapped him, and Cape realized that's exactly what she had done. She turned toward Cape as if Freddie was no longer in the room. He was dismissed.

"Anything else?" she asked.

Cape glanced at the man face down on the floor, then at Freddie, the black orb of his eye glowing darkly through the smoke. It wasn't the look of a cooperative man. Cape glanced at Sally and shook his head.

"Let's go find a decent restaurant."

They let themselves out, the guards tracking them down the stairs but making no move to stop them. Back on the street, Cape turned to Sally.

"What did you say to the son?"

"A Chinese epithet," she replied. "Loosely translated, I told him that if he spoke again I would inflict so much pain upon him that his ancestors—and all his descendants—would writhe in agony for a thousand years."

"He looked moved," said Cape.

"It's more poetic in Chinese," Sally assured him.

"He's obviously not a lover of poetry."

"He's young and bold," said Sally gravely, "but too inexperienced to take over from Freddie."

"But Freddie's getting old."

"Freddie's already old, but it takes more than old age to kill a reptile." They walked the next few blocks in silence. "You learn anything tonight?"

"Yeah," said Cape. "I've lost my appetite for Chinese food."

"How about Japanese?"

"Better—no fortune cookies."

"I know a place."

"Let's go," said Cape. "Maybe with some food in my stomach I'll be able to make sense of this case."

"I doubt it, but at least you won't die of hunger."

"At this rate, that's probably the only thing that won't kill me."

"See?" said Sally. "Things are looking up."

46

ANTHONY FELT LIKE AN intellectual without his gun.

He prided himself on his vocabulary and made this weekly trek to Stacey's Bookstore on Market regardless of the weather. The walk took him far enough from North Beach that he didn't have to worry about running into any of Frank's other goons, and he knew he wouldn't see them in a bookstore unless they'd stepped in to use the john. Most of them couldn't read the paper, let alone a book.

That was the hardest thing about working for Frank, the sheer banality of the conversations. *Fuckin'-this* and *fuckin'-that* all the time. It was like Frank had attended a training seminar called *How to Act Like a Wiseguy*, lessons in how to forget prepositions and shave your IQ in half by following a simple daily regimen.

But Anthony had a talent, a moral detachment, and lack of empathy that few professions rewarded except for certain branches of the military, and they didn't pay well enough. As crude as Frank Alessi might be, he was a businessman, a product of natural selection in the free market. He understood the value of talent, and

Anthony had a gift. He could look down his hawk-nose at a man and shoot him in the eye without blinking, then sleep like a baby. His work ethic was unencumbered by conscience, which made him very valuable to a man like Frank.

Anthony had picked out four new books and five periodicals, paid, and was just leaving the store as a short man in an nice-looking suit held the door for him, waiting until he could enter himself. Anthony nodded his thanks and moved onto the street as a large black man stepped from the curb and smiled as if they knew each other. Anthony's radar, suppressed during his bookstore reverie, kicked into gear too late. He felt the gun against his spine just as the black cop—he was sure they were cops—swung a lazy arm toward his solar plexus, clenching his fist at the last minute and knocking the wind out of him. Anthony doubled over and dropped his bag onto a pair of size-fifteen shoes.

"Nice of you to hold the door like that, Vinnie," said Beau pleasantly.

"We are public servants, after all," mused Vincent, bending over to grab Anthony by the collar. As he stood, coughing, Anthony noticed that a ridiculously large handgun had appeared in the black cop's right hand. Without a word, Anthony put his hands behind his head and waited to be frisked.

"Ain't you the cooperative one," said Beau.

"We'll see about that," said Vincent, pulling Anthony's arms down to cuff him. Some people were milling about, watching, but Beau gave them a look and they scattered. The two detectives led Anthony to their car.

Anthony twisted his head around and sighed in relief. The cop in the good suit had remembered his books. It occurred to him that going to jail would give him plenty of time to read.

Maybe today wasn't such a bad day, after all.

47

CAPE WAS NORTH OF the city when the earthquake hit San Francisco.

The Golden Gate Bridge had made it through the 1989 quake unscathed, but this time it was the first to fall. The people on the bridge never had a chance.

Traffic was light, a small blessing, but there were still over four hundred cars driving across the span when the first tremor hit. The surface of the road buckled and surged like a wave, sending cars slamming into each other. Before anyone realized what was happening, the bridge twisted from a second tremor so powerful it caused the unthinkable—one of the giant suspension cables snapped. The cable whipsawed back and forth, a giant snake scattering pedestrians and cars like leaves. As men and women plummeted toward the churning waves below, their screams were drowned by the shriek of twisting metal.

On the rugged hills overlooking the bridge from the north, a dark-haired woman watched helplessly as she clutched a young girl to her breast. She looked on in horror as an enormous shadow swept over them, blocking out the sun. The tidal wave was only seconds away.

Grace turned to Cape with a broad smile.

"Isn't it great?"

Cape was speechless as he watched the tidal wave sweep across the screen in the edit studio, washing away the bridge and crashing into the city near the Ferry Building. As the century-old clock tower broke in half and the wave devoured the streets south of Market, he turned to Grace with an indignant look on his face.

"You just destroyed my apartment."

Grace put a hand on his knee and gave it a reassuring squeeze.

"It wasn't personal," she replied. "I had to destroy the whole city."

"Oh, I guess that's OK then."

They were sitting in an edit suite at Industrial Light & Magic, the room dark except for the flickering light from the television monitors. Cape sat next to Grace on a black leather sofa about ten feet back from the screens, below which sat a young man with a goatee and a hoop earring. He moved his hands like a pianist across a mixing board covered with buttons, dials, and sliding knobs. After the city was reduced to churning rubble by the elemental fury of the ocean, he turned and looked questioningly at Grace.

"You want to see it again?"

"Absolutely," replied Grace. "Can you play it at half speed?"

When the earthquake struck again, Cape unconsciously gripped the arm of the sofa while Grace narrated.

"The asteroid has broken into fragments in space," she explained, "because the attempt to destroy it has failed. So a massive meteor shower is pummeling the Earth."

"And when is this supposed to take place?" asked Cape as he watched the suspension cable snap and twist across the bridge in slow motion.

Grace ignored the question, too caught up in her descriptions. "One of the bigger chunks hit the ocean about a hundred miles off the California coast, which triggered a massive earthquake and, of course, a deadly tidal wave."

"Of course," said Cape, forcing a smile.

"Jake," Grace called to the editor. "Freeze it there." The editor pushed a button. On the screen hundreds of people stood by their cars, clutched their loved ones, ran for safety, or simply stared impotently at their impending aquatic doom. Grace stepped to the monitor and circled some of the tragic figures with her index finger.

"See these people?" she asked.

Cape nodded, squinting at the screen.

"They're not real people."

"Of course they're not real people," replied Cape. "They're actors."

Grace shook her head. "They're not even that. One hundred percent digital, created one pixel at a time by a computer." She nodded at the editor, who pushed a button. The picture zoomed and started to move, one frame at a time.

Cape looked more closely. The people on the bridge looked as real as anyone he'd ever met, down to the smallest detail. One man's hair was tousled as if he'd just run his hands through it—you could see each strand move independently in the wind. Behind him a woman had lost her shoe. Cape could see a small hole in her sock and the tiny blister on her heel. Grace's finger traced the panicked crowd one by one, pointing out wrinkles, folds, even reflections in their eyes.

"Why pay extras when you can make them yourself?" She rested her hand on the editor's shoulder. "Thanks, Jake."

Cape was still studying the screen. "Incredible."

Grace smiled, obviously pleased to have impressed him.

"The CGI is cutting edge—sorry, *computer-generated imagery*. You saw the last three *Star Wars* movies?"

"Sure."

"Remember the winged alien with the elephant's nose?" she asked. "The one who owned Darth Vader's mother as a slave?"

"Yeah," said Cape. "He was blue."

Grace nodded. "He was completely digital, created by the artists here. All they did to complete the character was hire an actor to record his voice."

"I think I read an article about that."

"That was just one character, but now we can create hundreds."

"Must be expensive."

"Not as bad as casting calls and talent payments, by the time you're through," replied Grace. "And no problems with SAG, the actors' union. But it does get expensive, and time consuming. That's why I'm so excited—we're ahead of schedule with this scene." She turned back to the screen and frowned. "But I think the tidal wave needs more work. It needs to be ... *bigger*."

Cape looked hopeful. "Does that mean I'll have time to move into an apartment on top of one of the hills in Pacific Heights before the tidal wave hits?"

Grace smiled apologetically. "We're destroying the whole city."

Cape shrugged. "Then how about a last meal?"

"Good idea," replied Grace, checking her watch. "I'll buy."

The cafeteria was nicer than most restaurants in the city, plus it was relatively deserted. The producers, editors, and computer artists worked such odd hours that the typical lunchtime rush didn't occur. People came and went at all hours, sometimes just grabbing food to bring back to their editing bay.

Cape went for a turkey sandwich and chips while Grace loaded up on Cobb salad. Once the necessary condiments and utensils had been gathered, they sat down at an empty table some distance from anyone else.

"So how is it going?" Grace asked.

Cape hesitated by biting into his sandwich, trying to decide what to tell her. He'd given her regular updates, but now that he was sitting across from her, he realized that he'd omitted some details along the way. Grace knew he'd almost been killed in Ghirardelli Square, but he never mentioned his attackers were Russian. Similarly, he never told her about the Major's visit to his office, or about Ursa. Cape described his meetings at the Empire's offices but left out the Pole. All along he had edited himself instinctively, thinking he was being expedient, focusing on things that mattered directly to Grace. But now Cape wondered if his subconscious had other reasons.

He told himself Grace would only worry, or maybe even stop the investigation if she feared too much for his safety. A detective's job was to solve the case, not burden the client with his problems. But studying her now, as Grace looked at him expectantly, Cape wondered if some part of him didn't completely trust his own client. And after the past few days, he worried it might be impossible for him to trust anyone, period.

He shook himself from his reverie as Grace's expression changed to concern at his extended silence. "It's going just fine," he said reassuringly. "If discovering what you *don't* know is considered making progress, then I'm about to crack the case."

She smiled sympathetically. "You were looking for a connection to the drugs in Tom's room?"

"Yes," said Cape. "But I'm not sure that's the right angle. I talked to some of the characters involved in the local drug trade, and I didn't get the reactions I was expecting."

"But that doesn't mean they weren't involved."

"True." Cape nodded. "But suspecting a connection and establishing one are worlds apart. And unless that's the right angle, I'll never establish a motive. Without a motive, it's hard to track a killer."

Grace worked the muscles in her jaw. "Which means you won't find the people who killed Tom."

Cape studied the grim determination in her eyes, suddenly disgusted with himself for having doubts about her integrity.

"I'll find them," he said. "I just need a new angle."

"That's why you called about the movie's budget?"

"Yeah," he said. "How's it look?"

"It's a mess," replied Grace, pulling a folder from her bag and laying it on the table. "Frankly, I don't know what to make of it."

"Why not?" asked Cape. "You've handled the entire production budget on other films—isn't that what you told me?"

Grace shook her head. "That's not the problem. I understand the entries, but it doesn't make any sense. I thought Tom—" She hesitated before continuing. "I thought Tom would be more organized."

Cape leaned forward and opened the folder. "Give me an example."

Grace ran her finger down a column of numbers along the left side of the first page. "These are estimates," she explained. "Pretty standard entries for a film of this scale, separated into three broad categories: preproduction, production, and postproduction."

"Preproduction is scouting locations, that sort of thing?" asked Cape.

"Exactly," replied Grace. "Everything you do *before* you start shooting. Once the cameras start rolling and you're on location, then you're in production."

"And postproduction?" asked Cape. "Is that editing?"

Grace nodded. "Among other things—post can include editing, sound effects, film transfer, color correction, and special effects added to the film."

"Like the people on the bridge."

"In this case, yes," said Grace. "Sometimes special effects get classified as production if they're part of another scene you're actually shooting, but Tom separated all the digital effects into postproduction budgets."

"OK," said Cape. "So what's the problem?"

Grace turned to the next page and pointed to a table of line items and corresponding numbers. It looked like a standard spreadsheet program.

"These are *supposed* to be actuals," said Grace, frustration audible in her voice. "The real costs incurred so far on the film."

"So?"

"So according to this, we've already blown our budget," said Grace, "and we've spent money too early, where it shouldn't be spent yet."

"What do you mean by *yet*?"

"Look at this," said Grace, pointing at a number. "This is supposed to be the running total for computer effects, and it's already over budget. But when Tom did this sheet, I hadn't even started working with the guys here at ILM. That means Tom had already spent money on digital effects *before* I arrived."

"What effects?" asked Cape. "Early work on the bridge or the tidal wave?"

"That's what I thought, but nobody here seems to know," replied Grace in an exasperated voice. "Like I said, we're ahead of schedule on the effects, so maybe that's what happened."

"Maybe it's a billing error," suggested Cape, "or some of the costs were pre-billed to the studio."

"I've got the bill," replied Grace, "but it's short on details. Just some dates and studio time. If I can't determine what it's for, I'm going to make ILM eat the costs."

"Can you do that?'

Grace nodded. "I don't like to be a hard-ass, but a lot of production costs get swallowed by suppliers if you run over. So much of the actual cost is people's time and not hard costs, the accounting gets a little fuzzy sometimes."

Cape looked at the numbers, but they were meaningless to him. His experience told him to always follow the money, but he was in way over his head. He couldn't even do his own taxes. This case made more sense when people were shooting at him.

"What else?" he asked.

"Travel is over budget," said Grace. "Still tracking down receipts for that category, but it's almost triple what it should be."

Cape stared at the numbers as if they were tea leaves. "Anything else?"

"Talent costs are also out of whack."

"I thought you were creating virtual actors in the computer, not paying them," said Cape.

"That's the idea," said Grace. "Don't get me wrong—there are still *a lot* of real actors in this picture, like the woman watching the bridge collapse—the one holding the girl."

"She was in the last movie."

"Right," said Grace. "But Tom and I discussed keeping these costs down by going digital, so I have to find out why the original budget got blown."

"When can you do that?"

"Not while I'm finishing this movie," said Grace. "To track down all the actual bills and costs incurred so far, then separate fact from fiction…" She trailed off, shaking her head. "It will take weeks, if not months."

"Have you told the studio?" asked Cape.

"Of course," said Grace. "As soon as I saw how screwed up things were, I called Angelo, and he put me through to Adam."

"How did he react?"

"Not as pissed as I expected," replied Grace. "He said there's nothing we can do about the budget right now, but we're screwed if we don't finish this picture on time. And you know what, he's right."

Cape nodded but didn't say anything.

"But he wasn't sanguine about the situation, either," added Grace. "This is a big deal—if we've blown this budget, even the best opening weekend won't make back the money spent on this movie."

"Doesn't that affect people's percentages—the profit sharing?"

"For some people, absolutely," said Grace. "For me, and for Tom's share, it might be *adios*."

"Not Adam or Harry?" asked Cape. "Or the director?"

"Not necessarily," said Grace, a sarcastic smile creeping across her lips. "It's an old Hollywood trick—the senior people get a percentage of the gross, while the hired talent gets a percentage of the net."

"What's that mean in English?" asked Cape, wishing he hadn't slept through accounting.

"Some people get a percentage of how much money the movie generates at the box office—that's the *gross* of the picture."

"OK," said Cape tentatively.

"While some get a percentage of the *net*—that's how much money the movie makes—if it's profitable."

Cape thought for a moment before saying anything. "So if the movie loses money but still does well at the box office, then people like Harry and Adam still clean up?"

"Yup," said Grace.

"But the studio loses money," said Cape. "And they own the studio."

"That's the insidious part." Grace smiled. "It becomes a write-off for the studio, but Harry and Adam are listed as Executive Producers on the film—that's how they get their individual percentages. So they get rich even if their company loses money."

"So that's what an Executive Producer does," muttered Cape. "I always wondered about all those names at the beginning of a film. When you first told me you were a producer, I just assumed ..."

"That I didn't do a damn thing?" asked Grace lightly. "That's a running joke in the movie business—if you don't know what someone does on a film, just call them a producer."

"There certainly seem to be a lot of them."

Grace laughed. "The average movie has almost twelve different people with *producer* in their title—*Executive Producers, Associate Producers, Assistant Producers*, even *Co-Associate Producers*."

"What do they all do?"

"Honestly?" replied Grace. "Even I'm not sure sometimes. Some invested in the film, some contributed to the original story concept. And a few, like me, are real production people."

"Doing important things," said Cape, a teasing note to his voice.

"Don't patronize me," said Grace. "The only difference between George Lucas and Ed Wood was a good producer."

Cape held up his hands. "Just kidding, but they all get to be in the credits, don't they?"

"So?"

"The audience has to sit through an endless list of names before the film can start."

"Pretty boring, I'll admit," said Grace. "But giving people production credits keeps the price down. Some folks just want to be associated with films, maybe become famous, or impress their friends. So they'll take a smaller percentage, or maybe sell their idea to a studio for less money, simply because their name shows up on the big screen."

"I'd take the money and leave the fame for someone else."

"Smart guy," said Grace, squeezing his arm. "Just be glad you don't work in the movie business. You'd never survive with that lack of ego."

Cape leaned back in his chair and stretched. His head hurt. He was perfecting the art of learning a lot about nothing important. Maybe after a few hours of sifting, his brain could glean something useful from the information overload of the past two days, but he wasn't counting on it. "Thanks for the lesson in film accounting," he said, sighing. "The bottom line is that the movie might lose money, right?"

Grace nodded. "Unless I can curb costs during this final week of shooting, we'll go over budget."

"A lot of money?"

"Almost twenty million," said Grace sheepishly.

"That's a lot of money," replied Cape.

Grace shrugged. "Yeah, even for the movie business."

Cape forced a smile, not wanting to appear as frustrated as he felt.

"Did this help you at all?" asked Grace hopefully.

"I got a chance to eat," replied Cape. "And that always helps."

"What are you going to do next?"

"Move out of the city before you finish that tidal wave," said Cape. "Unless you'll reconsider and destroy L.A. instead?"

"Sorry," said Grace. "We have to destroy San Francisco."

"Why?"

"It's in the script."

Cape shrugged.

"That's as good a reason as any," he said.

48

SALLY SAT ALONE IN the dark and dreamt she was flying.

She was ten years old again, her teacher Xan leading her through the Mai Po marshes, a nature reserve consisting of shrimp ponds in the northwest corner of Hong Kong. It was a haven for migratory birds; when the shrimp ponds were drained each harvesting season, the birds feasted on tiny fish trapped in the mudflats. This time of year the ponds were full, but there were still plenty of birds for archery practice.

Rong was with them, but Sally ignored him. One of the younger instructors, he had become abusive with some of the other girls in Sally's class, hitting them when Master Xan wasn't looking. It angered Sally; she thought Xan missed nothing. The girls said nothing to him, and Rong was careful to never be out of shouting range of the older instructors. He knew what some of the girls would do if given the chance. It was a dangerous game, but Sally knew Rong couldn't help himself. She could always spot a sadist, even in a crowd of killers.

"Remember, *little dragon*," Xan said. "You must become the arrow." His voice was deep and resonant, almost affectionate. Sally walked a step behind and to his left, but still the scar was visible. When he turned to make eye contact it jumped across his face like a jagged bolt of lightning, from below his chin and across his eyes, straight up to his hairline. The black stubble of his scalp did nothing to hide its progress. The other girls told Sally a rival Triad leader had sent men to kill Xan many years ago. The scar was all that was left of them.

"Become the arrow," said Sally without conviction. Xan stopped their muddy march with an upraised hand.

"Am I wasting your time, little dragon?" Xan towered above her, lightning dancing as he spoke.

Sally bowed. "No, Master. It just—"

"—sounded like a load of Zen nonsense?"

Sally's eyes grew wide but she remained silent. She heard Rong off to the side, kicking at something in the long grass. Probably a small animal. Xan's eyes hardened, bringing her back to full attention.

"It is the same as striking a board," he said. "When you punch, what do you see?"

"The board breaking apart," said Sally without hesitation. "Before I hit it."

Xan nodded. "It is the same with the bow. See where you want the arrow to go in your mind, then fly with it."

Sally furrowed her brow, a look she perfected by age ten. "Fly with it?"

"Guide it," said Xan. "Make it follow your will to the target."

Sally bowed as Xan waved curtly at Rong, who jogged ahead to a small cluster of trees at the edge of the marsh. It was barely sunrise, a light fog drifting over the marsh. Not another soul in sight.

"When Rong hits the branches," said Xan, "the birds will take flight."

Sally nodded but didn't say anything. She held her arms loosely at her sides, the bow in her left hand, a quiver of hunting arrows across her back. She closed her eyes and waited for the cry of the birds.

A hundred screams shattered the still morning. Sally's hands flew, an arrow leaving the bow before the birds had cleared the trees. She fired a single arrow, turned to Xan, and bowed, a smile barely visible on her face. It was almost a full minute before the birds stopped squawking, but a scream continued to pierce the morning fog.

Xan looked across the marsh and saw Rong doubled over beneath the trees, clutching his right hand in his left, blood pouring across his forearm. That was the hand he used to hit the girls, but it would be a long while before the tendons healed, if they did at all. The tip of the hunting arrow was razor sharp and very wide, designed to tear through flesh and take some with it. Rong's cries echoed off the muddy ponds.

Xan turned to Sally, impassive. "What have you done?"

Sally held Xan's gaze and nodded, once. "I became the arrow, Master Xan."

Xan bowed, a smile flashing across his face.

"*Well done*, little dragon."

———————

Sally blinked and returned to the present. There wasn't much she missed about her childhood, but there was much she remembered.

She ran through the attack in Brighton Beach again. Cape was alive, and so was the Pole. But she had missed the man cloaked in shadows. She wasn't going to miss again.

She took a deep breath and stood, turning to face the target at the far end of her loft. The bow lay at her feet, a hundred hand-carved arrows feathered and ready to fly. She took one and notched it onto the string.

Time to fly.

49

"Are we there yet?"

After spending the morning sitting on his ass in an edit studio, Cape found the run to the bridge invigorating. It was the run back that was killing him.

"It's your office we came from," replied Beau, his breathing audible but not labored. "We're just running back and forth, so don't tell me you're lost."

They ran past Ghirardelli Square, with the island of Alcatraz just offshore, coming up on their left. The morning fog had burned off, giving the city a rare burst of undiluted sunshine with no wind. Cruising past Fisherman's Wharf, they made it to Pier 39, where they broke their stride and started walking, hands on their hips. The building where Cape's office was located stood across the street, broad windows flashing in the sun, beckoning them home to rest.

"Did I tell you how much I hate running?" asked Cape.

"Yeah, every step of the way for the last mile," replied Beau, "when you weren't wheezing."

"How far was that?"

"About ten miles," said Beau, blinking as sweat poured down his broad forehead.

"*Ten miles?*" said Cape, incredulous. "Whose idea was it to run ten miles?"

"Yours," said Beau. "You're the one suggested we go running—I said *sure*. You're the one said let's run to the bridge and back—I said *whatever*."

"I didn't realize it was ten miles," remarked Cape, looking back the way they had come.

"Should buy a map," suggested Beau. "If you was a cop, like me, you'd know what you were gettin' yourself into. Those of us in proper law enforcement jobs are expected to know the city we're protecting. Me—I know the city like the back of my hand."

"That's the problem," said Cape. "Your hands are bigger than mine."

"Ain't just my hands," replied Beau, chuckling.

"Was that some kind of racial remark?" asked Cape indignantly.

"Naw," said Beau, laughing. "I've seen you in the locker room."

"I'm flattered you looked," said Cape. "But I'm not interested."

"Just sizin' up the competition," replied Beau. "Sally ever mention me?"

Cape looked at his friend and shook his head sadly. "She said that if she were interested in any man in the city, then it would be you."

"For real?"

Cape hesitated. "I'm paraphrasing," he said. "Those are my words, not hers."

"You mean you're *exaggerating*," said Beau, his eyes narrowing.

"Actually, I should have said *lying*," replied Cape. "I was lying."

Beau shook his head. "Guess she'll never come to her senses."

"I'll tell her you said that."

"Don't tell her *that*," said Beau quickly.

"I won't use those exact words," said Cape reassuringly.

"You'll *paraphrase*, is that it?"

"Sure."

Beau shook his head, frowning. "Forget I said anything."

The light changed and they crossed the street. The three parking meters in front of the building were taken, an old convertible sandwiched between two SUVs. Cape idly ran his hand over the hood of the convertible as they walked to the front door.

The best thing about the dot-com boom, as far as Cape was concerned, was all the money Internet companies spent on their offices. That was one of many reasons most of them went bankrupt, believing their share price was money in the bank. And though they had long since abandoned their investors and vacated this building, they left behind a locker room and a full kitchen. Cape and the other tenants kept the kitchen stocked with items in the communal refrigerator usually marked. Beau pulled open the refrigerator and took out a large carton of orange juice, unopened.

"This yours?"

"Yeah," said Cape. "Glasses are behind you."

"Won't need a glass," replied Beau, cracking open the container and tilting his head back, draining it in one continuous gulp.

Cape reached past him and grabbed the last carton on the shelf, holding it protectively. "I'm going upstairs till I cool off," he said. "You need a shower?"

Beau shook his head. "Too tired," he said. "Let's go to your office and compare notes."

They went upstairs and Beau sat in one of the client chairs across from Cape, his feet on the desk.

"No sign of your Russian friends since you left town," he said. "It's been quiet."

"If we were in a movie," said Cape, "I'd say it's been *too quiet.*"

Beau scowled. "This ain't no movie."

"I know," said Cape. "I just wanted to say it."

"Whatever," said Beau, giving him a look. "You talk to Corelli?"

"Yeah."

"And?"

"He talked to a contact at the FBI, and they confirmed that Major Yuri Andropov is somewhere in the U.S."

Beau snorted. "Like that was something we didn't already know?"

"They think he came in from the Czech Republic," said Cape. "Got a clean passport and made a connection through the embassy. The feds call it *slipping through the net.*"

"Always worries me when they have a name for it," said Beau. "What else you learn?"

"Not much," said Cape. "Before coming here, they think he was in Chechnya, selling arms to the rebels."

"I thought he was Russian."

"Apparently the month before, he was in Moscow," replied Cape, "selling arms to the Russians."

"Nice guy, helping both sides kill each other."

"And probably getting rich doing it."

"Well, he's got a talent for keeping a low profile, 'cept when he's trying to kill you. We checked the typical scumbag haunts and came up empty."

"I don't think he's your typical scumbag."

"No shit," said Beau. "That's why we called the feds."

Cape sat up straighter. "FBI?"

"Me and Vinnie called everybody," replied Beau. "FBI, the INS, Customs, Port Authority, the ATF, and the Department of Homeland Security. Hell, I think we even called the DMV, but they put us on hold."

"You learn anything?"

Beau shook his head. "They all wanted to know if this guy was a terrorist."

"He's got me pretty terrified," said Cape.

"Not good enough," said Beau. "We said he's an arms dealer, drug dealer, murderer, plus he's in the country illegally."

"And what did the feds say to that?"

"They'd call us back in six to nine months when they have more manpower."

"*Six to nine months?*" said Cape. "I'll be dead by then."

Beau nodded. "Your tax dollars at work."

Cape sat back in his chair. "Guess I should've dropped the case when I had a chance."

Beau didn't say anything. They sat like that, listening to their own breathing and the tourists across the street, until Cape changed the subject.

"Were you able to check the lab reports?"

Beau's eyes shifted automatically to the cop stare he'd perfected over the years. "When you called this morning," he said slowly, "I considered telling you to go fuck yourself. I give you information, you gotta tell me something in return, friends or not. Last time you didn't have shit."

"That's 'cause I didn't know shit," replied Cape.

"And now you do?"

"You tell me."

Beau scowled. "You're an asshole," he said in a tired voice. "I checked the lab reports on the heroin we found in Otto's deli—the stuff in the sausages."

"And?"

"It's the same as the stuff we found in the producer's apartment."

"The same grade?" asked Cape. "Same quality?"

"I mean *exactly* the same," said Beau. "The levels of codeine and morphine match, along with everything else."

Cape nodded silently to himself.

"Your turn," said Beau, giving him the stare again.

Cape sighed. "I thought the movie production was a cover for the drugs."

"Yeah, so?"

"Now I think the drugs were a cover for the movie production."

"Is that a riddle?" said Beau testily. "Or one of them haikus?"

Cape shook his head. "I think they stole the smack from Otto, and killed him in the process."

"Your Russian friends or your movie friends?"

"My guess is the Russians stole the heroin to plant in the dead guy's apartment."

"Why?"

"To waste your time," replied Cape. "Throw us off the trail, so they could finish their real business. What have you and Vinnie been doing?"

"Sorting out a drug war," said Beau.

"What if there isn't a drug war?"

Beau didn't blink.

Cape leaned forward. "You assumed that Tom, the producer, was involved with drugs, right?"

"Seemed likely."

"Yeah," agreed Cape. "People get killed over drug deals all the time, and the idea of using a movie production as a front for distribution isn't half bad."

Beau dropped his feet to the floor.

"But it ain't half good, either," he said, nodding. "No permanent network, no way to move more than a few kilos of junk at a time."

Cape nodded. "Different players on every shoot."

"Hard to know who to trust."

"And I doubt Freddie Wang or Frank Alessi would sell a few kilos at a time to some producer they don't know," added Cape.

"You talked to them both, right?"

Cape nodded. "Frank first, then Freddie."

"We talked to both of them," said Beau. "Me and Vinnie were in an official capacity, so you might have had more luck. Frank's got so many connections, we can barely get the time of day from the fat fuck."

"I pushed some buttons with both of them, especially Frank," said Cape. "I find Freddie Wang harder to read."

"He's inscrutable," said Beau. "Chinese are like that."

"Bet that's what they say about you," replied Cape.

"Nah, they think we all look alike."

"You're bigger than most," said Cape. "I think you're right about the killings at the zoo and the bakery—they both reacted when I brought them up."

"You see a guy at Frank's looked like a hawk?"

Cape nodded. "Yeah, he's a pro. Had a gun on me the whole time I was there; his hand didn't shake once."

"Name's Anthony," said Beau. "We picked him up when he left Frank's place, got a tip he might've been the shooter at the zoo."

"He's definitely fired that gun before, judging from the way he holds it."

"He wasn't packing when he left Frank's," said Beau. "And a pro would've trashed the gun from the zoo anyway, gotten a new one." He shrugged, disgusted. "But what I think doesn't matter, 'cause he's back on the street again."

"How?"

"Vinnie and I kept him in the box for two hours," said Beau. "Got him talking, but not about the case—where'd you grow up, how long you been in the city, you want some more coffee—Anthony likes to hear himself talk, got a surprisingly big vocabulary. Then we take a break and crank the heat—that interrogation room is a fucking sauna, you get three guys in there with the thermostat up. Guy starts to sweat, shift around in his seat. We start asking tougher questions..." Beau frowned, reluctant to finish. "Then we get interrupted."

"By who—his lawyer?"

Beau smiled cynically. "Frank Alessi's lawyer, who happens to be Anthony's lawyer, who also happens to be the lawyer for a certain city councilman, whose campaign was heavily financed by donations from one of Frank's companies. Councilman calls the mayor, who calls the police chief, who calls our captain, who wants to know why the guy's lawyer hasn't been called."

"What did you say?"

"Told the captain the phone was broken," said Beau. "And it was, as soon as I pulled it out of the wall. Then we told him the thermostat in the interrogation room is all fucked up, he might want maintenance to take a look at it."

"But Anthony walked," said Cape in disbelief.

"Made bail," said Beau, nodding. "Which was a big number."

"He might've shot the guy at the zoo," said Cape, "but I don't think he killed Otto."

"Me neither." Beau sounded almost sad.

"Nobody wins if there's a war," said Cape. "You told me the system was working. Frank and Freddie Wang might hate each other, but they're both businessmen at heart, so why fuck up the business?"

"No reason," agreed Beau.

"That's why I think the Russians killed Otto," said Cape. "To steal just enough heroin to plant at the apartment. It wouldn't take long for a guy like the Major to figure out where the drug trade took place in this town."

"So we chase our own asses all week while you talk to the movie people 'bout drugs—instead of lookin' into their real business."

"Right."

"So what is their real business?"

"I'm not sure," admitted Cape, "but it has something to do with money—lots of money."

"Whose money?"

"The finances on the film are all fucked up," replied Cape. "They're way over budget, and Grace can't account for any of the overages."

Beau put his hands behind his head and stretched. "So maybe the dead guy was embezzling—or stealing money for somebody else—*or* someone was leaning on him."

Cape nodded. "Corelli said the Russian mob loves extortion rackets, so it's a definite possibility. The dead guy had a daughter—he'd make an easy mark."

Beau blew out his cheeks. "As good an angle as any," said Beau, "but if it's got nothin' to do with the drugs or the other murders, then it's got nothin' to do with me."

"What about the producer?"

Beau shook his head. "Officially still a suicide."

"Thanks for your support."

Beau shrugged. "Talk to the captain," he said. "Or find some evidence."

"The drugs aren't evidence?"

"Of a *murder*," said Beau. "That's the way it works in homicide, we investigate murders. Guy left a note."

Cape scoffed. "You can't call that a note—it said *I'm sorry.*"

"So am I," said Beau. "I think this whole thing stinks, you want the truth. But getting caught dealing drugs ain't the worst reason to jump off a bridge, either."

"But the Russians—"

"Are ghosts," said Beau emphatically. "Here and gone, no connection to anything except that target painted on your back."

"Swell."

Beau smiled sympathetically. "As a friend, I think you're onto something."

Cape nodded. "But as a cop ..."

"The whole things is circumstantial, hearsay, rumor—"

"And innuendo?"

"That, too," said Beau. "Nice theory, but show me the facts. I'm a civil servant, brother."

"You're not that civil."

Beau nodded and stretched. "That your convertible out front?"

"I take it you want a ride?"

"Bet your ass I do," replied Beau. "Too tired to shower, way too tired to walk."

"You didn't recognize my car?"

"Looks different—you get it washed or something?"

"I got the dent in the door fixed," said Cape. "The one on the driver's side."

"When did you have time to do that?"

"Dropped it off before I left for New York, just picked it up this morning."

"That dent gave the car character."

"I was sick of looking at it," said Cape. "Plus I had them install a new alarm while they were at it."

"What was wrong with the old one?"

"Kept draining the battery."

"Dead battery's one way to keep it from getting stolen," said Beau, "but not too practical. I always thought alarms on convertibles were kinda dumb—cut the roof and bye-bye radio."

Cape shrugged. "This one's connected to the ignition, so it's just to keep them from driving off with the car. Vintage rides are popular again."

"Vintage?" said Beau. "You mean old."

"I'm working on my image," said Cape. "Anyway, if the alarm goes off, it cuts off the engine and triggers a siren."

"Siren?" asked Beau, his eyebrows shooting upward.

Cape smiled. "Thought you'd like that. The guy who sold it to me said everyone ignores car alarms."

"True."

"But everybody freezes when they hear a siren. Sounds just like a cop car."

Beau shook his head, looking at Cape with a sad expression. "You, my friend, are an easy mark," he said. "I do believe you'd buy yourself a box of tampons if they came with the right sales pitch." He leaned forward, putting his hands on his knees as he started to stand up.

Cape opened the top drawer of his desk and took out his wallet and keys. He slid his thumb over a red button at the top of the car key. "This will convince you," he said. "Check it out." He held the key for Beau to examine as he pushed the button.

The explosion blew out the windows and knocked Cape backward over his chair. Beau was thrown like a rag doll across the desk as the building shook with concussive force. Glass was everywhere, wind-chime noises coming from shards splintering on impact and ricocheting off the walls.

As his head hit the floor, Cape caught a glimpse of his car spinning in mid-air outside the second-story window, tires on fire. A deafening crash of metal from the street below. The wailing of car alarms.

Beau landed head-first against Cape's chest, his feet sticking straight up behind the desk. Cape had the wind knocked out him for a second time and thought the collision with Beau might have been worse than the initial explosion.

Twisting around, Beau managed to shift his legs and fall completely to the floor with a loud grunt. He got his legs under him, then extended a hand to Cape. Neither man said anything as they brushed glass off their shoulders, then walked stiffly to the windows and looked down.

Tourists across the street on Pier 39 were shouting and taking pictures. Cape's car was upside down and on fire. It had landed on the SUV directly behind it and crushed the hood down to the engine. The SUV in front had jumped the curb and rolled almost twenty feet into the street. Both cars' alarms were howling in sympathy for Cape's demolished vehicle.

Beau put a hand under his chin and the other on his head, then twisted, cracking his neck the way you might crack your knuckles. He turned to Cape, who was still staring at the bottom of his car.

"If you don't catch these guys soon," said Beau sternly, "then I'll kill you myself. I'm *tired* of this shit."

Cape blinked, still in shock. "Imagine how I feel."

Beau reached out and brushed glass from Cape's shoulders, then patted him on the back. "It's stupid to have a convertible in San Francisco, anyway. The weather's too unreliable."

Cape nodded absently as the stench of burning rubber filled the air. He could hear sirens on their way. "Guess I'm not giving you a ride."

Beau shook his head. "Changed my mind—I'm walking."

50

THE MAJOR ENJOYED WORKING with his hands, even when they weren't covered in blood.

He lovingly ran his fingers over the remaining items from their shopping trip. They found the metal box and wires in the electrical section of a nearby hardware store, but they had to drive to a Home Depot in the suburbs for a big enough clamp. They got a good deal on the necessary tools—screwdriver, drill, metal screws. But the C-4 explosive, now that was expensive. Plastic explosives were a lot harder to find than in Russia, where the Soviet military had disbanded into a scattered mob of entrepreneurs.

Ursa looked on from a short distance, confident in the Major's ability to handle the explosive. The bomb on the detective's car had been a disappointment, but only because he wasn't in it. The explosion had been impressive.

The Major looked over his shoulder. "Do not fret, Ursa. Even a cat only has nine lives."

Ursa grunted. "What about the girl?"

The Major smiled. "If this doesn't work, comrade, then she's all yours."

51

"Why didn't you drive?"

Linda was waiting for him at the top of the stairs. She looked from the departing taxi toward Cape, a concerned look on her face. Her hair seemed suspicious.

"My car's in the shop," said Cape vaguely.

"What for?"

"Everything," said Cape. "Let's go inside."

The Sloth was sitting placidly in front of his computers, face lit by the shifting colors on the plasma screens. His mouth twitched in a half smile as Cape took the chair next to him. A heavy hand moved subtly across the keyboard as words scrolled across the screen directly in front of Cape.

YOU LOOKED BETTER WHEN YOU WERE DEAD.

"Thanks—I felt better, too," replied Cape. "I'm thinking about trying it full time, catch up on my rest."

Linda pulled up a chair. "Do you know anything?"

"Was that a general or specific question?" asked Cape. "Not that it matters, because the answer is probably a resounding *No* either way."

Linda's hair bounced in irritation. "About the case," she said. "Since we're looking for connections, it might be helpful if you filled us in *before* we got started."

Cape shrugged. "I don't think Tom was killed over drugs. The heroin was just a diversion."

"From what?"

"His real business," said Cape, "which had to do with money—maybe extortion. Maybe siphoning money from the movie's production budget to pay off the Russians, who were leaning on him. Or maybe the Russians are just muscle for someone else."

"That's a lot of *maybes*," remarked Linda.

"Tell me about it," said Cape. "That's why I'm here—I need to know if Tom had done this before on other films, and if he was acting alone."

Linda nodded. "This movie they're making now is losing money." Her tone made it clear she was stating a fact, not asking Cape to confirm a suspicion.

"How do you know that?" he asked. "I just reviewed the budgets with Grace this morning."

THEY ALL LOSE MONEY.

The letters glowed like a signpost in front of Cape.

"All?"

Linda glanced at a sheaf of notes before speaking. "All the movies Empire Studios has produced over the past two years have lost money."

"How is that possible?" asked Cape. "That astronaut film cleaned up at the box office."

Linda held up a hand. "These films *generated* lots of money. At the box office, internationally, on video and DVD—millions."

"So what's the problem?"

"The films generate cash, but they aren't *profitable*," replied Linda. "If you look at Empire's books, which we have, you'll see that every budget is in the red."

"You saw their books?"

Linda blushed slightly and her hair avoided eye contact altogether. "Their computer network doesn't have much of a firewall." She shrugged. "The Sloth hacked it."

The Sloth's hand jumped and the screens filled with spreadsheets similar to the ones Cape had seen that morning. At the top of each one was a movie title—Cape had gone to see most of them when they were released. The upper rows of numbers were green, the ones in the center yellow, and the bottom rows were all red. The first column was a series of categories that included *Gross Receipts, Distribution Costs, Deferments*, and *Net Profit*. Most of the columns were meaningless, but Cape certainly understood the progression from green to red.

"One or two movies I could understand," he said, shaking his head. "But most of these were hits. How could they stay in business, let alone be attractive for sale?"

Linda's hair bobbed forward with her in tow. "There are a couple of accounting techniques unique to the movie industry having to do with how people get paid."

"Grace mentioned that," said Cape, "whether you get paid from gross receipts or net profit. If you don't get your cut from the gross, you may not see very much cash."

Linda bounced in her chair. "Precisely, which means that if you're Empire, then it's to your advantage for the movie to actually *lose money on paper*, because then you don't have to pay off the investors."

"And that's legal?"

"If it's in a contract, then it's legal," replied Linda. "You see those yellow numbers?" She pointed at the rows of figures at the center of the screens.

"Yeah."

"Those are the studio's production costs for each film," she said. "In every case the initial costs of the studio were covered."

"So they didn't lose money," said Cape.

"Not initially," replied Linda, "and not on the studio's end. But they never closed the books. So long after the movie left the theaters, they kept billing expenses against the film."

"How?"

"Say someone at the studio takes a trip and talks about the movie during the flight," replied Linda. "Why not bill it to the movie they just made? Did someone mention it over dinner? While we're at it, shouldn't we charge the cost of dinner against the movie's budget?"

Cape leaned forward to scrutinize the screen. "So the studio covers its costs," he said, thinking out loud.

"Right."

"And the principals who get a percentage of the *gross* receipts," he continued, looking over at Linda, "they get paid."

"Right," said Linda. "A lot of money."

"People like Adam and Harry Berman," said Cape, "the executive producers, and maybe the director."

"Right."

"But if you *invested* in one of these films," Cape said, "then you got shafted."

"Bingo."

"Empire Studios can tell their investors that the films lost money, even though they were hits at the box office." Cape shook his head, not sure whether to be impressed or disgusted.

"I've been doing a lot of reading," said Linda. "Studios use terms like *rolling break even* and *deferments* to cover the necessary legal language, but if you don't know your way around movie contracts, you could easily lose your shirt."

"But we're talking tens of millions of dollars," said Cape. "What kind of investor would be that naïve?"

"That's the real question, isn't it?"

"Yeah," agreed Cape. "Who's been funding all of Empire's movies?"

"Way ahead of you," said Linda.

The Sloth slid his hand awkwardly the full length of the keyboard and the screens changed again. A list of ten names appeared, each followed by a series of numbers, each listed under the same movie titles as before.

"These are the individuals—and companies—who invested in films produced over the past two years." Linda and her hair had started to bounce in an asynchronous rhythm, so Cape knew this wasn't just another group of figures.

"Anyone stand out?" he said.

"I was hoping you'd ask that." Her hair practically reached out for a hug.

"These two," said Linda. As she pointed, the Sloth made two names expand to fill the screen. "They invested in every film in progressively greater amounts."

Cape read aloud. "Tactical Machinery Corporation of Hoboken, New Jersey, and GDS of Bonn, Switzerland," he said. "What does GDS stand for?"

"General Defense Systems."

"And they not only invested in all the movies, they increased their involvement with each successive film?"

"Yup." Linda was practically vibrating with excitement.

"That leads to two questions," said Cape. "Who runs the companies, and what business are they in?"

Linda looked at her notes again. "They're both subsidiaries of larger companies based in Eastern Europe. It took me an entire day with Sloth's help to trace the connections from these companies to all the firms they supposedly do business with around the world. But the two companies listed here, as far as I can tell, are just mailboxes—charters of incorporation, pieces of paper—that's it."

"You mean they're shell companies?"

Linda nodded vigorously. "The Sloth couldn't find any trace of these companies anywhere online *except* for their dealings with Empire Studios."

Cape nodded. "What about overseas?"

"That's a different story," said Linda, "and it doesn't have a happy ending. They're involved in the manufacturing of machine parts, some transportation systems, but mostly—when you cut through all the miscellaneous crap—they're in the weapons business."

Cape turned to face her, wondering if his hair was bobbing up and down. "You're positive?"

"Almost 80 percent of their transactions are to—and from—defense contractors around the world."

Cape chewed at his lower lip as he asked the next question, but he already knew the answer. "Who owns the companies?"

"Lots of people," said Linda, "if you look at all the subsidiaries around the world." She paused. "But one name is associated with virtually all of them."

"Yuri Andropov," said Cape quietly.

"You already knew."

"I should have said *Major* Yuri Andropov," replied Cape. "The man who's been trying to kill me on a daily basis."

"There's something else," said Linda tentatively.

Cape looked from her to the Sloth. "It gets better?"

"In order to establish the shell company here in the States," said Linda, "there had to be a U.S. resident listed as a principal owner."

"The one in Hoboken?"

"Yes," replied Linda. "Andropov is listed as an executive, but someone else you know is the president."

"Who?" asked Cape, suspecting the answer but not willing to commit.

"Harry Berman," said Linda.

Cape blinked. "You mean Adam."

Linda shook her head. "No, I checked. It's Harry Berman—the older brother. The company was incorporated almost two years ago. Adam's the Vice President—they're in it together."

Cape leaned back in his chair and exhaled loudly. "Fuck me."

"We haven't been able to trace all the money," added Linda, "but the investments from Andropov have been legal, as far as we can tell. But these movies are shitty investments. And the business here in the States and the one in Switzerland can't be connected to any illegal activity either—they're both clean."

"That's the point," Cape nearly spat. "They're *clean.*"

"What do you mean?"

"They're laundering money," he said, suddenly pissed at himself. "I should have guessed when Grace first told me about the budget."

Linda looked questioningly at the Sloth.

WILL TAKE TIME TO TRACE, BUT SEEMS LIKELY.

"Don't bother." Cape squeezed the Sloth on the shoulder. "And thanks, old friend." He stood and faced Linda. "It's the only explanation—millions of dollars flowing through bogus companies into films that don't turn a profit. The studio covers their costs, the two brothers get rich, and the Major probably gets a kickback."

Linda nodded. "Makes sense."

"More sense than heroin smuggling," said Cape disgustedly. "It's classic money laundering on a grand scale, in an industry that no federal agency would even look at twice."

"Why not?"

"Productions are too transient to monitor easily," replied Cape. "Grace said every movie is like a new business starting from scratch, with different investors—movie production is better than a shell company, because it's a moving target that's totally legit. I'm amazed more studios don't run scams like this."

"Maybe they do."

"All I care about is Empire," said Cape, adding, "and Grace."

"What are you going to tell her?"

"I need to find her first," replied Cape. "She's supposed to be shooting the final scene today—she's downtown, near the Ferry Building."

Linda noticed his expression. "You think she's in danger?"

"She submitted her numbers to Tom right before he was killed," said Cape, "and now she's the only one looking at the total budget."

Linda finished his thought. "And she's started asking the studio questions."

"Yeah," replied Cape. "Just like Tom."

"Wait," said Linda. "There's one thing that doesn't make sense to me."

"What?" asked Cape, already heading for the door.

"If the scam is working, why would the Bermans want to sell the company?"

Cape shrugged. "My guess is the Major is a demanding business partner. You said the investments had increased with each new film, right?"

Linda nodded.

"Then I'll bet the Major has increased his demands."

"To what?" asked Linda.

"I'm not sure I want to know," said Cape. "But somehow I'm going to find out."

52

"ARE WE DONE HERE?"

Angelo was close enough to Adam Berman to smell the booze on his breath, which simply meant he was in the same room. He was sitting across the desk from him, which was closer than his usual safe distance at the door. Paperwork had many hazards associated with it, such as getting impaled by a letter opener during one of your boss's bipolar moments.

"Almost done," replied Angelo. "You said you wanted to review the shooting schedule."

"Did I?" asked Adam suspiciously.

Angelo nodded. He pulled a calendar from a file folder and turned it around so Adam could read it. "You said you wanted to know our final day of shooting."

Adam's eyes cleared momentarily. "Yeah, when is it?"

"Today, actually." Angelo pointed to a square on the calendar.

Adam leaned forward. "After today, it's just editing and finishing?"

"Pretty much."

"And we've got an editor."

Angelo nodded emphatically. "One of the best."

"So we don't need Grace anymore."

Angelo blinked. "Well, she's going to supervise—"

Adam cut him off with an angry wave. "I know what she *could* be doing, dipshit. But we don't need her, right? I mean, worst-case scenario, we could still finish the film."

Angelo hesitated, until he saw Adam's hand drift idly toward a paperweight. It looked just heavy enough to hurt. "Right, I guess—if we had to."

Adam's hand withdrew to a neutral spot on the desk, a demilitarized zone between the paperweight and the stapler.

"Then get rid of her," he said evenly.

Angelo's brow furrowed. "You mean fire her?"

"What did I just say?" asked Adam testily. "Weren't you the *putz* explaining how the percentages work on this picture?"

"Yes," said Angelo, realizing too late he'd copped to being a putz. "We reviewed the contracts yesterday."

"So if we get rid of Grace after today, we don't have to pay her shares," said Adam definitively.

Angelo hesitated but now realized why Adam had wanted to meet. "Yes, that's right, Mr. Berman."

Adam nodded, satisfied.

"Then fuck her," he said.

53

THE PEOPLE GATHERED AROUND the clock tower were scared shitless.

That was the idea, anyway. They were supposed to be watching a cataclysmic tidal wave as it swept inexorably toward them. Some were holding hands, others weeping. Many simply stared in shock, unable to run for higher ground. But now they were all looking at their shoes to avoid eye contact with the man holding the bullhorn.

"*THAT WAS REALLY PITIFUL,*" boomed the amplified voice.

The actors shifted uncomfortably as the director stomped back and forth. He had longish hair, a high forehead, and pale gray eyes. His mouth twisted into a sneer of contempt. He wore a black T-shirt, studded belt, frayed jeans, and black boots that came to impossibly sharp points at the toes, which were capped with silver. The actors eyed the boots warily, as if the young director was prone to kicking fits.

He thumbed the switch on the electric bullhorn. Though he stood close enough to be heard without it, the bullhorn had become an extension of his body, a film prop used to inflict his personality on the cast and crew.

"*THAT WAS TAKE—,*" he turned to a young woman hovering nervously nearby, holding a clipboard. She quickly read off a number in a nervous whisper.

"*THAT WAS TAKE FIFTEEN.*" He paused, letting them feel the weight of the number. "*AND IT SUCKED.*"

He scanned the crowd to gauge the effects of his motivational speech. No one moved. "*WE ARE LOSING THE LIGHT, PEOPLE.*" His voice echoed off the walls of the Ferry Building. "*APOCALYPTIC DESTRUCTION IS ONLY MOMENTS AWAY…A WALL OF WATER TALLER THAN THIS CLOCK TOWER IS COMING…*" He lowered the bullhorn to give the cluster of actors a baleful stare.

"*YOU ARE SUPPOSED TO BE ACTORS,*" he shouted. "*SO ACT!*" Brusquely handing the bullhorn to the woman with the clipboard, he stalked away.

There were two cameras working the scene. The first was in fixed position thirty feet from the crowd, pointing toward the clock tower of the Ferry Building, San Francisco Bay in the background. The second was a steady-cam, a hydraulic contraption attached to the waist of a cameraman, enabling him to carry a full size camera and keep the image stable as he moved among the actors shooting close-ups. The first camera would pan across the crowd just behind the second cameraman's movements to avoid catching him in the frame.

Grace was standing twenty feet away between two large video monitors. The one on her left showed the image from the first camera; the monitor on her right displayed the steady cam's perspective.

She was looking at her watch and tapping her foot anxiously when Cape came up behind her.

"Isn't the sun taking direction today?" he asked. "Just tell it to work overtime."

Grace whirled around with a stern expression on her face that morphed into a brilliant smile. She rolled her eyes toward the director as he stomped back toward the monitors. "If he wants to be the center of attention so badly," she muttered, "then he should just put himself in the scene."

Cape smiled and put a hand on her arm. "I know this is probably a bad time, but can you talk?"

Grace glanced quickly over her shoulder.

"Not really," she began, then noticed the look in Cape's eyes. "How about between takes?"

"Fair enough." Cape scanned the scene and nodded. "Did you drive yourself here?"

Grace nodded. "Why, didn't you?"

"I took a cab," said Cape as he looked past her at their surroundings. "We'll both take one out of here."

"Why wouldn't—," Grace began. The director's voice jumped at them from ten feet away, sounding strident without the bullhorn, the cry of a spoiled child.

"Grace, you mind socializing on your own time?" He looked at Cape and added, "And who the fuck is this?"

Cape calmly looked the director in the eye and stood very still, a placid expression on his face. Neither intimidated nor impressed, and it showed. Most people can't stand absolutely still for very long, especially while making eye contact with someone else. It's unnatural and vaguely intimidating, at some deep subconscious level. The director started to say something but thought better of it, breaking eye contact and turning his ire back on Grace.

"Are we ready?" he asked testily.

"When you are, Michael," Grace replied. She did her best not to smirk as the director swiveled around.

Everyone turned toward the monitors. A man sitting in front of the first monitor put on a pair of headphones, as did a woman next to the other monitor. Members of the production crew scurried back and forth between the cameras, the monitors, and the actors—checking distances, testing cables, reading light meters. Grace watched them all like an attentive mother. A moment later the director raised his bullhorn.

"ACTION!"

Cape took advantage of the distraction to reach under his jacket and check his belt. At the small of his back was the revolver, on his right hip the oversized can of pepper mace. He didn't expect trouble during the shoot, but he hadn't expected his car to get launched into orbit, either. He had told Sally where to meet him but couldn't spot her; he usually didn't unless the situation warranted it.

Cape glanced idly at the monitor on the left. The camera panned slowly across the crowd of actors to the clock tower, its white surface reflecting diffuse afternoon light, casting a halo over the crowd. The clock tower was two hundred and forty feet high, the clock faces on each of its four sides twenty-two feet in diameter. It was designed to be seen from a distance at sea when it was built in 1898. Today it was scheduled for destruction by a tidal wave, according to the director, though Cape had his doubts. Modeled after a twelfth-century tower in Seville, Spain, the Ferry Building had survived the 1906 earthquake and fire that left the city in ruins. Decades later, it defied the 1989 earthquake that obliterated the street in front of it and tore down buildings all over the city. Cape suspected it would outlast them all, even Hollywood.

Above the clock was a balustrade surrounding antique bells that chimed every half-hour. The columns rose in layers to the peak of the tower, their gentle curves reminiscent of a Colonial porch. Behind the columns, the bells were hidden in shadow, a stark contrast to the gleaming white exterior of the tower.

Cape switched his attention to Grace, who methodically looked from one monitor to the other, then raised her head to scan the overall scene. She seemed relaxed and in control, totally at ease in this surreal environment. He followed her gaze to the monitor on the right—as the second cameraman moved through the crowd, a slow parade of faces appeared. Cape recognized one or two as actors from the first asteroid movie. He assumed the others were extras.

A woman clutched a young girl, her lower lip trembling. Behind them, an older man pointed in the direction of the make-believe wave, tears running down his cheeks. Cape wondered if he was crying because it was in the script, or because of a sudden realization that his acting career had come to this—pointing at a mythic tidal wave for hours so an asshole with a bullhorn could yell at him.

Cape was turning away from the monitor when the camera focused on the next man in the crowd. Slick black hair and an aquiline nose turned toward the imaginary wave as the man pointed, his black eyes narrowed in mock concern. Even the distance of the camera couldn't dim the cruel inner light of those eyes. The man looked as afraid as a shark at a swim meet.

Major Yuri Andropov was a very bad actor.

"*What balls,*" Cape muttered. "The bastard put himself in the movie." As he stared at the face on the screen, transfixed, Cape heard the Pole's voice echo through his memory.

I think the Major wants to be famous.

Cape grabbed Grace so hard she cried out.

"Do you know who that is?" he whispered fiercely, pointing at the monitor.

Grace looked from the screen to Cape and shook her head. She waved brusquely at the young woman with the clipboard, who left the director's side and bounced over to them. "Amy, do you have the call sheet?" she asked in a subdued voice. "And the head shots?"

Amy nodded eagerly, jaws working overtime on her gum.

"Find him," said Grace, pointing at the screen. Amy looked just in time to see the Major before the camera panned the next extra, an athletic-looking man in a wheelchair holding a dog.

Cape scanned the cluster of actors in the distance, trying to pinpoint the Major. He spotted him toward the back, only fifteen feet from the base of the clock tower. The guy with the steady cam had shot almost all the extras—Cape figured he had maybe ten to go, presuming the plan was to shoot them all and edit the footage later. He looked at the left monitor and saw the fixed camera pull back for a wide shot of the entire crowd. He guessed this scene required another five minutes of shooting, tops.

Amy looked up from her clipboard with a triumphant smile. She started to blow a bubble to celebrate her discovery but caught herself, glancing nervously over her shoulder at the director. He was standing near the left monitor, wearing a pair of headphones. Amy turned her attention back to Grace and read aloud from a white sheet of paper attached to a black-and-white photograph.

"His name is Igor Stravinsky," she said brightly, "from Des Moines, Iowa. He's just an extra—we're paying him scale, the standard day rate. He's only in this scene, as far as I know." Amy looked expectantly at Grace, who cringed when she heard the name.

"*Igor Stravinsky from Des Moines?*" Cape said in disbelief. "Didn't that strike anyone as odd?"

Amy nodded, working her gum as if it were her cud.

"Funny name, huh?"

Cape looked at Grace, who sheepishly waved Amy back toward the director. When she was out of earshot, Cape pulled Grace even closer.

"You wanted to know who killed Tom," he said. "You're paying him scale—the standard day rate."

Grace gasped, her knees buckling. Cape caught her arms and shook her gently.

"I want you to keep shooting until I get close to him," he said.

Grace nodded, stealing a glance at the mass of actors only a short distance away. She looked like she might get sick. Cape touched her lightly on the cheek, then turned and ran.

Almost thirty feet behind the crowd, a line of yellow tape marked the boundary of the shooting area. Another twenty feet beyond, four white trucks blocked the road. One truck housed catering; the next was makeup, wardrobe, and a few bathrooms and showers. The next was a mobile production office, the last held four private dressing rooms. There was roughly six feet of clear space between each pair of trucks, an alley running from the street into the heart of the production. Taking one last look around the area, Cape couldn't see another way in.

He assumed all eyes remained focused on the nonexistent tidal wave, so he didn't give himself a very wide berth or take it slow—he made it to the back of the trucks in less than a minute. Four doors were spaced evenly along the side of each truck, giving access to the various rooms and offices. Hoping to stay hidden as long as possible, Cape moved quickly between the second and third trucks.

The vehicles were seventy feet long. When he was halfway down the alley he could see the actors, their backs to him. He recognized the shiny black hair of the Major as the crowd shifted.

Twenty feet from the end of the trucks, Cape broke into a light run. He heard a door creak open on worn hinges as he passed, but he didn't slow down. He kept his eyes focused on the Major. As he cleared the trucks, he reached behind his back and pulled the revolver without breaking stride.

Cape was nearing the yellow tape when he heard a sound like a jet engine, the sudden displacement of air caused by a huge object moving at high speed. He turned too late. A massive impact knocked the wind out of him and sent him flying. His first thought was that he'd been hit by a car, but in the back of his mind knew that was wishful thinking. As he hit the ground, he heard a bellowing roar.

Ursa had finally caught up with him.

Cape rolled, but the landing was still hard. Grimacing, he twisted onto his back in time to see Ursa lumbering toward him, head down like an angry rhino. Cape instinctively extended his right hand, but it was empty. He had lost his gun.

The great bear was only four angry strides away.

Forcing a breath, Cape rolled toward Ursa, hoping he timed it right. As the giant took a final step to close the gap, it looked as though he might stomp Cape into the ground.

Cape scissored his legs violently, catching Ursa behind the left ankle just as he was about to plant his right foot onto Cape's skull. Ursa fell forward and sideways, collapsing into a sitting position at Cape's feet. Cape cocked his right leg and kicked heel-first. The cartilage of Ursa's nose sounded like crunching Styrofoam.

Cape heard yelling and knew the crowd wasn't following the script. They had seen the fight and were running. He briefly wondered if the cameras were still rolling. He wanted to look for the Major but knew he couldn't risk turning away from the golem at his feet.

Ursa shook his head and coughed, blood streaming from his nose into the crevasses of his hideous scars. One red river found its way to his mouth and Ursa smacked his lips and smiled. With a maniacal gleam in his good eye, Ursa started to laugh.

"Screw this." Cape grabbed the pepper spray from his belt. He was still on the ground only inches away from Ursa. Leaning forward, he thumbed the safety off and held down the spray button. A thin but powerful stream hit Ursa square in the face. Cape squeezed until the spray trickled to nothing. Even from a several feet away, he could feel the burn in his nostrils as his own eyes started to water.

Ursa howled, his right hand smacking his face as if it had caught on fire. He snarled in guttural Russian and lashed out with his enormous left hand, grabbing Cape's right leg. Cape wasn't prepared for the speed of the larger man and gasped from the sudden jolt of pain—Ursa's hand was a vice, his fingers wrapping completely around Cape's leg as if he were a child. The giant hand was molding his shin like clay, grinding against the bone.

Cape tried to put leverage behind his other leg but only managed to twist around and face in the other direction. He kicked his way around in a semi-circle, but Ursa turned with him and kept gripping his leg mercilessly, blinking and spitting away the mace.

Ursa was completely blind, eyes squeezed shut. But he'd stopped clawing at his face. Using his free hand, he snared Cape's other leg at the knee, digging in his fingers as he methodically climbed Cape's body, one excruciating rung at a time. With only half of Ursa's weight upon him, Cape could barely move.

Cape was on his back, the clock tower soaring into the twilight. Ursa's disfigured sneer rose up as he tried throwing his weight to one side, completely obscuring the tower and blotting out the dying sun. The three channels of scar tissue running across Ursa's face were flowing with blood and mace, bitter drops falling into Cape's mouth as he gasped for air.

Ursa raised his head and opened his milky eye against the pain, the ghastly orb swiveling to find Cape. Keeping the other eye squeezed shut, Ursa moved his arms from Cape's legs to his torso, digging into Cape's sides as he tried to slip his arms around him. Cape knew what was coming—a bear hug that would be his last.

Ursa shifted his weight and Cape kicked sideways, rocking to his left and freeing his right arm. He managed a right hook to the face, but it had no momentum. Ursa chuckled and spat in Cape's face.

Cape knew he wasn't strong enough to punch his way out of this. Time to fight dirty.

Hooking his thumb around Ursa's right eye socket, he jabbed. Ursa howled in rage but held on, squinting hard against the pressure of Cape's thumb. Cape tried to get a sharper angle on the giant's eye but his hand slipped, unable to maintain pressure against Ursa's bloody cheek.

Ursa had his right arm halfway under Cape, who could feel the pressure building against his rib cage. He tasted blood but wasn't sure if it was his or Ursa's. Frantically he rocked back and forth, trying to free his left arm. He was getting weak. His breathing was already labored, his vision starting to blur. He could almost see the clock tower and wondered what time it was. Pretty soon it wouldn't matter.

Cape heard a wet cracking sound—one of his ribs must have popped. *This will be over soon, one way or another.* He ignored the pain and lurched sideways—Ursa's right arm pulled away and Cape managed to bend his left arm at the elbow. Swinging his right as hard as he could, he punched Ursa repeatedly in the right eye, rolling sideways after every punch until he managed to free his left arm completely. He heard another *crack* as he desperately raised both hands above Ursa's head, hoping to box the giant's ears hard enough to shatter the eardrums.

Before Cape could deliver the strike, another *crack* preceded a sudden sharp pain in his neck. Instinctively he snapped his head backward, banging the back of his skull against the pavement. White spots appeared as he blinked—he was desperate to stay focused on Ursa but was struggling to remain conscious.

Ursa's head lolled to the left, his thick tongue protruding from a mouth rimmed with blood. Both eyes were open and rolled backward, the sclera veined and red. A gurgling sound as Cape felt something hot and viscous spread across his chest. He was pretty sure it wasn't molasses.

Cape blinked sweat from his eyes. His body was numb, his arms lead weights. Using both hands, he grabbed Ursa's skull and pushed, raising the enormous head with no small effort.

The head of a barbed arrow protruded almost three inches through the front of Ursa's neck, the black shaft shiny with the same blood pooling across Cape's chest. Craning his neck around, Cape saw two more arrows sticking out of Ursa's back, their feathered shafts pointing back toward the top of the clock tower. Cape thought he saw a cloaked figure disappear behind the columns, but he couldn't be sure at this distance.

Ursa was dead weight. With a final heave, Cape managed to roll out from under the once-great bear. He crawled onto his hands and knees and stayed there, trying to get his breathing under control. After a long minute, he sat on his heels, raising a tentative hand to his neck. A shallow cut ran just below his Adam's apple, where the head of the killing arrow had penetrated through Ursa's neck. If it left a scar, it would be one he could live with.

Getting his legs under him, Cape stood shakily and looked around. The actors were all gone—back to their trailers, hotels, agents, or lawyers—or wherever it was that actors ran. A small group of production staff were still standing by the monitors, a safe distance from the mayhem. They were still getting close-ups via the monitor on the left, which showed the image from the fixed camera. It was focused on the area at the base of the tower. The right monitor was blank, the guy with the steady cam having long since fled for safer ground.

Cape looked to his right and saw Grace coming toward him, her expression shifting between relief and panic with every stride. The brash young director was nowhere to be seen.

Major Yuri Andropov was long gone.

Cape felt faint and sat down heavily on the pavement. He heard sirens in the distance.

It was a sound he was getting used to.

54

"I THOUGHT YOU WEREN'T allowed to leave town."

Grace sat next to Cape in an exit row of the Airbus. The flight was only half full, mostly with business travelers, cell phones and PDAs at the ready in holsters on their belts, just in case the pilot had to make an emergency landing and they could turn them on again. As the plane reached altitude, laptops sprouted in front of them like toadstools. There wasn't a paperback book in sight.

As he absently touched the bandage on his neck, Cape concluded the lives of his fellow passengers were far more stressful than his own, despite the occasional risk of getting killed by a human bear.

"I'm not *supposed* to leave town," said Cape. "It's the difference between *could* and *should*."

"You think the police will see it that way?"

Cape shrugged. "Technically, I'm supposed to be available for further questioning," he said. "With any luck, I'll be back before they can think of any more questions."

"What about your … friend?" said Grace hesitantly, not sure how to describe someone who sent Death flying from the upper reaches of a clock tower. *Guardian angel* didn't seem to fit.

Cape cocked an eyebrow. "You didn't see anyone besides me and the unfriendly giant, did you?"

Grace shook her head.

"Neither did anyone else."

"But the arrows—"

"Can't be traced," replied Cape. "Now, I do have a friend that's a martial arts instructor who happens to be good with a bow, but there are twenty people in Chinatown who swear she was teaching a class when Ursa was killed. The cops could question them, but none of them speak English, so it might take a while."

Grace watched him for a long moment without speaking.

"Don't you ever worry about breaking the law?"

"The cops I know are much more interested in justice than the law," said Cape. "They want to catch the guys who killed your friend Tom. Now they have one less to worry about."

"You're lucky you have friends on the force," said Grace.

"I'm lucky I have friends, period," said Cape. "That's something I never take for granted."

Grace smiled briefly, then turned to look out the window. A thick blanket of cumulus clouds obscured the landscape, making every-thing below look nice and clean. Too bad it wasn't that way on the ground.

"I can't believe Harry is laundering money," she said quietly, still glancing at the beckoning clouds.

"I had trouble with that, too," said Cape gently, "and I don't know him the way you do. He's the one that hired you, isn't he?"

Grace nodded. "I originally went to work at Empire because of Harry."

"But things changed."

"I ended up working for Adam," said Grace, her voice tinged with regret. "I figured it was good to get experience working on big productions."

"Hasn't it been?"

"I've learned a lot…" Her voice trailed off as she studied the pristine world beyond the plane's wing.

Cape resisted the urge to touch her but to no avail. Without turning away from the window, Grace moved her hand onto the arm rest and found his. Before he could react she had intertwined their fingers and squeezed.

"Thanks for saving my life," she said quietly.

Cape squeezed back but didn't say anything.

"Sorry about your car," she added.

"Glad they found the bomb attached to yours," replied Cape.

"Yeah, but mine was a rental."

She ran her thumb across the back of his hand. Her skin was warm and smooth. Cape gave her profile the attention it deserved— the strong lines of her face, her black hair lustrous in the dim light of the plane, the gentle curve of her neck. It was a nice view.

After several minutes, Grace turned to look Cape in the eye with a renewed determination, as if she'd just made an important decision—it reminded Cape of when she'd first stepped into his office.

"I lost the faith," she said simply.

"What do you mean?"

343

"I got into this business because I love movies," she said. "But after a while I started to care more about gross receipts than plot lines."

"It's a business," said Cape.

"But it's a self-fulfilling prophecy," replied Grace with sudden fervor. "Good movies can make money, but bad movies—properly marketed and launched on the right weekend—can also make money. It's your choice."

Cape didn't say anything. He knew something about choices, but she wasn't really talking to him. This was something she needed to hear herself say.

"Somewhere along the way, I got caught up in the *business* of the movie business," said Grace.

"Maybe that's what happened to Harry."

"Maybe," said Grace, her voice regaining a note of melancholy. "But making a bad sequel to a summer blockbuster is a far cry from a Russian gangster laundering money through your studio. If Harry strayed that far from the path, I'm not sure he was ever on it."

"Maybe he's just a good actor," suggested Cape.

"There are no *good* actors," replied Grace. "Only great actors and bad actors, the latter owing their success entirely to the director, cameraman, and producer."

"Spoken like someone who really loves movies."

Grace blushed.

Cape squeezed her hand. "Nice to have you back."

"So what do you want me to do?" Grace slid her hand away and took a deep breath, getting back to business. The intimate moment passed as if it had never occurred. Cape managed not to whine or grind his teeth, but he did consider asking the flight attendant for a cup of ice.

"You talked to Angelo already?" he asked.

Grace nodded. "Told him there was an incident on the set but we got the final shot; we can still make the schedule."

"The Major might have contacted someone at Empire, but I doubt it," said Cape. "I think he has them over a barrel and exploits the relationship when he can. Right now he's probably laying low, trying to decide when to resurface."

"But you're not worried Adam or Harry will be suspicious?"

"It doesn't matter," said Cape. "The smartest thing the Bermans could do—in fact the only thing, unless they want to leave the country—is to show up for work and act like nothing's wrong."

"And maybe shred a few documents," added Grace.

"That would be the smart move," Cape agreed. "Make any connections to the Major disappear."

"So you have a plan?"

"Not really."

Grace waited for the punch line. When it didn't arrive, she asked, "Do you ever?"

Cape considered the question. "I prefer to improvise."

"You should have been an actor."

"In my next life," said Cape. "They don't know you're flying out, do they?"

Grace shook her head. "I told Angelo I'd call him from the set tomorrow—he thinks I'm still in San Francisco."

"Then I want you to walk in on Harry and demand that he resign."

Grace gave a sigh that was almost a gasp. She worked the muscles in her jaw and nodded. "OK—what are you going to do?"

Cape smiled. "I'm going to prove something, once and for all."

"What?"

"That real life is never like it is in the movies."

55

GRACE STRODE ACROSS THE lobby of Empire Studios as if she owned the place.

"Celene, put down that phone," she commanded. The pierced receptionist sat frozen beneath the halogen lights, her studs, hoops, and rings sparkling like shards of diamond embedded in her flesh.

Grace led Cape to the elevator. Once inside she let her guard down, releasing a deep breath she didn't know she was holding.

"Nervous?"

"About confronting Harry?" asked Grace. "I was sad at first—then nervous—but now I'm working up to getting royally pissed."

"How's it coming?"

"Any minute now."

The elevator doors opened on the fifth floor and Cape peered around the corner. The hallway was empty in both directions. As they walked quietly along the thick carpet, Cape scanned the ceiling and molding for cameras. Just because he couldn't see any didn't mean they weren't there, so he kept looking.

The light on the intercom glowed faintly like a dying star, its pale yellow surface pitted and worn. Cape wondered how many thousands of times it had been pushed over the past two years.

"Harry, it's Grace." She spoke clearly, her thumb pressed hard against the button. She managed to find her anger, and it was about to be unleashed. A minute passed before a mellifluous voice washed over them.

"You're in New York?" said Harry pleasantly. "What a wonderful surprise. Do come in, Grace." The door unlocked with an audible click.

As Grace turned the handle she spared a quick glance over her shoulder. Cape was pressed against the wall next to the intercom. He winked at her as she closed the door.

"What brings you home early, Grace?"

Cape could hear Harry's rich tenor through the door. Grace said something in return—he couldn't quite catch it, but it sounded like the word *truth* had a role in her opening volley. Cape smiled as he jogged down the hall to Adam Berman's office.

The door was locked. Dropping to his knees, Cape saw there was no deadbolt, just a simple latch. He took a small folded strip of metal about the size of a money clip from his wallet and straightened it out. After two careful jabs the latch popped.

The office was empty. Closing the door behind him, Cape scanned the room. The same collection of trophies and plaques lined the wall, the same couch and chairs filled the room. The bookcases behind the desk held the same assortment of books, magazines, and the occasional framed photograph.

Cape moved to the desk. Papers littered its surface, along with a few paperweights and two small statues, but nothing seemed more significant than anything else. The phone seemed to be working, the red message light pulsing. Cape sat down and put his hands on the desk, looking at the room from Adam's perspective.

As he rocked in the chair, Cape saw something he'd missed while standing. A glass half filled with bourbon and ice sat just under the shadow of an Emmy award. The ice had yet to melt, and there was barely any ring around its base. Someone had been sitting here moments before he picked the lock. Cape ran his hands under the desk, feeling for a button or latch.

Nothing.

Pushing back in the chair, Cape pulled out the top drawer and froze.

Adam Berman's voice was directly behind him.

Cape stood and turned, facing the bookcases that lined the wall. The voice was muffled but unmistakably Adam's. He sounded angry—random words had enough velocity behind them to penetrate the wall. *Dare... outrage... integrity.* Cape moved closer to the bookcase and bent his legs, trying to look at it from Adam's height.

The shelf held roughly thirty books, and Cape grabbed each in turn and pulled on them gently. Each tilted back on its spine as any normal book would. The last item on the shelf was an Oscar, standing as mute witness to Cape's incursion.

"That would be too obvious," muttered Cape. Peering closely, he saw there wasn't any dust on the statue. Shrugging, he wrapped his hand around the gold man and pulled.

The statue tilted forward on a spring mechanism mounted in its base, and the bookcase sprang forward and sideways, the only sound a gentle rolling noise as it slid along a wheeled track.

"Very Indiana Jones." Cape took a step back as the bookcase came to a halt and found himself on the threshold of a secret chamber.

The room was a near-perfect cube ten feet on a side with no windows. On the facing wall were three flat-screen televisions. On the first was an image of Harry Berman, his benevolent face looking unusually stern. The second had a view of the ocean as seen through a living room window. Taped to the wall below the second TV was a numbered list of places that included New York, Paris, and San Francisco—all the places the Bermans had property. On the third screen was Grace, her face flushed as she pointed accusingly into the camera.

In the center of the room was a chair mounted to the floor, cables running along its base to a row of computers. Lights flashed as computers hummed in fits and starts, responding to the demands of the man in the chair.

Adam Berman couldn't see Cape because of the helmet he was wearing. Cables ran from its top, and two small electrodes were taped to Adam's cheeks just above his mouth. A darkened visor covered his eyes. Cape guessed from the reflected light on Adam's face that it was some kind of backlit display, and the screens on the wall were back-up for when he wasn't wearing the helmet. On his right hand was a glove, each finger controlling an independent cable running to the bank of computers. As Adam gesticulated wildly in the chair, the image of his brother Harry gestured emphatically on the screen.

Cape could hear Grace's voice leaking from headphones mounted inside of the helmet and was reminded of the computer-generated actors she had shown him. How much had this cost, and which film's budget had paid for it? He watched Adam shift back and forth, muttering into a microphone just below his chin. The cable from the microphone ran to a separate computer—Cape assumed it was some kind of voice synthesizer. He'd seen primitive versions at toy stores last Christmas.

Cape strode over to the voice-computer and yanked the cable from its socket. On the big screen, Grace leaned forward and shook her head, holding a hand to her ear. Cape walked down the row of computers and pulled cables at every stop, looking over his shoulder as the image of Harry Berman broke into pixels and ragged chunks on the small screen. He saw Grace on-screen, staring, then suddenly she walked off camera. Cape stepped over to Adam, who was still rocking back and forth, oblivious.

Cape set his right foot against Adam's hip and knocked him off the chair.

Adam landed in a tangle of cable with a loud *ooooff*, helmet askew. It fell off completely as he scrambled backward, away from Cape.

"Hi, Adam. Remember me?"

Cape heard knocking from the office behind him. Adam looked as if he were in shock. He wasn't going anywhere. Cape ran quickly across the office to open the door for Grace, then jogged back to the hidden room. Adam was still crouched in the corner, his eyes those of a frightened child. Grace gasped as she came into the room. She'd seen the technology before.

Adam wrapped his arms around his knees, tears streaming down his cheeks, right hand still clad in its high-tech glove. He looked at them with an expression of infinite sadness. "I loved my brother," he said miserably. "I loved him."

Cape squatted down to be at eye level before saying anything.

"He's dead, isn't he, Adam?"

Adam wailed and hid his head between his legs, rolling onto his side. Heavy sobs racked his pudgy frame as his feet kicked the computers, the sounds all the more pitiful in the confined space. Cape sat on the floor next to him and put a hand on his back. Adam's breathing slowed gradually but his eyes were squeezed shut. He wasn't going to be coherent anytime soon.

"Oh, my God."

Angelo stood in the doorway, mouth open. His eyes jumped from one inexplicable thing to the next, trying to piece it all together. Cape gestured at the chair in the center of the room.

"Have a seat, Angelo," he said. "There are some things you ought to know."

56

CAPE COULD TELL WHEN he wasn't wanted. Getting shot, lied to, and almost blown up in one week was bad enough. But getting evicted was more than he could handle.

He came straight to his office from the airport and found the letter under his door. It hurt just to pick it up—he was bruised down to the bone from his fight with Ursa, and his side burned where the bullet had grazed his ribs. His neck was still bandaged. From any angle he looked and felt like shit.

He sat down heavily behind his desk and read. The letter was a petition to his landlord, signed by his fellow tenants, demanding that Cape be evicted. While they were sensitive to the demands and risks of his profession and had tolerated a *plethora of unsavory visitors* over the years, the exploding car was the last straw.

Cape had done some work for his landlord last year pro bono—only a day's worth of running around, but Cape figured he earned some goodwill. That and the sagging economy might mean the difference between moving to a new office or just paying to have the windows replaced. He crumpled the memo into a ball and threw it into the hallway.

"Littering is against the law," boomed a familiar voice.

Beau stepped into the doorway and threw the paper back to Cape.

"Big fine, anyway," he added.

Cape gestured toward the client chair. "You must be one of a plethora of unsavory visitors."

Beau frowned. "Come again?"

"Never mind—hope you don't mind the broken-glass decor."

Beau crunched his way across the floor, glancing at the plastic sheets taped over the windows as they billowed in the breeze. "When you gonna clean up?"

"I've been busy."

"Makes two of us," said Beau. "Remember the shooter in Frank's office, guy looked like a hawk?"

Cape nodded. "Anthony, right?"

"He was definitely the shooter," said Beau.

"Forensics came through?"

Beau sighed. "No, but Frank did," he said miserably. "Harbor patrol found Anthony bobbing like a buoy near Pier 23, face down in the water. Which was just as well, 'cause the shot to the back of his head took most of his face with it."

Cape recalled his visit with Frank, the portly charm of the man a thin disguise for the animal inside. "You'll never pin it on Frank."

"Tell me something I don't know," said Beau. "I'll get the fat bastard another day, on something else."

Cape nodded absently. "Nothing left but dead ends."

"Nothing but dead bodies," replied Beau. "I talked to Corelli, who talked to Interpol. Thought you'd want to know there's been no sign of the Major."

Cape shrugged. "I'm not surprised. He slipped into the country easily enough. No doubt he could sneak out without attracting too much attention."

"Unless he wanted to finish what he started," said Beau, looking intently at Cape.

"Yeah, I thought of that," said Cape. "But there's no profit in killing me now, and I think he's an opportunist. Besides, what am I supposed to do?"

"Move?"

Cape shook his head. "Not a chance."

"Change your name to something like Joe or John," said Beau. "Something anonymous—save you the trouble of spelling your real name."

"Thanks," said Cape. "Not interested."

"Just thought I'd mention it."

"Where's your partner on all of this?"

Beau shrugged. "Busy wrapping up the paperwork on that string of bodies you left behind. And Vinnie's a stickler for details—drives me crazy sometimes."

"You're starting to sound like half of an old married couple."

"Watch it."

"Ever think about going back to Narcotics?"

"Nah," said Beau. "Sometimes—not really. Figure with Homicide I'm dealin' with a better class of people."

"You mean dead people?"

"Exactly," said Beau. "It's the scumbags that are still walkin' and talkin' that get you down."

"Never thought of it that way," said Cape.

Both men turned as footsteps echoed down the hall, paused, then resumed. A moment later a young man stood in the doorway. He was about six feet tall with long dark hair and brooding eyes. He looked from Beau to Cape with an impassive stare.

"You are Cape Weathers?"

Cape nodded. There was something about the young man that wasn't right. Beau clearly registered the same thing; he shifted in his chair to make the gun on his hip obvious. The young man seemed unfazed.

"Your phone is going to ring," he said.

Before Cape could respond, the young man turned and walked back down the hallway. The echo of his last footstep had died just as the phone started to ring. Both Cape and Beau started, looking at the phone as if it were about to explode. Cape grabbed it on the third ring.

An indistinct voice whispered across the line.

"You have a delivery ... from a friend."

Cape stared at the dead phone before returning it to its cradle. Beau started to say something but Cape held up his hand, stood, walked to the door, and peered around the jamb into the hallway. A large cardboard box sat on the floor, precisely at the point where the young man might have left it when they heard his footsteps pause.

Cape gingerly placed a hand on each side of the box and tested its weight. He guessed around ten pounds. When he was positive there were no wires attached to the bottom, he carried the box into the office and placed it gently on the desk.

Beau eyed the box suspiciously. "If that's another bomb, our friendship is officially over." The box was sixteen inches on a side, a simple cube of brown cardboard wrapped with twine.

Cape smiled as he studied the address label.

"Relax," he said. "It's from a friend." He pulled at the twine to release the cardboard flaps on top. Nothing exploded. He and Beau leaned forward together, almost bumping heads as they peered inside.

A blue plastic bag filled the cardboard box, twisted closed at the top and held fast by heavy string. Looking across the box at Beau, Cape pulled the string deliberately.

"Boom," he said.

Beau scowled.

The stench hit hard, knocking them back onto their seats. Cape's eyes started to water and Beau coughed as he brought his hand to his nose. Both men looked at each other with a somber expression before standing and risking another glance inside.

"It was addressed to you," said Beau evenly. "You deal with it."

"Is that a dare?"

"Call it what you want," replied Beau, "but I ain't puttin' my hand in there."

Cape held his breath as he reached inside. He wrapped his fingers around what felt like cold spaghetti and slowly raised his arm, fighting the urge to gag. He stared unblinking in anticipation of what he was about to see only an arm's length away.

Major Yuri Andropov stared back at him, his eyes lifeless orbs sunken into their sockets. His jaw was slack, the teeth crooked and yellow, and a dried trail of blood ran from one nostril. His neck was ragged; gangrenous pus oozed slowly along its edge before dripping into the box.

In the center of his forehead was a hole barely wider than a pencil, just above and between his eyes. It looked deep red inside but black around the edges. There was no exit wound or gaping hole in the back of the skull, suggesting a small caliber gun had been used, maybe a .22.

The Major's head was surprisingly heavy.

Cape dropped it into the box and sat down, wiping his hand on his thigh. "Beau, I'd like you to meet the Major—the murder suspect you and Vinnie have been looking for."

Beau looked like he was considering putting Cape's head in a box of its own.

"A friend sent you that?"

Cape looked again at the address label, hand-written in perfect block letters. Next to his name was a small pen-and-ink drawing of a chess piece—a white knight. In the upper left corner where the return address would normally be printed, there was a similar sketch of a black king.

The memory of a shark's grin flashed before his eyes, and Cape shook his head and smiled. "Yeah," he said. "A friend I didn't know I had."

"You and your friends," Beau said in a tired voice, knowing he was on the list. "I gotta call Vinnie—he's gonna *love* this."

57

"Harry's been dead two years."

Cape walked slowly beside Grace as she delivered the news. The Golden Gate Bridge dominated the view ahead as they walked along the beach at Crissy Field. Kids were flying kites and yelling, dogs barking. One stalwart family waded into the surf, turned blue, and ran for their towels. With every step the scene of Tom's murder loomed closer, but Grace seemed oddly at peace. Somehow knowing the truth brought calm, if not comfort.

The fog had faded like a bad hangover, revealing the sun but leaving behind an ocean breeze just cold enough to remind you to stay out of the shadows. That was something Cape had already taken to heart. He squinted against the wind and shook his head in disbelief.

"Two years."

Grace nodded. "His disappearance coincides with the start of Yuri Andropov's investments with Empire. I guess Adam needed Harry out of the way before he could take the Major's money."

"That's when Harry supposedly developed sociophobia, right?"

Grace nodded, eyes unfocused as she stared out to sea. "Hard to believe we all fell for that one."

"Isn't the movie business run by powerful eccentrics?" asked Cape gently. "I think you told me that once."

Grace forced a smile. "I also told you Harry had become strange, even by Hollywood standards."

"So maybe deep down, you knew," said Cape.

"Building a virtual Harry would cost a fortune."

"That might explain why your special effects budget was blown."

Grace nodded. "You knew, didn't you?"

Cape shrugged. "I didn't know what to expect when I went into Adam's office," he said, "but there were stupid discrepancies that bothered me."

"Such as?"

"Harry knew who I was from the moment I stepped into his office," said Cape. "I was supposed to be dead, and he was a little too cool about it all, even for a guy hiding behind a screen. I had just been with Adam, so I started to wonder how close the brothers really were. Like maybe they were talking."

"What else?"

"Everyone, including Adam, told me how important awards and critical acclaim were to Harry, but all the statues and plaques were in Adam's office, beautifully displayed. Harry's office was barren— Adam had hoarded all the trophies for himself."

"I'm an idiot," said Grace.

"You were too close to the situation," replied Cape. "You were there to talk to them about movie production, I was there to notice things."

Grace nodded absently as she wondered what else she'd taken for granted. "There's more, isn't there?"

"Adam was supposedly the brother interested in money," said Cape, "but Harry bragged about arranging the sale. Not the artistic visionary everyone had described."

"I never believed Harry would sell the company."

"The language Adam and Harry used to describe each other was similar," said Cape. "They both reflexively used the phrase *I love my brother*, almost like a mantra."

Grace recalled the image of Adam Berman crying on the floor. "Maybe Adam really did love Harry."

"I think he did."

"Yet he killed him," said Grace sadly.

Cape shook his head. "I don't think so—my bet's the Major killed Harry after he discovered Adam was turning the studio into a money-laundering operation." He turned to look at Grace. "I think the same thing happened to your friend Tom."

"You don't think Tom was involved at all?" Grace asked hopefully.

Cape shook his head. "I think Tom noticed the same discrepancies in the budget you did, and he started asking questions. The Major was getting cocky—he even put himself in the movie. I'll bet the accounting was getting sloppy, too."

Grace stopped walking and stared at the magnificent bridge, a mute witness to so many lives. So many deaths. After a long moment Grace sighed, as if releasing a great weight.

They stood silently for several minutes, watching sunlight skip across the crests of waves. When Grace turned to face him, Cape noticed the years around her eyes had disappeared, the lines erased by silver light coming off the water.

"What do you think will happen to Adam?" she asked.

"That's a tough one," said Cape as they resumed their walk. "After his brother was killed he obviously snapped, taking on both personalities inside that bald head of his. He couldn't let go of his greedy self, but he also adopted the benevolent persona of his older brother."

"You really believe that?"

"I don't think Adam was ever the most stable individual on the planet."

"That's an understatement," agreed Grace.

"Then it doesn't matter what I think," said Cape. "What matters is what a judge will believe."

Grace nodded but didn't say anything.

"How about you?" asked Cape.

Grace smiled self-consciously. "I've got a film to produce."

"So you're going to finish the movie?"

"Yes, I am," replied Grace. "There were other investors besides the Major, and the studio stands to lose more if we scrap the production than if we release the film. With any luck, box office receipts will make up for the budget overages."

"Whose decision was that?"

Grace smiled again. "Angelo."

"He's your new boss?" Cape laughed.

"With Harry and Adam out of the picture, he's in charge," said Grace. "We had a long talk yesterday—he asked me to finish the film. I never thought I'd say this, but I have a feeling he's a different person without Adam kicking him in the balls on a daily basis."

"That would certainly affect my outlook."

"I'll finish the film, and then I'll tell you what I really think of him."

"And after that?"

Grace looked at Cape with a bittersweet expression, smile warm but her eyes a little sad. "I think I'm going to take some time off after this job," she said. "I want to remember *why* I wanted to make movies in the first place—I want to have that feeling again."

"Maybe you should try going to the movies instead of making them."

Grace stopped walking. "Are you asking me out?"

"Of course not," said Cape a little too quickly. "I never date my clients."

"I thought you were through with this case," replied Grace.

"I haven't sent you my bill," replied Cape. "Besides, I don't even know what movies are playing."

"I'll check the paper," said Grace, "just in case you change your mind."

Cape cocked an eyebrow. "I thought you were slow to commit."

"Maybe it's time I tried something different."

Cape shrugged and looked toward the bridge, wondering if he should change the subject. "Where are you headed now?"

"To the baseball stadium," said Grace. "The one on the Embarcadero where the Giants play—we're going to destroy it tomorrow afternoon."

"You're destroying the baseball stadium?" said Cape. "That's great news."

"You don't like baseball?"

"Nothing against the team, but the games have been screwing up traffic ever since they built that thing—I liked it better when they played at Candlestick."

"I'm afraid it's only temporary," said Grace. "Special effects."

"That's OK," said Cape. "I'm not sure I'm ready for anything permanent right now."

"Are we still talking about the stadium?"

"What else would we be talking about?" asked Cape.

"I'll be in town for another week," said Grace.

"OK," said Cape cautiously. "But you're still a client."

Grace leaned forward and kissed him lightly on the lips.

"You're fired."

She smiled before turning and walking slowly toward the parking lot.

Cape stood and watched her until she drove away, the ocean at his back, the bridge farther away than it looked. He licked his lips and tasted strawberries.

"I'll have to remember to send her a bill."

ACKNOWLEDGMENTS

Writing may be a solitary pursuit, but no one writes a book by himself. I'd like to thank everyone who inspired, guided, and redirected this book as I was struggling to bring it to life.

My tenacious agent, Jill Grosjean. Barbara Moore at Midnight Ink for believing in these characters. Karl Anderson, my keen-eyed editor. Pamela Cannon, bulletproof publicist. The Independent Mystery Booksellers and their amazing customers. The delightful gang of murderers and thieves at the Book Passage Mystery Writers Conference.

Most importantly, I'd like to thank my family. My wife, Kathryn, for convincing me that I'm easier to live with when I'm writing. Clare Ruth Maleeny and Helen Grace Maleeny—two smart, creative, and funny girls who make the sun rise every day.

ABOUT THE AUTHOR

Tim Maleeny is the author of *Stealing the Dragon*, a novel that Lee Child called "a perfect thriller debut," which was named a "Killer Book" by the Independent Mystery Booksellers Association.

His short fiction has been nominated for the Macavity Award and appears in *Alfred Hitchcock's Mystery Magazine* and *Death Do Us Part*, an anthology edited by Harlan Coben for the Mystery Writers of America.

A graduate of Dartmouth College and Columbia University, Tim currently lives in San Francisco with his wife and daughters. To contact him or learn more about his writing, visit www.timmaleeny.com

WWW.MIDNIGHTINKBOOKS.COM

From the gritty streets of New York City to sacred tombs in the Middle East, it's always midnight somewhere. Join us online at any hour for fresh new voices in mystery fiction, book club questions, author information, mystery resources, and more.

Midnight Ink promises a wild ride filled with cunning villains, conflicted heroes, hilarious hazards, mind-bending puzzles, and enough twists and turns to keep readers on the edge of their seats.

MIDNIGHT INK ORDERING INFORMATION

Order by Phone:

- Call toll-free within the U.S. and Canada at
  1-888-NITEINK (1-888-648-3465)
- We accept VISA, MasterCard, and American Express

Order by Mail:

Send the full price of your order (MN residents add 6.5% sales tax) in U.S. funds, plus postage & handling to:

> Midnight Ink
> 2143 Wooddale Drive, H115
> Woodbury, MN 55125-2989

Postage & Handling:

Standard (U.S., Mexico, & Canada). If your order is:
> $24.99 and under, add $3.00
> $25.00 and over, FREE STANDARD SHIPPING

AK, HI, PR: $15.00 for one book plus $1.00 for each additional book.

International Orders (airmail only):
> $16.00 for one book plus $3.00 for each additional book

Orders are processed within 2 business days. Please allow for normal shipping time. Postage and handling rates subject to change.